ALLURE
OF DECEIT

ALSO BY
SUSAN FROETSCHEL

Fear of Beauty

A Novel

ALLURE
OF DECEIT

SUSAN FROETSCHEL

SEVENTH STREET BOOKS®
AN IMPRINT OF PROMETHEUS BOOKS
59 JOHN GLENN DRIVE • AMHERST, NY 14228
www.seventhstreetbooks.com

Published 2015 by Seventh Street Books®, an imprint of Prometheus Books

Cover image © Emilio Morenatti / AP / Corbis
Cover design by Jacqueline Nasso Cooke

Inquiries should be addressed to
Seventh Street Books
59 John Glenn Drive
Amherst, New York 14228
VOICE: 716-691-0133 • FAX: 716-691-0137
WWW.SEVENTHSTREETBOOKS.COM

19 18 17 16 15 • 5 4 3 2 1

Library of Congress Cataloging-in-Publication Data

Froetschel, Susan.
    Allure of deceit / Susan Froetschel.
        pages ; cm
    ISBN 978-1-61614-017-5 (softcover) — ISBN 978-1-61614-037-3 (ebook)
    1. Americans—Afghanistan—Fiction. 2. Culture conflict—Afghanistan—
Fiction. 3. Charities—Fiction. I. Title.

PS3556.R59353A82 2015
813'.54—dc23
                                                                        2014032081

Printed in the United States of America

For my sisters—Terri, Laurie, and Joyce

PART 1

This is the hell which the guilty called a lie.
                                                    —Koran 55:43

CHAPTER 1

Lime, peacock, moss, sea mist, forest, and fern—gowns in every shade of green swirled about the ballroom floor. Aromas of mint and rosemary drifted from all-green centerpieces. Leading policymakers, academics, corporate executives, journalists, and celebrities gathered in small groups, their voices low and earnest, discussing extremists massacring students in Africa, indiscriminate dumping of toxins into waterways and cancer spikes for Asia, the lack of schools and work for refugees scattered throughout the Middle East, and the countless cruelties exacted on impoverished children everywhere.

Everyone in the ballroom had a worthy cause and hoped to attract the attention of the evening's hostess, Lydia Sendry, the woman who controlled GlobalConnect, the world's largest charitable foundation.

Pearl Hanson was nervous, still in disbelief that her tiny organization, based in rural Texas, had received a cherished invitation to the spring event. Conservatives from Texas were not the typical guests of such events hosted by major foundations, designed to match the nation's leading opinion makers with new applicants like Pearl. She pinched her arm once more.

Her group had a track record for training women in rigorous natural family planning. For women with willing partners, the program was about 80 percent effective in providing birth control. For the inevitable mishaps, the group provided a year or two of support for families that could not afford to feed and clothe a newborn. Or adoptions could be arranged.

Pearl Hanson wanted to go global and submitted her proposal to GlobalConnect. The plan—head to Afghanistan and provide training in natural family planning while organizing orphanages as backup.

In the end, GlobalConnect would choose only a fraction of the applicants. The invitation alone marked applicants as global players.

"Be yourself," Annie Johnson, GlobalConnect's executive director, had advised. "Lydia is warm and easy to talk with. You don't need to say a lot, and she will have loads of questions. Be candid and be prepared." Annie also confided that Pearl's group was a frontrunner for the first phase of funding, including travel grants for finding local partners.

Pearl waited her turn. Taller than most of the other guests, she observed the woman who controlled the world's most powerful foundation. Lydia Sendry was reserved, sitting in the corner and studying the ballroom. Her soft silvery hair was swept to one side, and a walker was tucked out of the way. From all appearances, Lydia was the gentle grandmother type beloved by family and friends.

But the woman's eyes were neither old nor distracted. Her gaze was intense as applicants and their escorts filed by her table for brief chats. She did not delegate responsibility in distributing hundreds of millions of dollars each year. Only a fraction of the proposals could be funded, and all were approved by the small board led by Lydia.

And when Lydia sat alone, waiting for the next applicant to step forward, her dark eyes darted about, studying the room's occupants in a keen, even wrathful way.

Lydia Sendry wanted to leave behind a better world.

~~~~~

Paul Reichart wandered the ballroom, thinking about the foundation's ridiculous rules. Board members and executive staff had to attend at least one event annually, cheering on the desperate requests for money. Like others, he was uncomfortable, and not because of the formality. Paul was unusual among foundation staff, constantly reminded that he lacked big foundation experience. Snide murmurs followed that the global development director had obtained the job only because of his long ties with the Sendry family.

The grumbling was unfair. Every employee lacked experience

---

because GlobalConnect was so massive, with more assets than any other private foundation in the world. Annie Johnson and the other executives insisted the work of making connections was crucial, that elaborate displays demonstrated powerful connections.

Yet they envied Paul's connections with Lydia.

He couldn't wait for the evening to end and to get on a plane back to Asia. The board approved Paul's working from offices in India and Afghanistan, target nations for the foundation. As development director, he constantly traveled, training new staff and overseeing GlobalConnect programs.

Paul liked to think that Lydia trusted him. He felt lucky to work far from the bureaucracy in New York.

The New York events were phony and conceited. Staff planned every detail, always on the lookout for symbols that reflected high-minded ideals and Lydia's preferences. For example, the staff knew how much Lydia abhorred waste. The meal was vegetarian, with ridiculously delicate portion sizes for the salads, fruit, and grilled vegetables. Top-shelf brands of alcohol flowed freely, one of Lydia's little tests. Decisions about money were constantly being made, despite the celebratory atmosphere, and the smart guests avoided alcoholic beverages. Donors and recipients had to stay sharp, assessing attitudes and the nuances of need, excess, and hurt feelings.

Such attention to detail did not prevent the wrong people from making decisions or the wrong groups from receiving awards.

Paul kept his criticism to himself. Best he stayed far from the States. The executive staff quickly marginalized employees who posed too many questions or suggestions. Paul owed Lydia and her only son everything, and he had no other plans but to dedicate his life to a foundation that almost failed to materialize. More than once, Annie reminded staff that plans for the foundation had not been finalized before the premature death of Michael Sendry, the founder of Photizonet, who was Lydia's son and Paul's best friend. A select few understood Michael's vision, or so she intimated.

If she only knew... For Annie, the foundation was wealthy,

influential, and adored, and she was a stubborn bulldozer against all criticism.

The evening's speeches had ended, and guests maneuvered about the room. A young man, college-aged and blond, trim in an expensive tuxedo made to fit an athletic build, zigzagged through the crowd, affable as he approached Lydia's table, where a security perimeter protected her from unwanted, unreasonable pleas. The man was too young, too unknown. A member of Lydia's security team, also in tuxedo, leaped forward, issuing a reminder that guests needed an appointment and designated escort to approach Lydia's table.

Like a magician, the intruder waved his hand and released what appeared to be a yellow scarf flowing from his sleeve. A petite woman in a turquoise silk sheath stepped forward and stretched the banner wide, the words in blood red: FAMILY PLANNING SAVES LIVES; DO MORE AT HOME, GLOBALCONNECT.

Security ripped the banner away and escorted the young couple from the ballroom, but not before photographers captured the image— Lydia with her head turned, reading the message.

Hiding her fury, Annie excused herself from a small group of executives and headed back to the podium. First, a brisk apology for the interruption from what she described as "the foundation's young and enthusiastic supporters" and then the well-practiced summary of statistics on the millions donated by GlobalConnect to worthy causes over the past year.

Then she paused, ensuring that she had the crowd's attention. "We represent civil society, but our organization is not a democracy," she said. "Our role has been approved by voters in our democratic society time and time again. They have placed their trust in visionaries of our society to set priorities on needs and provide funding. The late Michael Sendry was among the greatest of these visionaries. His life, cut short, was so full. He innovated tirelessly without complaint and set goals for us. It's his vision we honor every day."

The audience cheered wildly.

Annie moved close to the microphone and spoke over the

applause, her voice strong and firm, to point out how the protests were self-defeating. "As many of you know, GlobalConnect has a unique set of governing policies. Michael emphasized tolerance, compromise. He believed that opponents can work together, and many paths can lead to the same goal. Unseemly demands for funding in one area only prompt GlobalConnect to locate and fund organizations with opposite goals."

Leaving the podium, Annie cast a sheepish look in Lydia's direction. The board's chair would not want to hear excuses. The security team would be disciplined the next day. Some members would lose their jobs.

Paul was nauseated and could not hide his disgust. He left the ballroom, ready to return to Asia. He could not bear to hear others talking about Michael, especially Annie. She had never even met the tech wizard.

GlobalConnect was not a democracy. Rather than define, identify, and emphasize global problems and leading solutions, the board relied on a scattershot approach, spreading resources too far and forcing programs to compete. Grant applicants and policymakers played games, and staff wasted Michael's money, all weakening GlobalConnect's sense of purpose. Paul didn't blame Lydia. She cared, but she wasn't tough enough to see how people manipulated the grant process. He hated to admit it, but Michael's wife might have been right. The executive staff was too controlling, yet too timid to make decisive, radical plans to overhaul all of society.

Lydia had lost her way.

~~~~~

The hostess of the charitable ball, Lydia Sendry, observed the crowd with a mix of pleasure, calculation, and regret. Mostly regret. Ever lurking in the back of her mind was escape, the desire to return home to Michigan and her memories of Michael. She kept a low profile at such public events. Her simple dress in forest green was indistinguishable among the black tuxedos. Near seventy years of age, she pretended to be feeble, using a walker in public, even though it was shoved into a closet at home. She encouraged vague rumors about ill health.

Her table was positioned so she could survey the entire room and guest exchanges. In turn, guests constantly glanced Lydia's way, checking for reactions from the woman who controlled the board, the policies, and the huge and unending flow of funding.

Annie's blunt reminders about democracy were true but troubling.

The foundation honoring her son was vast. Although relatively new, it operated in more than thirty developing nations and could be counted on to distribute at least $400 million annually for a mix of organizations. GlobalConnect was influential, yet it limited support to some fifty groups per year. Competition was intense.

Lydia's thoughts could not help but drift to Michael. He would have enjoyed the party, but not judging the passions of others. She certainly did not relish the role. She despised controlling the money inherited after the death of her only son.

Such an inheritance was unnatural. The young man had started his own tech company in his early twenties, piggybacking on German research and developing an affordable system that allowed Internet data to travel with light waves. The system, low-cost and fast, required no elaborate infrastructure. For the first time, communities could set up their own intranet around a chain of solar-powered lighting.

As with any revolutionary innovation, the system destroyed entire industries, upending the world's most powerful cable, satellite, and telecommunications companies. The traditionalists resisted the new technology. So, Michael had bypassed American and European markets, sending startup teams to the least developed countries in the world. His firm, Photizonet, went public six years later, and he became the richest man in the world.

Michael married his college sweetheart. No one had known that Rose, his young wife, was pregnant as the couple set off for a honeymoon in India, a brief stay at the Oberoi Amarvilas in Agra before heading off to hike in Nagarkot. A prep meeting was organized for Rose to discuss preferences on hiking routes and guides. At the last minute,

Michael decided to skip a company conference call and accompany his wife to the luncheon meeting.

As the couple headed into the restaurant, a young man in neat Western attire shouted a greeting before he tossed a small package their way. Michael stepped in front of his wife and caught the explosive device.

Indian news media had quickly identified the victims, and Lydia learned about the deaths from news shows the next morning. The corporation contacted her, explaining how they had already dispatched her son's longtime friend, employee, and best man to Agra. Paul Reichart was not a tech wizard. Instead, he had worked for Photizonet's cultural development department, organizing teams that profiled and prepared communities throughout Asia before arranging installations. Lydia would never forget the distraught call from Paul—his voice broken, as he prepared to accompany the remains home. Representing the family, Paul had acted as an intermediary with the Indian police.

Police quickly tracked the attacker, who had distinctive scars from burns on one side of his face. A large, ornate dagger was tucked inside the man's belt, and police killed him on the spot. Later, the officers determined that the troubled man was from northern Helmand Province, Afghanistan, and had been living in India illegally. The drifter had little education and no work experience. All that was known was that he had described himself as an orphan, the son of house servants who had died years earlier in a horrific fire.

The thirty-year-old inventor, his wife, and their unborn child had died less than a week after the marriage. Only their attorney knew about the inkling plan for a foundation.

The day after the couple's funeral, Michael's attorney had met with Lydia. Her son had reached out to Henry Strohn while in graduate school. The gruff man had advised Michael throughout the tech startup and then served as his personal attorney. Reading from neat notes, Henry quickly described his last meeting with the couple and the numerous documents signed, including the couple's wills and a living trust. Toward the end of the meeting, Michael mentioned an intention to start a charitable trust or foundation. He asked Henry to investigate several key areas—family planning, education, environmental protection, human rights, and citizenship as related to curtailing poverty.

"The discussion was brief," Henry had admitted. He turned to a pile of folders and extracted a piece of notebook paper. "This was the last instruction I received from your son."

Lydia had held the paper, dazed, as Henry continued. As far as he knew, no one else had known about the couple's plans. The primary beneficiaries of their living trust, Michael and Rose, were dead. "Children, yet unnamed, of Michael and Rose Sendry" were listed as a secondary beneficiary along with Lydia.

She was sole heir to her son's majority share in the corporation and his wealth, as well as the notion of a foundation—with little guidance other than a handwritten mission statement scrawled on what looked like a piece of scrap paper.

"As far as we can determine, that paper is all that exists regarding the foundation," Henry had explained. No board of directors had been appointed, no funds designated or distributed. Official forms had not been signed or filed. "We began research and were waiting for a final review from your son. From the company's point of view, the statement and plans are vague." Henry paused. He asked if Lydia had known anything about Michael's plans to start a foundation with his share of Photizonet profits.

She shook her head. "Not a clue. Though I'm not surprised. He was so generous."

"And frugal," Henry added. He didn't have to tell Lydia. Michael had adored Rose for sharing his enthusiasm to live far below their means. The two had shopped at thrift stores and farmers' markets. He took pride at the high mileage on his 2005 Corolla, and she enjoyed growing vegetables and cooking for friends at home. "Too frugal. Their bungalow in Redwood City? No security. Three bedrooms, one and half baths."

"They were so happy there." Tears burned her eyes. "There are no other beneficiaries on the trust? And what about Rose's parents?"

"Unlike the foundation, the intentions for the living trust are clear. As you know, Michael rejected a prenuptial agreement, refusing to accept my advice or Rose's, for that matter. He also wanted to list her parents as a beneficiary, but Rose was firm. She asked that he leave her parents out of the trust for the time being until the two sides of the family got to know each other better."

Every sentence pointed to the couple's desire to live simply and practice generosity with their wealth.

"Lydia, I must say something before we go on." Henry took the scrap from her hands and placed it on the desk between them. "As far as I can tell, you and perhaps Rose's parents are the only candidates with reason to resist this last-minute addition in their estate plans."

Lydia had felt like a fool for not immediately understanding. Of course, a proposed foundation locked up Michael's vast fortune.

"But you're his mother," he had continued in his soft, businesslike way. "He could make colleagues laugh with his stories about thrifty parents, but he trusted your good sense implicitly. He would trust your instincts." He pointed to the note. "It's your decision whether we proceed on a foundation."

He advised there was no need for her to hurry. "I suspect that no one else knows about this piece of paper. And even if they do, you don't need to act. The courts would agree. The foundation was proposed, not finalized. Or, we can file the paperwork for a foundation."

Lydia remembered staring at the paper with its ragged edge and re-reading the words. The writing was tight, unevenly spaced, like a young boy's work in elementary school. There was no doubt that the crooked writing belonged to her son. She asked if Michael had been alone when he handed over the paper. Henry shook his head.

"Rose was in the room. He drafted it himself and handed it over to me." The attorney looked down at his hands. "I can only guess, but I would presume they had talked about this plan beforehand."

Lydia had no more questions. Ignoring a final wish from her son was unthinkable. She told Henry to continue work on the foundation, relying on the mission statement supplied by her son.

He nodded. "You are the best judge of Michael's wishes. You can shape the foundation and its rules to guide future leaders."

A hands-off approach was so tempting and would have been the healthiest option for her. She could live her life, trust others to make decisions, and walk away from the headaches associated with so much money.

Instead, Lydia took active control from the start. She based the foundation in Michigan. She wanted a small board of directors and a long list of strict rules. She asked that the announcement be delayed until absolutely necessary. When news of GlobalConnect was released, the reaction was unanimous surprise. Apparently, Michael and Rose had not confided in any friends or colleagues at work.

Lydia had her reasons for tight control. She was sure, even months later, that Michael's death was not a random act of terrorism. She spent a small fortune on investigations of hotel staff in India, Photizonet staff and competitors, the tourist agency, and the guides. Early on, the investigation covered Rose's family as well as the couple's closest friends, including Henry Strohn and Paul Reichart. Photizonet work had required frequent travel by employees to Asia, but the investigators unearthed no connections with the killer. Young people in the region could be easily tricked into carrying such packages for a small fee. Anyone might have co-opted the man to toss the package at the couple.

The list of those with reason to envy Michael was endless. His innovations had disrupted the tech world. But leads dwindled. Investigators could not determine whether a stranger had instigated the attack or the young man had acted on his own.

The investigators warned that her son may not have been the target.

Her desire for answers was stronger than ever, but Lydia kept the obsession to herself. She used the foundation to observe and test interactions of staff, critics, Photizonet colleagues, and grant recipients. GlobalConnect was her best tool for asking questions, maybe learning the reasons behind the senseless deaths of her son and daughter-in-law.

Lydia could not rest. She no longer trusted her judgment about others' motivations. She constantly pored over possible reasons why anyone might want to harm Michael.

A hand touched her shoulder, interrupting the memories. Annie gently asked about resuming the parade of grant applicants, and Lydia nodded. Annie was a strict organizer, scheduling every minute of Lydia's time at such events. Conversations with the potential grant recipients typically lasted about ten minutes. If Lydia fingered the pearl clip holding her hair back, she needed more time. If she sipped her drink, grapefruit juice with a touch of salt, an aide stepped in to halt the meeting.

More often than not, Lydia cut the meetings short.

"It's been the most delightful evening," said the director of a powerful health nonprofit, as he bowed and kissed her hand. One of Annie's assistants hovered nearby, timing the conversation. The executive thanked her for a recent check and outlined new initiatives as she sipped the grapefruit juice.

Next was the director of a small group that ran natural-family-planning programs in rural Texas. Pearl Hanson was a Texas conservative, practical and stubborn. Despite limited tools and her brash ways, her program had raised awareness about the economic benefits of small families. The link between wealth and family planning prompted even devout women to pursue methods of contraception on their own. Pearl understood and didn't cast blame.

She was ambitious, seeking to leapfrog national expansion by expanding the program to developing nations, starting with Afghanistan. She was eager to work with Islamist groups. One of her goals was to change attitudes in Islamic nations about long-term guardianships for children.

"Not adoption?" Lydia asked.

Hanson shook her head. "Islamic family law does not allow adoption there. There are provisions for guardianship, but many children are treated poorly and forced to work." She went on to suggest the need for regulating guardianships—while convincing Afghans to think the plans were their idea all the while.

"It would be like adoption with more regulation," Hanson explained. She hoped to run a pilot study, encouraging the value of smaller families, increasing appreciation of unwanted children, and involving men in family planning.

The board typically valued programs that aimed for big social change, and Lydia, ever on the lookout for the possibility of new details about her son's death, preferred programs that put people on the ground in Afghanistan and India. She asked Hanson the usual questions and liked the answers. "Your next step is finding local Afghan partners."

The tall woman was worried and pointed out how few shared her group's approach.

"Better to find a group not at all like yours." Lydia explained how GlobalConnect tended to fund innovative programs, and diverse teams produced more innovation. GlobalConnect went one step further, forcing opposite groups to work together. To attract funding, the groups had to resist polarization and hate. This meant approaching men on women's rights, collecting the opinions of elders on education for children, finding small businesses that protected the environment, and encouraging environmental groups to support business startups. The process was time-consuming, but it produced sustainable results.

"It's why your proposal stood out," Lydia noted.

She promised Pearl that GlobalConnect could help with contacts in Afghanistan. Hanson leaned forward and interrupted, asking to meet Paul Reichart. "He's a legend among the aid groups in Afghanistan."

Typically grant applicants praised her son's foresight. Few mentioned staff members like Paul. Lydia straightened the hair clip and asked what the woman knew about Paul.

Pearl hurried on about developing close ties to small villages, delivering supplies, organizing health groups. "He developed quite the network among villages. The leaders trust him." She then talked about a particular village, how more than one organization referred to Laashekoh as a role model for managing relationships. "It's a small village, but Paul Reichart worked magic in Laashekoh."

GlobalConnect staff members were not supposed to take credit for program successes. The policy directed that all focus remain on grant recipients. Annie did not trust self-evaluations from staff, and any boasting could jeopardize Paul's position at GlobalConnect. Lydia advised Pearl to seek an Islamic group as a partner. "That will strengthen your application."

An assistant hovered nearby. Pearl Hanson thanked Lydia and vowed to do whatever was necessary to contribute to the GlobalConnect mission.

Lydia then asked to borrow another assistant's cell phone to call Henry. He was a member of the GlobalConnect board, but Lydia still regarded him as her son's attorney. He answered after the first ring. "Nice to know I'm needed."

"Always." She asked him to pull research on a village named Laashekoh and Paul's activities. "But don't tell Paul."

"For a specific grant?"

"Pending," she said.

"Historical or current?"

"Since Michael's death."

He went silent. "What did you hear?" She relayed the scrap of information.

Henry warned her that information on a remote village in a country of thirty million people would be limited.

It was her turn for silence and a reminder that she would never give up on finding out why Michael had died.

CHAPTER 2

Parsaa slipped out of bed and donned extra layers of clothes. The family kept their shoes by the doorway in specific order, and he needed no light to retrieve his. He opened the door slowly, trying not to disturb his family.

Daybreak was hours away. Sleep was elusive. As soon as he stepped outdoors, he thought about returning to his wife's side and wrapping his arms around her, wishing for sleep to arrive and waiting for worries he could not always identify to vanish. Family, home, faith, the natural world—a man should want no more.

Long ago he had recited familiar prayers to fight the thoughts darting through his head, but over the years he felt less comfortable using passages from the Koran for that selfish purpose. Instead, when sleep failed and weather allowed, he walked the familiar path outlining the perimeter of the village to order his thoughts. He relished how some parts of the village never changed—the curving path underneath his feet, the soft rattle of branches and scurrying noises of mice, the silhouettes of mountains that blocked the strongest winds from the northwest. But time also marked patterns. Shadows of trees lengthened, rocks tumbled away from the walls surrounding the village, and the stars shifted ever westward in the sky over Laashekoh.

The sound of his footsteps, however soft, should have alerted a sentry on duty near the road leading to the village, but a string of days with no fighting or visitors had made the village complacent. Parsaa and the other leaders should have scolded older boys for building a temporary shelter of mud and branches for protection against rain or snow. The sentry was probably sleeping inside. Parsaa would remind Ahmed in the morning to speak to the boys.

In truth, Parsaa, didn't mind being alone with his thoughts. The darkness masked constant reminders that his eyesight was less keen than it had been only a few years earlier.

For a long time, Parsaa had denied his difficulties with seeing. The deficit was gradual, and he did not tell others. With four sons, he had no need to hunt and no one noticed that his aim was off for shooting. And he could still read the Koran to his sons at night. His family made no comment one night when he repositioned the lantern, aiming light directly to the page. They knew he had committed the words to memory, but not that he used the light to test his sight. No matter how much he blinked and tried to focus, a fog covered the words. Increasingly, he asked a son to take over reading, and Parsaa worried about the day when the swirls and waves of letters lost their meaning.

He envied the vigor of his offspring. His father and the other men of the village must have once felt the same. Yet they never spoke of such feelings, and neither would he.

Stone walls twisted around the village, and Parsaa walked the outer edge until he reached an open section looking out over folds of mountains and a large valley. The isolated village rested on a plateau, with tiers etched into the mountainside. Fruit trees surrounded the village, and beyond were fields for grain and vegetable crops. Multiple springs fed a small river nearby that in turn rushed into the large river below. The moon waited behind a mass of clouds. The mountains, even those tall enough to catch the earliest of snows, blended with the night sky. As he stood at the village's edge, the rest of the world seemed at once distant and close. He stared into the soft black distance and was pleased to detect the gray strip of the river, perhaps because glare from the moon and stars did not interfere. He wondered if his sons could detect the individual clouds passing overhead.

He was not ready to ask such questions. Those who could not see were forced to trust the descriptions of others.

The cool night air signaled winter's approach. Except for the sleeping sentry, Parsaa could count on being alone. He pulled a wool shawl tight to his chest and sat on the stone wall to wait for the clouds to tumble past the moon. Alone, he found it easier to focus. He enjoyed training his mind on a task that needed to be completed the next day, allowing a vision to unfold moment by moment. The habit relaxed him.

His eyes stared into the night, but his mind was intent on a burst of gold afternoon sun and thoughts of slashing at the last of the winter wheat. He imagined his younger sons helping stack and secure the piles while pelting him with questions. Parsaa smiled. The youngest boys assumed that parents possessed all the world's answers, while Saddiq, the oldest, posed questions that often could not be answered.

Saddiq was old enough to leave for the school his older brother never had a chance to attend. Parsaa's oldest son had died the previous year, and the parents agreed to a brief delay for the next son. In the meantime, his mother, Sofi, tried to convince the boy to prepare and try reading on his own.

Saddiq was stubborn and insisted that school was for children. He saw no need for lessons and asked his parents why he couldn't stay at home and work in the village fields instead. Sofi was upset, but Parsaa refused to worry. Such fear was natural.

"If you scold him, he will resent reading," Parsaa had warned his wife many times. "He worries about leaving home, too. And if he sees the younger ones reading and using these skills at the market . . ." The man shrugged. "Then he will want to catch up." The boys would be adults soon enough and had to learn to make decisions for themselves.

In the meantime, Parsaa kept Saddiq busy with unpleasant tasks the older men did not want to do. Even on rainy days, the boy worked at tasks. The work in the fields was nearing an end, but as winter approached, the village could always use more wood. Saddiq willingly set out from the village, looking for fallen trees, chopping and dragging wood while his brothers sat by a warm fire and listened to Sofi read stories.

The family read together after dinner, and the younger boys giggled when Saddiq struggled or missed a word.

"The younger boys are doing well, and Saddiq pretends not to notice," Sofi said. "His bad habits will take control."

She pressed when Parsaa did not answer. "How long will you let him stay away from school?"

"Until he is ready to go without being forced." He ordered his wife not to complain or compare the boy with the younger children. "Force yourself not to care, and he will start to care for himself." Parsaa could only hope he was right, though he did not understand the reasoning from a boy who was normally so curious.

The moon teased, glowing silver behind a moving cloud, before vanishing again. That's when a bouncing light in the valley below caught his eye. Parsaa stood, comparing the light's movement in relationship to the river.

The light moved away from Laashekoh and toward a hidden canyon.

Far from the road, the canyon was deceptively narrow before widening into a dead-end. The eastern side had two entrances. One was a narrow road, supposed to be under watch by Laashekoh's sentries and mostly unused, except for old trucks delivering supplies every few months. Two men were required. The driver steered while the other walked ahead, shouting directions on intricate turns to avoid wedging the vehicle between the canyon walls. The road continued toward a lush field, and waiting at the very end was a small compound surrounded by trees and sheer cliffs.

The second access was a treacherous path beginning along the canyon's edge and descending diagonally to the canyon floor and the family compound.

The compound's setting had been selected for the purpose of defense. One man could keep watch over the narrow entrance and easily pick off intruders. The compound's caretaker deliberately encouraged thick brush near both entrances, and a stranger would not accidentally stumble upon either one. Travelers had to know about a special detour and then backtrack along a rocky stretch. Few locals, even in Laashekoh, knew much about the compound at the end of the canyon.

Parsaa worried the light might not be real, and he blinked several times. The light still dipped up and down with the curves of the land-

scape—an individual carrying a strong, battery-powered torch and not
a lantern bouncing with a wagon. The canyon road was an hour away by
foot, and he could only imagine the sound of trudging footsteps along
the rocky path.

Visitors to the compound were rare. The owners, a married couple
without children, were self-absorbed eccentrics. The caretaker and his
wife fretted over security, more because of their advancing age rather
than because of real dangers. The occupants had little to do with neighboring villages, and Parsaa assisted the small and ornery group with
security.

Parsaa studied the light until it moved out of sight and wondered
about a woman who had been his closest friend in childhood and why
a traveler headed to the compound so late at night.

~~~~~~

The late crop of wheat took on a golden glow in the morning light,
ready for harvest, and the wind pushed at the strands in gentle waves.
The men of Laashekoh scattered throughout the small field to cut the
stalks away. The young boys followed in the men's footsteps, gathering
and tying the strands into bundles before moving them into storage.

The field was large enough to provide the village with bread for
the winter, but some villagers wanted to expand the boundaries. Parsaa
reluctantly agreed, though he worried about the vagaries of weather
and human nature. The villagers could invest long hours in the new
field, and a sudden windstorm or drought would destroy a large harvest
overnight.

The small field had thrived under the attention of many. More
wheat to sell, more money for the village, would mean less attention
for the crops.

The field was edged by rocks and bramble bushes, and as Parsaa
approached, a gray *sar-khorak* trilled before going quiet. The bird
waited patiently for the humans to disturb the creatures that dug holes
throughout the field and stole grain. Parsaa did not let up swinging the

scythe, carving gentle arcs into the field, the wheat falling in line on either side, while keeping his eyes on the shrike. Suddenly, the bird dove into a nearby section of uncut wheat and emerged with a plump mouse. Clamping its beak tight, the shrike returned to the edge area. Once there, the bird took careful aim and impaled the mouse against a long thorn. Stepping back, the shrike leisurely pecked at its writhing meal.

With every swing of the blade, Parsaa was a co-conspirator. He tried to focus on etching crescent patterns onto the field, rather than disrupting routines and driving small creatures to their death.

Someone shouted his name from the other side of the field long before the midday meal. A few women waved their arms, signaling the men to return to the village center. Other men had already hurried away from the field.

A moan from the east turned into a growl and then a roaring chopping noise. A helicopter approached, its blades beating the air. Parsaa stared upward as the machine circled overhead, sweeping dangerously close to the village and kicking up stinging dust. Women and men held on to head covers. The machine backed away and tried another pass over Laashekoh before slowing and dropping out of sight to land in the river valley below.

The children of Laashekoh waited near the stone wall, leaping, waving, and pointing below. Ahmed shouted for his wife to prepare hot water for tea.

Parsaa glanced back at the shrub, where part of the mouse still dangled. The bird had abandoned its meal, hiding in a nearby tree and waiting for the noise to end. Predators could become prey, too.

The villagers had hoped to complete the harvest before sunset, and Parsaa regretted walking away from the field. His clothes were covered with dust and bits of stalk, and his skin itched. His wife hurried to his side, handing over a damp rag, and together they walked to the wall.

"Are the Americans returning?" Sofi asked.

Wiping the grit from his face, he shook his head. "Not the soldiers. This helicopter is too small, and they would not have flown over the village."

She looked disappointed and he teased her. "They will climb the hill like everyone else, and you'll know soon enough who they are."

And what they want from us, he thought to himself.

~~~~~

Two foreign women with loose headscarves stepped through the village gate, followed by a nervous young man. The three carried backpacks and panted from the climb. The tall, older woman led the group. Curls escaped her headscarf and framed a face lined with what must have been years of work in the sun.

The other woman, stout and soaked in sweat despite the cool air, dropped her pack to the ground and sat on a mat by the fire. She pulled at her *perahaan* to keep it from sticking to her skin. A child handed over a mug with water, and the woman drank without pause.

The older woman smiled at the circle of villagers. She crouched down to open one pack and extracted a small, fluffy toy. She offered the animal to the nearest child, but the little girl backed away. The woman pulled out another animal, cradling one in each hand. The youngest children stared at Parsaa, expecting a decision, and he directed Ahmed to examine the creatures.

Typically, visitors checked with parents before distributing gifts, and Parsaa wondered how long the group had been in Afghanistan.

Ahmed held a toy up, laughing. He asked if it was a dog or monkey.

"Not any stuffed dog!" At last, the younger woman caught her breath and used Dari. "Gund Boo—and all are brand-new." She explained that there should be enough gifts for all the village children.

"Boo!" the older woman shouted. Curious children huddled around the woman while the older boys stood back with the men.

Parsaa didn't understand most of what she said, and not because the woman's Dari was rough. Ahmed's wife snapped orders. The children could accept the gifts, she directed, but must wait and follow the visitor's instructions. Then she added sternly, "Only children whose parents are here and approve."

Village parents typically did not mind strangers distributing a few sweets or toys. Such occasions were rare, and the boundaries were clear. Children could not expect their parents to provide similar gifts. But these gifts were more for the visitors' pleasure. The tall one beamed, moving about like a nervous songbird, pushing her hair underneath the headscarf and rubbing the skin along her neck and near her eyes. Her *perahaan* was stiff, probably new, and instead of traditional pants, she wore jeans that were increasingly available in the markets. The clothes made scratching noises with every move.

He had heard about such women, impatient and sure, unaccustomed to hearing no.

The woman plucked the animals from the pack and held them out high before handing them over. Suddenly, the man aimed a cell phone at the group.

"*Ne!*" Ahmed rushed forward to block a photograph.

The villagers had agreed long ago. They did not want images of their children leaving the village.

His companion, the tall woman, shouted in anger, and the young man dropped his arm. She confiscated the phone, tapping buttons before placing it in her pocket. The younger woman apologized. "He should not have tried taking a photograph without asking permission."

The older woman pointed to the gate, and the man left the village without a word. Only then, the women introduced themselves, but the names did not register for Parsaa. He did not ask the women to repeat the muddle of harsh English vowels that sounded like noises made by insects during a hot summer night. Instead he thought of the two as *Bacha* and *Pir*, young and old.

The women explained that they ran an orphanage, but Bacha's tone was strange, almost gleeful. "We are based in Kabul, and do not distribute used or old goods." She shouted as if trying to convince the whole village. "We love children and are here to help them!"

She suggested the region was a troubled place, but that Laashekoh could help nearby villages and even cities. Parsaa tried to follow the conversation, but the children were rowdy—the boys tossing the animals about like balls, the girls giggling as they rubbed the fur against their cheeks.

Bacha used the end of her head cover to wipe her brow and spoke in slow Dari. "We work with an organization in Kabul. Hope for Children. And we can help you."

Typically, Parsaa waited and listened. But he had to correct her swiftly. Otherwise, the women would press on with whatever plans they had for Laashekoh. The strangers were too brash, and that was not good for the village children to see.

He held his hand up. "But we don't need help."

The woman rushed to speak. "But we have read about your village. We heard about children in need of our care."

Parsaa was firm. "You are thinking of another village. For now, we drink tea and do not discuss such matters in front of our children."

A group of children delivered hot water and tea leaves, a tray with cups, warm bread, sliced apples, and goat's milk. One of the girls was Thara, whose parents no longer lived in the village. She lived with Ahmed and Karimah, who cared for her. Like other children in Laashekoh, the girl was well fed.

The village needed no help from outsiders. Surely, the strangers would lose interest and leave Laashekoh alone.

The visitors whispered among themselves and accepted plates of food. The women reached for the milk. Bacha took gulps, and Pir made a comment, followed by a laugh. Parsaa worried that the milk was sour and tried some. The milk tasted fine.

Pir drained her cup and asked for more. Ahmed poured and politely asked where the women were from. Bacha answered at once: "America."

Pir spoke up. "Tex-is." Bacha repeated the word slowly, "Tex-is." She asked if the villagers had heard of the place.

Ahmed shook his head, and Pir chided her partner. Bacha quickly chewed her naan and swallowed. "Can the women join us, too?"

Parsaa and Ahmed were not surprised, and Ahmed immediately waved for the wives to join the gathering. Before leaving, American soldiers once stationed in a nearby outpost had warned the village to expect more foreign visitors.

"Charity workers will travel all over Afghanistan and soon find Laashekoh," the soldier had confided. "Most aid workers mean well and will abide by your wishes. But others . . ." His voice had drifted off, as if he did not know how to explain.

Parsaa had found it difficult to believe that people thousands of miles away wanted to donate money for a village they had never seen.

"Some work outside the cities to avoid the government inspections," the soldier had explained. "They collect money and take advantage of generous hearts, but use the larger share for their own benefit. They talk about need in Afghanistan to collect more funds and keep their own jobs. Others are looking for adventure, fame . . ."

The soldier was firm, warning Parsaa to check the offers closely. "Do not sign documents that you do not understand."

The soldier had also advised that such encounters would go more smoothly if the men included village women in the meetings. "Especially if the visitors are women," he added. "I understand it's not your way, but including more villagers can discourage the most persistent. Women have little choice but to accept the answers of other women."

The two women were more controlling than the soldier had described, and Parsaa hoped that the American soldier was right. Karimah chased the children away from the meeting, still muttering about how the gifts should have been left near the gate.

The two visitors smiled, and yet they had a way of passing their gaze over the wives as if the women couldn't possibly make decisions. Pir and Bacha knew who was in charge and kept their eyes on Parsaa. In turn, Parsaa studied Pir.

American women were used to getting their way. Parsaa didn't know what the two wanted, but he was patient.

The story slowly unwound. Bacha explained that they had heard news reports about a group of traffickers intercepted nearby while transporting children from small Afghan villages to Pakistan. "We offer rewards for villages that turn over children in need of care," she said. "We take them off your hands and provide them with a safe home."

Parsaa put his cup down and expressed his regret that the women had traveled so far on a misunderstanding. The village had already handled the matter. "We returned the children to their families. The American soldiers helped." The visitors need not know that a few children without parents remained in the village.

Bacha's shoulders slumped with disappointment. "A shame."

"Not at all." Parsaa kept his voice stern. "The children have parents, brothers, aunts and uncles, communities."

The two women murmured. The exchange sounded like arguing. Quickly, Bacha switched back to Dari. "Do you think more children will pass through here?"

"We hope not," Parsaa replied. "Children belong in their villages with families."

Bacha rushed to talk about family planning, supporting children in need of homes, finding guardians and working with a sharia family court that reviewed all placements. Then she raised her voice, an effort to make Parsaa understand. Or perhaps she wanted the entire village to hear. "We agree with you. Though sometimes parents cannot care for their children, and some children are happier in an orphanage. There are benefits you cannot imagine! And we offer generous rewards. Finder fees." She asked if the village wanted to partner with the group.

Once again, Parsaa remembered advice from the soldier. End tiresome visits with the briefest of responses. Sign no documents. He simply offered more tea and milk.

"My friend worries about children trapped in unhappy places, neglected and unwanted," Bacha said.

"That is not the case here." The women of Laashekoh nodded.

Pir offered a comment in English and kept her eyes on Parsaa. Then she pointed to the river and Bacha translated. "No one in sight for as far as the eye can see. My friend says she feels as if she fell into a painting."

The two women pressed on with questions for the village women. Karimah and Sofi followed Parsaa's lead and kept their answers short.

Then the visitors asked about the history of Laashekoh. Parsaa didn't want to answer the question in front of other villagers. He was the only one in the village who understood the entanglements and promises made over the years, and he waved his hand to dismiss the question.

Bacha pressed, asking about property ownership, whether Laashekoh was owned as a collective or by individual families. Parsaa was vague. "The village settled with the permission of a tribal chief."

"But the agreement was with you, Parsaa? Before 1995?"

"A village is not about one man," he said softly. Questions about the land in Laashekoh made him nervous. The woman already seemed to know the answers though none of the villagers, even his wife, knew of the true arrangements.

Bacha continued posing questions as Pir stood, pacing back and forth, gazing toward the river and mountains.

"My friend likes you very much, and our organization would like to help this village. We receive many donations, and a major donor has taken notice of our work." She paused, as if realizing the explanation might be too much, too fast. "We could do more. So many families were displaced by the war—especially children."

"We have been fortunate," Parsaa said. "Allah willing." He wanted the questions to stop, but he also wanted the women to understand. Laashekoh did not need help.

"We are in need of local partners. You could help us, and we would pay you. The donors want Afghans involved in the decision making." She reached inside her pack and extracted papers. Forms for a partnership. "All you need to do is sign. We would handle most matters in the city. We would run ideas by you. Or, not bother you much at all."

Parsaa shook his head. The village would not sign the forms. "Orphans are a family responsibility. Aunts and uncles in the village provide care and spiritual guidance."

Another sharp question came from Pir, the older woman. Bacha spoke more gently, asking if the village had help returning the children from the trafficking operation. He told her about the soldiers at the outpost, and she asked about Paul Reichart, an aid worker.

"He's from GlobalConnect," Bacha said flatly. She asked if Paul had handled property matters for the children or village.

"He helped return children to their families." Parsaa was curt and hid his puzzlement. "There was no property."

She pleaded with him, explaining her group had access to funding, too. "Has Paul told you how much money is available for villages like yours?"

Parsaa pointed out that the villagers did not discuss money with Paul. Bacha glanced at her colleague and spoke softly. Then she shook her head. "You are making a mistake."

"It should not be easy for Afghan families to give up their children." Parsaa stood and asked if the women worked with Paul.

"Not yet," Bacha said, adding that they were trying to arrange a meeting with him. He was supposed to provide contacts. "But he doesn't want others working in this area." In the meantime, the women were assisting children of women serving prison sentences. "One of the women is from Laashekoh," she added. "Leila?"

At hearing the name, the other villagers were no longer restless and listened closely. Sofi, his wife, made a small choking noise, and leaned against Karimah. Leila, the daughter of his dearest and lifelong friend who had since died. Her delayed marriage had disrupted the village. A woman whose beauty was destroyed overnight with an acid attack even as her marriage contract was under negotiation. She, along with her parents and husband, had helped organize a trafficking ring, shipping children to Pakistan.

Leila had also shoved his oldest son off a cliff the night before Ali was supposed to leave for school.

Parsaa didn't stop the woman, though he didn't want to listen.

"She has an attorney who advises her, and they have welcomed our support. Leila's attorney advised us that there were too many girls here for a small village to handle."

The woman referred to "girls," not Leila's sisters who were being raised by village families. A relief. Sofi would be panicked about losing Komal, the youngest of the sisters. But Leila had already been convicted and was in prison. She had no claim and couldn't know how the villagers felt about her sisters. Parsaa didn't understand her need for an attorney. He wanted to shout, explain how Leila deserved no assistance or comfort, but instead he moved close to Bacha and kept his voice low. Only Ahmed, Sofi, and Karimah could hear. "Have you spoken with Leila?"

Bacha was eager and did not wait for Pir. "Do you know her? We are not allowed near her. Not yet. Her attorney describes her as a hero. She was trying to rescue the children and give them a better future."

"You cannot believe all that you hear." Parsaa's laugh was harsh. "Her attorney should look into her other crimes."

"Many donors want to help her." Bacha looked around. "They would help here, too, but only if you let them."

Laashekoh would have nothing to do with groups that supported Leila, and Parsaa offered a warning. "Leila is young, but she is treacherous. The attorney, anyone else who deals with her, should be careful."

Pir's pale eyes sharpened as Bacha translated. "My friend claims you don't want the children hearing us talk about Leila," Bacha said. "Do others in the village feel the same about her?"

Karimah spoke up. "If anything, he is too kind. She is evil, and we do not speak her name."

The visitors were stubborn. "Villages often find it too easy to blame a young woman," Bacha said. "Refusing to talk buries truth."

Parsaa leaned in close. "The American soldiers investigated and that is why she is in prison. You can check on this."

"But the Americans are not here anymore, are they? We heard her story and only wanted to help the girls she described."

"She did not tell you her entire story," Parsaa retorted.

"Perhaps men are too impatient to listen."

He was weary of twisting words back and forth and refused to prove her point with harsh words. The best response for fools was silence. The conversation stalled, and Parsaa explained that he needed to return to harvesting wheat. Bacha asked if the village would sell them vegetables. She explained the orphanage's policy—to rely on Afghans for as many supplies as possible. "We pay well," she added.

Ahmed offered carrots, cauliflower, potatoes, and other root crops and asked how many crates they needed.

"The pilot always worries about overloading the helicopter." Bacha sighed. "And we have one more stop nearby before returning to the city."

The helicopter had an empty seat, and it was decided that three crates of vegetables could safely fill the empty space. Older boys ran to fill the crates before showing them to the women. Letting loose a happy noise, Pir pulled a sweet potato from a pile and tucked it into her bag.

"Her dinner tonight!" Bacha announced. Parsaa and Ahmed, followed by boys lugging the crates, accompanied the women to the waiting helicopter. As the group approached, the young pilot, the man who had attempted to take pictures, looked upset by the additional load. He did not argue, though, and stacked the crates on the one empty seat, binding them in place with thick straps.

The women then thanked the village men and children, exchanging farewells as if all were close friends. The engine roared, and the helicopter lifted, hesitated, and then banked toward the north with a chugging roar.

Ahmed bantered with the boys as they climbed the hill. Once the village gate was in sight, the boys raced ahead. "I hope the women don't return," the younger man said.

Parsaa agreed but offered no other comment. His goals had once seemed so simple, so reasonable—providing for his family with a comfortable home and harvests, encouraging others in the village to do the same, while keeping Laashekoh secure. For too many, home, food, and safety no longer offered enough.

There would be more visitors, and he wondered, how long would Laashekoh say no? He often sensed that others, even his own wife and children, wanted more. The worst part was that deep inside he yearned for more, too. Not more money or success with farming. Not more friends or another woman.

Perhaps it was less change. Or at least, the power of knowing what the future held.

He shook his head. He was not old enough for such vague fears. Like the steady shift of the sun, the water pouring down the mountainside, the lines on a human face, nothing on earth had real permanence. Parsaa kept his worries to himself. No need to worry Ahmed. Strangers would pass through the village quickly, spreading ideas like dust whipped by the swirling helicopter blades.

CHAPTER 3

Only two people knew who owned the property surrounding Laashekoh.

Parsaa had an urge to talk with Zahira, a friend since childhood, and tell her about the visitors. Her home at the canyon's end was centered amid the stretches of land owned by Laashekoh. Her father had been one of the region's fiercest warlords, cultivating a reputation for ruthlessness and swift justice. The man was brutal but knew how to apply a kind word for lasting influence. Blacker built his militia by offering protection to the most desperate of refugees, families who longed for homes and safety. He had invited groups of refugees, including Parsaa's father, to build small villages and farm the best land. Blacker allowed villagers to keep most of their harvests, and in exchange, the families raised their sons to train in his militia and respond to any command from the man.

It was a small price to pay. The sense of permanency and security was priceless.

But Blacker was long dead. His militia disbanded, many of the lieutenants had scattered, looking for new battles with foreign fighters. Zahira, his only child, remained at the compound after a life of contradictions. Her father claimed to fight for Afghan traditions, but he surrounded his daughter with western comforts. She had left Afghanistan to study medicine, but she saw few patients and lived as a hermit. The warlord who expected unquestioning obedience from his deputies had cherished his daughter as an adviser, treating her as equal.

Happiness eluded her because Zahira had always wanted more. Parsaa had known her father well and regretted that the old memories were not part of their friendship.

The walk along the river and the descent into the canyon took about two hours. Parsaa paused at the compound's edge. He wanted to speak with Zahira alone and would not approach the house until he was sure that her husband was inside his workshop at the far end of the compound.

The compound had about twenty buildings, most in disrepair. Only a few lights gleamed from the main house, though Zahira's husband, Arhaan, could be anywhere. The blind man had no use for light. Others could not be sure if he was working or prowling the grounds.

Over the years, Arhaan spent more time in his workshop, one wall of which was lined with cages for his mynas. The man ate and slept there and devoted the rest of his hours to studying the birds, taking each for long walks, and training them to converse. The mynas studied the man and every twitch of his mouth.

Parsaa was grateful to arrive at night and not see the overgrown fields, the faded carvings, walls in need of patching, and other reminders of how time and weather wore at the compound.

The place was quiet except for a plaintive mewing. A cat with a swollen belly waited outside the main house. The door opened and the desperate creature stumbled inside.

Parsaa waited, listening for sounds of the blind husband. Once, Parsaa had envied Arhaan and regretted his own marriage, arranged when he was a child, but only for a short while. Over the years, he had come to appreciate his parents' wisdom. Parsaa was not so foolish to talk about such feelings with one woman or the other. The tightest connection for families was loyalty. His relationship with his wife was better for not talking much about the meetings with Zahira.

If anything, the years and secrets had strained the friendship with Zahira. He was content with his life and marriage, and she was not.

~~~~~

After sundown, Zahira let the mother cat inside. Ready to give birth, the old yellow cat headed for a worn blanket in a dark corner to wait out the contractions alone. One by one, four kittens slipped out into the world. Zahira tried reading by the fire, but the cries made it hard to concentrate. Ignoring glares from the anxious mother, Zahira approached the blanket to watch the activity. As expected, the first kitten was toughest, and each one born afterward was smaller and weaker than its predecessor.

Zahira kept the cat to irritate her husband, and she would keep the yellow kittens, too.

The mother cat was spent after giving birth but had enough energy to twist away from the desperate pink mouths of her two smallest kittens. Impatient with their ineptitude, she blocked them from getting near her belly. One squirming kitten squealed with fear.

The cat was livid about another creature witnessing the indignities associated with giving birth. Zahira had seen such hostility from women before. Crouching, Zahira slowly reached for the unwanted offspring, gently placing them closer to the swollen teats. Irritated, the mother swatted at Zahira's hand, and the firstborn kitten moved on to another teat, filling its stomach and ignoring mews from the neglected pair. Zahira tried again—one managed to get a taste, enough to know what it was missing—and the provoked mother hissed.

Zahira chided the old cat and rearranged the kittens. "It's up to you," she said, then hurried to her bedroom. There, she checked the baby girl, who was sleeping in a basket, before climbing into her own bed nearby.

Moments later, a slight tap came from outside—a sound she had not heard in months. Her stomach turned and she wondered if her ears played tricks. Then another pebble struck the outer wall. Zahira called Aza, more like an aunt than a house servant, from another part of the house, and Zahira pointed to the basket. "He must not know about the child," she whispered. "Keep her quiet until I return."

Zahira snatched an oversized wool scarf, wrapping it tightly around her head and shoulders, before heading to the outer room and opening the door.

And there was Parsaa. They had not talked alone in months, and she held his stare. "I need your advice," he whispered.

She stepped aside and let him enter. A tiny mew interrupted, and Parsaa approached the blanket. The mother cat was alert with two kittens nestled between her legs. The other two had moved away from the blanket. One was still and the other crawled helplessly along the edge.

"I already tried." Zahira spoke up. "She won't accept them."

Of course, he took that as a challenge, kneeling to poke the rejected kitten. Then he held the back of the mother cat's neck and pinched her teat. The cat flattened her ears and opened her mouth with a long hiss. But Parsaa pinched again, before rubbing his damp fingers against the kitten's mouth and guiding it into position. The frantic kitten latched on with aggressive new hope.

The weary cat glared but did not roll away. Zahira didn't like being wrong. Not with him. "She may still refuse the kitten later. We should not intervene."

Parsaa stood. "We must talk. Two foreign women came to the village today."

She put her finger to her mouth. "You are sure Arhaan did not hear you?"

Worry was contagious. Parsaa looked guilty, explaining how he had spoken with Mohan, the caretaker and Aza's husband. "He will signal if Arhaan steps away from the workshop."

Still she worried. Her husband had ways of sensing what she did not want him to hear, and Mohan and Aza did not like her meeting with other men in the house. She waved her hand for Parsaa to leave the house and wait by the clinic door. Then she circled the perimeter of the home, checking whether her husband or others lurked and listened nearby.

Parsaa was foolish to trust Mohan, who had lived more than seven decades. Arhaan knew the compound well. His hearing was keen enough to hear another man breathing. The compound was small, yet she and her husband lived in separate worlds. She had once admired his academic pursuits, but the work had become so narrow and strange over the years. The two no longer understood each other.

As she turned the corner toward the clinic, she studied the dark workshop where Arhaan spent most of his hours. At night, her husband had every advantage over her.

Zahira unlocked the clinic doorway with the only key, careful about cupping her hands around the lock to muffle the clicking noise. She held the door open and Parsaa emerged from the shadows. Once inside, she turned the deadbolt, switched on the desk lamp, and crossed her arms. He waited by the door, uncomfortable in the modern structure with its tile floor, stainless surfaces, and shiny cabinets.

There was no place like the clinic within a day's walk, yet most villagers resisted seeking care from Zahira. She heard what they said about her. She was eccentric and, if she were so skilled, they wondered, why did she remain in the remote area? Those with the best skills should not return home, or so the myth went. Then there were the rumors about abortions, though Parsaa had never spoken about those with her.

"Our meetings upset Mohan and Aza," Zahira said. "It doesn't matter how long we have known each other." She glanced back at him. He was sheepish or impatient, but it didn't matter. Parsaa only visited when he needed something from her. Foreigners visited, and he wanted advice. A child fell ill, and he asked for medicine. He purchased ammunition, and then arranged for secret shipments to her compound. He had questions and asked her to check the computer.

She could not admit it out loud, but Zahira missed her father. He knew how to control others. Unfortunately, Blacker had trusted Parsaa more than he did his own daughter. Parsaa owed his livelihood, his home, his comfortable existence to Blacker. And all that was based on her assessment of a man's loyalty years ago.

Parsaa was no longer a loyal friend. He wasn't disloyal, but such was the problem of old friendships—memories softened by age were cherished more than recent encounters.

She pointedly asked how long it had been since his last visit, though she knew exactly the number of weeks. Parsaa ignored her question. "Did two foreign women stop here today?" he asked. "Did you see the helicopter?"

She shook her head quickly.

"They are from an orphanage and are looking for children."

"So why would they come here?" she snapped.

"They mentioned a nearby stop." He leaned over the counter. "I thought you could check on them with the computer."

"The computer," she said bitterly. She did not hurry to turn on the machine, run by a special terminal and equipment purchased with funds from a foreign charity. Parsaa often asked Zahira to look up news about the government, fighting, the weather. He was curious about everything but her. During his last visit, she had coolly reminded him that he could afford similar equipment, but he dismissed that notion. He was hypocritical, seeking access to the modern world while denying it for the rest of the village.

The argument had kept him away for months. She didn't want to argue again.

Zahira tried to assure him. "If you told them there are no orphans, they will leave quickly. Women around here do not hand their infants over to strangers!"

But Parsaa suspected the women wanted something other than children. "They have read about Laashekoh on the Internet. I need to know what has been said and remove any mentions of the village."

Zahira felt sorry for him and told him that what he asked was impossible. "Sometimes you can pull down what you have said, but not what others have said about a village." She asked where the women were from, and he told her a place named Texas in the United States.

She grimaced. "They are probably Christians. They think they can control the destiny of our souls."

He asked how they could know so much about the area, and she was impatient, pointing out the same way he read stories about other parts of the world. "An outpost with nearly a hundred people was stationed nearby. Who knows what any of them have said about the village online?"

Laashekoh had no cell phones, no computers, and Parsaa still assumed that he could restrict the information's flow to one direction.

"Did they ask about me or the clinic?" To avoid eye contact, she started the computer.

He shook his head, and she dismissed his worries. "They came and you sent them away."

"They had questions about the land, who owns it and when the transaction took place. I thought they might question you and Arhaan."

She typed search terms before showing him photos of adults and Afghan children. "Would you recognize them?"

He shook his head, and she tried more phrases. "No," he said.

She pointed out the government continued to sort out quarrels over land transactions that took place between 1996 and 2001, when the Taliban were in control. "That is not our transaction. Besides, we have a proper deed, and we have had no quarrels about ownership."

"So there should be no questions for Laashekoh about the land?"

He had always cared more about the village than he did about her. She was but an extension of Laashekoh. "No," Zahira said wearily. "The property deed is valid. The exchange was registered in 1990."

"Is that enough?" he pressed.

"For you," she retorted, and then she quickly controlled herself. The time was not right for her to press a claim. Others in Laashekoh had no idea who really owned the surrounding land.

She stood and let him sit before the computer. "Parsaa, all these years and you do not feel secure. No level of security is enough if someone wants what belongs to another."

His long fingers jabbed at the keyboard with its overlay for Dari, and he asked for reminders because he used the computer so irregularly. How to search, how to use Google Translate, how to navigate among the pages. He was intent on knowing what was said about Laashekoh and did not notice her reticence.

Zahira felt foolish for how much she had once longed for Parsaa. The match had seemed so logical when she convinced her father to delay her marriage arrangements.

~~~~~~

Blacker had one child and explained to his lieutenants that the strategy was to avoid making a compact and eliminating opportunities for an alliance. The marriage plans would not be finalized until she neared completion of her medical degree. Besides, Blacker wanted his daughter to be happy. Plenty of suitors were willing to wait for the prize—not Blacker's demanding daughter but rather the land and militia.

Afghanistan's political future was unclear. The ability of warlords to control a territory and its governance was slipping away. Larger forces could change the country overnight. But that was true in other lands, too. Blacker was torn between hoping his only daughter would live near the compound or leave the country for her safety, hoping she married a strong man who kept her in line or a weak man who welcomed her control. A young woman with no husband, brothers, uncles, or sons was vulnerable and could not control large tracts of land. No woman could oversee the militia Blacker had developed over the years.

Blacker wanted to extend his control far into the future, preserving the land for his daughter and her children. The husband didn't matter. Before approving a marriage, Blacker needed a better sense of where the country was headed. Many Afghans resented those who had cooperated with the Russians. The clerics prayed and griped, blaming arrogant and loose women for the fast-changing world beyond Afghanistan's borders.

It was no secret that Zahira had studied in Russia. Blacker dismissed criticism, noting that women had no interest in politics.

But his daughter was intelligent, raised by a man who rejected religious superstition and laws based on such nonsense. Any man linked to Zahira would struggle to hold on to the land. Blacker kept such thoughts to himself even as he looked for loopholes in the sharia inheritance laws. Blacker did not want his land to pass to another man simply because he had married his daughter. An outsider would lack the will to fight for the land.

Also, Blacker could not forget that his own wife had died giving birth to his only child and could not shake off fear of a similar fate for Zahira. The invisible, unyielding bonds of childhood were the best seal to such transactions.

Blacker had laid out his fears and plans to Zahira. If something happened to him, the property could be confiscated in a matter of weeks. "Parsaa owes our family much," her father advised. "He won't forget. Besides, you will have more control over him as landowner than husband. Allah willing."

Months before Zahira's marriage, Blacker had secretly arranged a debt with Parsaa's father. A signed document suggested that Blacker owed the other man a large sum of money in exchange for unspecified services over the years—and Blacker's land was transferred for payment. For Blacker, the imaginary debt was ideal. The deal eliminated criticisms about his daughter's education and rural interpretations of inheritance laws that eventually directed all his holdings to his daughter's spouse.

Blacker had died shortly before the Taliban took control of the nearby cities, closed schools, and imposed restrictions for women from previous centuries. And while the Taliban leaders ignored many poor, remote villages, including Laashekoh, women could not study or work. Travel was difficult. Airline flights were disrupted. Men with weapons set up random checkpoints along the highways, charging tolls and taking what they wanted from passersby.

When the Taliban were in control, Zahira relied on Mohan and other lieutenants loyal to Blacker to smuggle items to the compound. Weapons, books, electronics, tanks of fuel, and medical supplies were hidden in wagonloads brimming with produce, rags, scrap metal, birdseed, or copies of the Koran.

The land transfer had taken place years earlier, and as Blacker expected, it protected the property. The men of Laashekoh were tough, devout, and widely respected. The greediest and most ignorant Taliban were not about to fight a man with an entire village who would back his claim. Blacker did not inform Zahira's blind husband about the debt or property transfer. Arhaan did not question the brief marriage contract that specified wealth and "land surrounding the compound."

But rules around property ownership were as tenuous as the country's politics. The Afghan government was deeply divided, and Americans who enforced many laws were withdrawing troops. Rules could be broken.

~~~~~~

Parsaa fumbled with the computer, and Zahira held off from offering assistance. It was the only way he would learn how much he needed her. "Did they ask specifically about ownership?" she asked.

With a sigh, he noted the foreign women knew more about the land than he would have expected. She lowered her voice. "You must tell no one about their visit. Arhaan assumes that this land belongs to us—to him. It's not a good time to let him or anyone else think otherwise. He despises you and would raise a fuss." She asked if others knew about Blacker's arrangement.

"No one in the village knows," he said.

"Not even your sons?" Zahira questioned.

Parsaa shook his head. "They are better off not knowing."

Zahira closed her eyes. "Do not talk about the foreign women," she urged.

Parsaa wasn't sure that was enough. "These women are persistent. They could ask questions of others, here or at the property offices. They have more resources than we do."

She frowned. "They always have more resources. But the exchange was legal." Parsaa did not argue, but he did not look relieved either.

"They underestimate us," she insisted. "You have no reason to worry."

"They are dangerous if they know more about our land than we do," he replied. He stood, ready to leave.

"We will fight this together," she promised. "Say nothing about their visit or their questions. They will forget about Laashekoh."

He nodded but seemed distracted by promises made years ago.

Or, he was upset by the secrecy. To keep peace and minimize questions among villagers, he couldn't claim the land as his. Her father had predicted that the feelings for Parsaa would fade, yet he had not mentioned that the same could happen with loyalty.

The signed and secret contract stated that Zahira, Arhaan, and their descendants could use the compound indefinitely. Blacker told her about another unwritten agreement: If Zahira had children, Parsaa would organize another debt and return at least half the land over to her family.

There should be no hard feelings. The village used but a fraction of Blacker's land.

Parsaa did not know about the child living at the compound. His family would not view the child as Zahira's daughter and would balk at transferring land rights to the child. Sharia law did not recognize adoption or inheritance rights for unrelated children. The infant was not Zahira's daughter in Afghanistan and never would be. Parsaa might promise that his sons and other villagers would abide by the terms of the contract. But once in the grave, men could not ensure such commitments were kept. Parsaa's sons could decide they wanted more. They would put the interests of their own children ahead of hers. They could leave Laashekoh and forget about protecting a woman they did not know. They could sell the land.

Her life and the compound stood on unsteady ground. She did not want her daughter growing up amid uncertainty. Zahira no longer wanted to stay in Afghanistan, but relocating would be complicated and expensive. Most foreigners did not trust Afghans after the long war.

After quietly examining a few websites, he commented that the search did not offer answers to his questions.

"You must change how you search," she said.

He stood. "Do you really think every answer can be found?"

"Maybe not," she said.

As Parsaa opened the door, a wail from the main house pierced the night and then was abruptly muffled.

"One of Arhaan's birds," Zahira lied. "It's ill."

Parsaa looked troubled.

"You should pity me," she said. "Arhaan loves his birds more than he loves me."

Parsaa didn't understand her marriage or perhaps he did not

care. His passion for the land around Laashekoh probably no longer included her and the childhood friendship they shared.

Zahira wasn't sure she understood the arrangement, so she refused to talk about her husband or admit that the marriage was a mistake. During Parsaa's visits, she yearned to touch him and invite him to reciprocate. But that was too great a risk. She could not bear his rejection. So many years had passed, and he had made no move, its own rebuff. If she did reach for his arm, hint at intimacy, Parsaa would not return to the compound. Instead, he would send another villager to check on the lonely place.

Weary of discussing problems, she wanted to check on the child.

Parsaa started to walk away and then turned. "Life seemed so easy back then, didn't it?"

"Only because we were young," she said.

He hurried off into the night. Her father had taught Zahira to care for herself, and she intended to teach her child the same.

CHAPTER 4

Parsaa headed back to Laashekoh later than he had intended. He could have taken the direct route out of the canyon, the one used by wagons and newcomers, but instead he stayed with the path along the canyon's higher edge. Clouds obscured the stars and the expansive view of the valley beyond the river. He relied on his walking stick though the low clouds and damp night air almost felt like a protective shield against the rocks waiting below. One misstep in the deceptive shadows could send him tumbling to his death.

He should have been relieved to exit the cliff walk, but he did not enjoy being alone with his thoughts after visits with Zahira. He suspected she sought more than friendship. A constant battle raged inside as he compared Zahira and his wife, Sofi. Parsaa had sworn to Blacker that he would protect the man's daughter. Over time the sacred duty had transformed into a burden while a wife who had once seemed dull surprised him with her ideas and spirit.

Such thoughts should not be spoken aloud.

The path gently rolled alongside the river, and with every step, he shed guilt. Still far from Laashekoh, he rounded a sharp curve along the path. The smell of smoke put him on alert, though he could not see the source. Crouching low, he stepped away from the path, moving slowly to check the other side of the river.

A gleam emerged from a cluster of boulders, a small fire across the river. Parsaa heard no noise other than the river racing over the rocks.

A family or a group of refugees, traders, or bandits would make more noise. One person probably waited by the fire, and the person might not want to be seen from Laashekoh.

The person who made the fire was either sleeping or kept his gaze focused on the flames. Parsaa studied the scene across the river, the placement of boulders, to determine the best approach to the campsite. He took a wide detour away from the river before returning to the path and walking until he found a wide section where the water spread and the current lost its strength. He no longer smelled smoke nor saw the firelight.

Kneeling on the ground, Parsaa reached his hand into the icy water and felt the thick layer of gravel. He hid his pack and rolled his loose pant legs high, but kept his boots on, ready to run or fight in the frigid water.

A few dry rocks led to the center stretch, where he stepped into water up to his knees. Parsaa gasped. The undercurrent pulled at his ankles. Leaning into the flow, with knees bent, he moved deliberately, pressing his boots into the gravel and using his walking stick to test the water's depth with every step.

Once on the other side, he was cautious. A guard could wait at the camp's perimeter. Parsaa caught a whiff of smoke and decided against moving too close. His own feet ached from the cold water. The fire was dying. One person, nervously watching for an intruder, could be as dangerous as many.

A long sigh broke the silence. A man stood, passing by the fire and walking away from the boulders and the river to relieve himself. The gait was familiar, and the light confirmed the identity. Paul Reichart, the aid worker who had helped with returning orphans to their homes in the north. Covered in dust, he moved sluggishly as if exhausted.

Paul returned and stood over the fire to warm his hands before wrapping a sleeping bag around his shoulders and settling amid the boulders.

Parsaa almost called out.

Suddenly, Paul leaned forward. He dropped his head to his knees and groaned as if in pain. Parsaa slowly backed away. The aid worker presented no danger and was welcome in Laashekoh. Paul had his reasons for wanting to be alone.

~~~~~

When Parsaa reached Laashekoh, the courtyard was empty. Even the men in no hurry to join their wives, those who stayed close to the fire pit and fed logs to the leaping flames, had retired. A breeze sweeping through the valley had been too much for the fire, and the last of its embers gave off a ghostly glow.

Sleep should have come easy after the long day. The strange visitors, their news of Leila and eagerness to find orphans, troubled Parsaa, and he wondered if villages elsewhere in Afghanistan had to deal with such disruptions. Or was Laashekoh cursed because an American outpost had once been stationed nearby?

The wet boots were tight, and he removed them outside. Standing in the darkness, beyond the entrance to his bedroom, he disrobed and waited for his breathing to slow. Only then, he slowly lifted the layers of covers and slipped beside Sofi.

Parsaa resisted the temptation to curl his arm around her waist, to press his aching feet against her legs. Sofi was an unusual woman, one who did not ask many questions. Still, she was curious, vigilant with a sharp sense for her husband's worries. Best not to wake her. By morning, the visit with Zahira would seem like a distant memory.

Anxious, Parsaa forced himself to lie still and stare toward the ceiling, wishing for a few hours of relief from thinking about the strangers' questions. He kept his breath even and imagined resting on a cloud. Only then he closed his eyes.

An odd noise—a faint scuffing noise in the other room—pushed him awake. Alert, Parsaa was determined to keep surprise on his side. Night disturbances were rare, except for the occasional illness or night-mare among his children or others in neighboring homes. Children burst awake with tears or shouts, and the women hurried to their sides, offering comfort and quickly restoring quiet. Children did not move with stealth.

Parsaa waited and studied familiar shapes in the darkness. His wife was still. The mound of blankets in the corner of the room was Baby Komal. The toddler was not their daughter and could not sleep with

Parsaa's other children, all boys. Instead, she had her own bundle of blankets in the corner of the bedroom within reach of Sofi's arm.

Both were sound sleepers and did not move. The noise seemed to come from the opposite direction—the common area or perhaps the room where his sons slept.

Normally, the source of a random noise at night quickly became apparent—adults murmuring in nearby homes, a mouse stealing crumbs in the kitchen, trees creaking in protest against the wind. Parsaa could check the kitchen, ensuring that no embers had escaped the stove. But the very absence of noise alerted Parsaa that something was wrong. He sensed a presence—someone fighting to control every breath.

The next footstep was light, followed by another long pause.

Parsaa moved his hand slowly, slowly, to reach for a small, loaded Glock. Such pistols were once rare in Afghanistan, and Parsaa was surprised and grateful for the gift from one of the Afghan soldiers before the team vacated the nearby outpost. The man promised the weapon was sure. He also pointed out that the markets would soon offer more ammunition as the foreign troops returned home and more pistols were left behind.

The pistol was convenient for the bedroom's tight space. Parsaa wrapped his hand around the grip and pulled his hand back underneath the blanket, aiming the pistol toward a doorway he could not see.

Parsaa thought about his options. He could storm the other room, but the person might get away. He could fire the pistol into the darkness, but miss, and the person could shoot back in return. Or, he could wait for the approach and then tackle the intruder.

A black shape glided into the bedroom. The figure was small, but not one of the children. No, the boys would dash into the room and squirm between their parents. No one other than his sons had reason to enter the space. The figure was too cautious, with a long pause between every step, so long Parsaa wondered if his mind wasn't playing tricks.

The shadow moved again, edging along the wall on the other side of the room. Sofi's side. Soon, Parsaa would have to shift position to see the intruder.

Parsaa prepared to move and place his body squarely between the person and Sofi. Steeling himself, he took slow, deep breaths and hoped for a footstep, a clue to the intruder's position.

And then it came—a soft footfall near his wife's head, the sound of a hand reaching about in the darkness.

In a single move, Parsaa lunged over his wife, grasping at cloth and then a small leg. He pulled hard, but the leg swung his way, kicking him in the head. Hard. On one elbow and one knee, Parsaa lost his grip as the person pulled away.

"Stop!" he ordered and reached in the tangle of covers for the pistol. Without a word, Sofi crawled out from underneath him.

Parsaa stood, shouting again and reaching for a wall to find the doorway as Sofi fumbled with a lantern.

But he didn't need the lantern. An orange glow beckoned him. The intruder knelt before the stove, shoving an object into the flames. Sparks flared and hit the floor. There was a whiff of burning flesh.

Before Parsaa could cross the room, one of his sons emerged from the darkness, wrapping an arm around the intruder's neck and pulling the person to the floor with a thud.

A girl groaned and twisted to one side but did not resist.

Saddiq, Parsaa's oldest son, quickly removed his hands and stood, staring at the girl and then at the tongues of fire curling and swelling around the flat object in the stove.

Sofi approached, holding the lantern high.

Najwa. The girl had arrived in Laashekoh with other children, gathered by traffickers to be sold in Pakistan. Parsaa and American soldiers, with the help of Paul Reichart, had returned the children to their homes in a province just north of Helmand. But the men had never found Najwa's home. The other children did not know her and could not remember when she had joined the group. "She may have been among the first," offered one of the older boys before leaving to reunite with his family.

The soldiers, the aid worker, and Laashekoh women had questioned the girl.

Sofi placed the lantern on the floor. She poured what was left of the day's water into a bowl, gathered clean rags, and began gently dabbing at the burns on the girl's hands. Sofi urged Saddiq to go outside and collect extra water stored in a large cylinder.

Parsaa examined the fire, poking at the object with a stick.

"It's a book," Sofi murmured. "The one we were reading."

An old copy of *The Historical Geography of Afghanistan*. It was too late to rescue the book from the flames.

Najwa did not move and stared off to the side of the room with a strange expression, as if in a satisfied trance. Saddiq placed a bucket of water next to his mother, and she sprinkled drops on the loose bandages. Parsaa crouched next to the girl. "What are you doing in here?" he demanded.

She stared at Saddiq and then at Parsaa, before turning her head, trying to hide behind her headscarf. "I meant no harm," she said softly. "I am awake now."

The story was strange and short. Najwa insisted she did not know how she found her way into the house, let alone the bedroom. Parsaa asked Sofi to search the girl. His wife complied and found a *peshkabz* tucked in the roll of one sleeve. The knife's curved blade was honed to a vicious point and the handle was lapis lazuli. Sofi held it up wordlessly and then handed it over to her husband.

Parsaa told Saddiq to check his brothers. The group waited in silence until he returned and advised his father the other boys were fine and sleeping soundly. His father then sent Saddiq off to wake the family who had been keeping Najwa. Before long, Saddiq returned with Talibah, who was shaken about being woken in the middle of the night. She glared at Najwa, and Parsaa showed her the weapon. She shook her head.

"She must have brought it with her," Parsaa said.

Bending over, Talibah struck Najwa about the head, shouting that the girl could not be trusted. Parsaa pulled the woman away. Still, Talibah refused to allow Najwa to return to the small room that the family had set aside for her, and Sofi nodded in agreement.

So others could feel secure, Parsaa locked Najwa inside a storage shed, along with plenty of covers, food, water, and a pot so the girl could relieve herself. Sofi promised to change the girl's bandages in the morning.

When Parsaa returned, Saddiq waited by the dying fire, staring at the thin layers of gray ash. The father placed a hand on his son's shoulder. "Try to get some sleep." The boy looked troubled and turned away without a word.

Parsaa returned to the bedroom, where Sofi was straightening Komal's covers. His wife's hand lingered on the child's soft hair before she joined him under the wool covers.

"Do you think Najwa intended harm?" Sofi whispered.

Parsaa didn't think so. He wrapped his arms around his wife and reminded her that many women and boys carried knives for work.

"Perhaps Najwa grabbed the book to defend herself? Could she have been after Komal and changed her mind?"

Parsaa murmured that the girl reached for the book and not the child. "She was walking in her sleep."

Sofi asked about the struggle. "But why didn't she wake up when you reached for her in the bedroom? Why did she rush to the stove?"

Parsaa couldn't answer. He agreed that it was strange.

"The girl is sneaky. You must take her away."

"Soon," Parsaa promised.

"The village women are angry," Sofi insisted. "Tomorrow."

~~~~~~

After the disturbance, Parsaa and Sofi did not sleep well. Both awoke long before dawn, and Komal squirmed and whimpered soon afterward. The boys were still asleep, and Parsaa retrieved more wood for the fire, warming the kitchen, while his wife wrapped Komal snugly in a blanket and placed her near the stove.

Cold weather was coming, and the village could not keep a young girl inside a storage shed. Once again, his wife warned him that everyone in the village would soon hear about the girl wandering about at night and entering another family's bedroom. The village women would expect Parsaa to remove her quickly. If not, every misfortune would be blamed on Najwa.

They would not give her another chance.

The complaints were many. Since her arrival in Laashekoh, the girl had not spoken much, yet she exuded a boldness that was odd for a stranger. Neither the children nor the adults of Laashekoh trusted her or liked her. Most families refused to allow Najwa into their homes. The women prohibited letting her work alongside the older village children or caring for younger ones. They would not let her join them when cooking or washing clothes. Instead, they sent her to work in the fields for long hours alone during the day, and at night she cleaned the heavy cookware and beat rugs.

The girl worked hard and did not complain, though her eyes narrowed with angry judgment. She often lingered behind walls and corners, listening to conversations not intended for her ears. Najwa frightened the other children.

With her awkward ways, she truly seemed to be an orphan. Orphans were expected to work hard and save for the future, and for girls, that meant securing a good marriage, but Najwa lacked both a dowry and pleasant appearance. Slight in build, she was shorter than other girls her age, but she appeared older than her eleven or twelve years. Her hair was dry and uncombed, and her face was marked with blotches and a few old scars. Clenched teeth gave her mouth a stubborn edge, as if she anticipated disagreement. She could not see well and squinted even when directly facing others, as if she could not trust their words.

The commotion in the middle of the night confirmed the village women's worries. Najwa was trouble. It didn't matter if she was locked away in the shed, out of sight. Parsaa couldn't blame the women for wanting a return to normality. The village was burdened by caring for too many girls without parents. Najwa was one problem too many.

Once the fire was blazing, Parsaa reached for his wife's hand and pulled her to sit with him before she prepared the breakfast. Parsaa went over the options with Sofi, as Komal amused herself by chewing on a rag soaked in goat's milk.

Najwa was old enough for a marriage contract. The village could send her to live with the groom's family and wait for marriage. But few families would allow their sons to enter such a partnership—not without knowing more about her family background. Parsaa could provide a suitable amount for a dowry, but planning marriages took time. Families were suspicious about hasty arrangements that involved excessive sums. He should travel alone to make initial arrangements and negotiate as carefully as he would for a daughter. If he brought Najwa along during the first trip, the negotiators would understand that he was desperate.

Besides, her parents might have already promised her to a groom, and it was a crime to provide a girl already promised for marriage to another man. That could be a reason why Najwa was not eager to return to her home and parents. But then she wasn't keen on cooperating with the residents of Laashekoh.

Regardless of what the girl wanted, Laashekoh was too small to absorb strangers for very long, especially girls with no fathers, uncles, husbands, or brothers to watch over them.

Parsaa had wanted to keep trying to locate the girl's family. Paul Reichart, the aid worker who had helped return other children from the traffickers to their homes, had promised to investigate. Parsaa had also asked around at the market about families in need of a servant, but with no success. Most villages had plenty of children and did not need another mouth to feed. He thought about taking her to one of the larger towns and paying a fee so that brokers would find her a servant's position.

Sofi shook her head. "She won't be easy to place. They will send her back before the next full moon."

He sighed. "It would be best for all concerned if we found her family."

"Don't be foolish," Sofi chided him softly. She no longer believed Najwa and her claims about not knowing the whereabouts of her own family. Many villagers had questioned her, and all Najwa could say was that she was from Qarya, a small village in northern Ghōr. But that was of little help. *Qarya* meant "small village," and even the Americans with their maps could not locate the place. When asked to describe her home, Najwa rambled on about three hills nearby.

Most Afghan villages could count three hills nearby.

Parsaa had long advised villagers to keep asking questions and listen closely. Najwa had to remember more.

But her stories were vague, the details varying with listeners. She couldn't describe roads or waterways or markets with specifics. One day, she suggested her parents did not own their own land, and her father had left for long periods to do odd jobs. With another, she explained that her father left and vanished. Her mother worked in fields belonging to a family whose name she could not recall. Then, she talked about a mother near death after bearing too many children. Yes, she had brothers. None had attended school, and all had left to fight in wars.

There were no uncles, she told Sofi.

To the aid worker, she explained that her parents had lived in one village all their lives. With Parsaa, she suggested that her parents had moved about in Ghōr more than once.

When asked if she had already been promised to another family for marriage, all Najwa could say was she did not know.

Sofi interrupted his thoughts. "You have spent far too long searching for a family that may not exist."

"The girl could be afraid to return." Parsaa also suspected Najwa knew more about her background. "Perhaps they were cruel."

His wife was impatient. "She does not show fear."

"Why would a child lie?" He appealed to his wife. "Why would she act in ways that jeopardize her future?"

"Perhaps they wanted nothing to do with her."

Women could be hard on other women.

Sofi poured more hot water and leaned close to his ear. "Najwa does not like us. She does not want to be here."

"We cannot hand our problem to another village," he said.

"She needs training," Sofi agreed. "But that is no longer possible here."

Parsaa asked about Najwa's skills with chores, and Sofi thought a moment. "As good as one can expect at that age," she admitted. "Granted, the women have been hard on her lately. But she does what she's told."

"Has Najwa stolen others' belongings?"

Sofi shook her head. "But she should not be near other children."

He pulled a thread at the edge of the wool carpet. "Think about it," his wife urged. "The foreign women came. They spoke loudly about offering rewards for finding orphans. And not long afterward, Najwa was in our bedroom. I fear she has picked up dangerous ideas."

"She would abduct a child?" he asked.

Komal chortled from the corner of the room. The little girl tossed her rag and squirmed to escape the cover. Smiling, Sofi retrieved the toddler and returned to Parsaa's side. Time alone with her husband was rare with five children in the house and so much work.

Sofi tucked Komal between the two adults and placed her hand so the child could bend and play with the fingers. "I'm not sure she wanted just any child."

They quietly played with the youngest sister of Leila. Parsaa worried about his wife's attachment to the little girl for many reasons. Komal's mother and her older sister, Leila, were serving prison sentences for trafficking, and after the arrests, Leila's sisters were divided among village families. The years would pass quickly. The child's mother could leave prison and retrieve her daughters. Raising another woman's child was like tending a neighbor's garden, and love did not ensure control.

Early on, Sofi and Parsaa had tried keeping a distance, but the child seemed so cheerful and content to be away from her sisters that it was unthinkable that evil pulsed through her veins. Perhaps Shaitan had overlooked the little one. Baby Komal was easy, watching Sofi as she worked in the fields, laughing and trying to keep up with the boys during the evening. The child did not complain or demand attention. If left alone, she fingered strands of grass or folded and refolded the edge of her *perahaan*, her eyes wide as if listening intently to conversations she could not understand.

Parsaa had warned his wife that the family had no claim over Komal. Sofi had little to say other than insisting that was not a reason to deny her love.

Other villagers would not approve. Parents wanted their children to know that Leila's crimes had shamed an entire family. Ostracizing the girls was the best hope for preventing a repeat of wrongdoings in the small village. Parsaa, Sofi, and the boys engaged in playful activities with Komal in the privacy of their own home. Parsaa often wondered if Sofi would love Komal as much when the girl was older.

Sofi interrupted his thoughts. "Najwa might not be a problem in a place with few families, a small home with no children," she mused.

An idea slipped into his head. Or, perhaps that was his wife's intention.

He could take Najwa to Zahira's compound, he explained. The place was too much work for Aza and Mohan, who were getting older and should have had help long ago, and Najwa would be in a remote location with no children or young adults. Four adults could give her assignments and monitor her work. What trouble could she get into? "But only if I can assure Zahira that the girl won't steal or cause other problems."

His wife cast a long look at her husband. None of the women of Laashekoh, including Sofi, liked Zahira well. They never offered to include her in village celebrations or activities.

"Mixing two troubles does not make a problem go away," she said. "Najwa could drive someone mad."

"What other options do we have?" Parsaa said. "The compound is far enough away. That would satisfy women here. Yet it's close enough for us to provide guidance and Zahira to reach out for help."

Sofi was not convinced.

"She could leave today," he added. "And I could still search for another home."

There was no other option, and Sofi agreed to pack meals and Najwa's meager belongings that morning. Zahira could check the girl's burns.

"It's the best an orphan girl could hope for." Parsaa was impatient for Laashekoh to return to normal routines.

PART 2

And spend in the way of Allah and cast not yourselves
to perdition with your own hands, and do good [to
others]; surely Allah loves the doers of good.
                                            —Koran 2:195

CHAPTER 5

The table was set three days before Canadian Thanksgiving—all that was left to add was a small bouquet, candlelight, and, of course, the meal itself.

Lydia last met her daughter-in-law's parents at the memorial service that followed much too soon after the wedding. So much time had passed, but she impulsively sent an e-mail, tentatively suggesting the gathering in East Lansing, and the couple surprised her with their eagerness. They also agreed to bring photographs.

The three parents shared a bond. Lydia's only son had married an only daughter. Michael and Rose each had an independent streak, ready to separate from their parents and find a love that would rival that of their parents. Michael had once admitted to feeling like the odd man out, growing up with parents who had remained the best of friends: "It was lonely at times because both of you were so close." He wanted nothing more than to follow his parents in finding his own best friend for sharing dreams, secrets, and love.

Sitting in a dark room, with a glass of wine, Lydia remembered so many conversations and jotted notes on what she should share. The memories were bittersweet, and the plans offered a hint of anticipation that she had once felt when waiting to join her husband at the end of the workday or receive a telephone call from her son.

~~~~~~

Rose's parents, Rebecca and Tim, drove from Toronto to spend Monday with Lydia. The turkey was in the oven, the rest of the meal was prepared, and Lydia just had to switch on burners. The sky was perfect, the air crisp as leaves danced about the streets. Lydia had borrowed extra bikes from friends for a quick tour of campus and the small town before tackling final preparations for the meal. The streets were free of traffic, though plenty of people their age were out, taking advantage of one of the year's last golden days. Trails linked a charming campus with meadows and parks, and the couple expressed pleased surprise over the small-town atmosphere and the solid oaks, maples, hickories, and beech arching over the Red Cedar River and Grand River Avenue.

Returning home, they opened champagne and shared tasks of chopping, slicing, spreading, and mashing—and all three admitted their amazement that it wasn't so hard to talk for hours about memories of two grown children.

Rebecca mentioned that Thanksgiving was Rose's favorite holiday and Lydia smiled. "Michael's, too," she said. "And when Rose told him it was her favorite, Michael said that was when he knew she was the one."

Tears glistened in their eyes more than once, but there were also plenty of smiles. The dinner was perfect, delicious, the cleanup fast. Tim tended the fire. They piled photograph albums on the coffee table and took turns slowly turning pages that documented their children's lives. Most of Michael's shots were outdoors, the boy muddy, climbing trees, or organizing a group of neighborhood children for parades, alien battles, or hiking expeditions. A tiny Rose was featured in modern dance recitals, choral groups, reading competitions with a dreamy attitude that later gave way to a steely determination in graduate school.

More than once, the parents murmured how the two were a perfect couple, lucky to have met one another and enjoyed success. "We should have done this sooner." Rebecca was abrupt, apologizing to Lydia for not extending their own invitation and not taking a more active interest in the foundation named after the couple.

Lydia understood the reticence and shook her head. "There is no need for an apology. We needed time." She did not bring up her failure to invite them to participate in the foundation or her resentment. Rebecca and Tim still had each other while she was completely alone. She gently steered the subject in another direction. "I was surprised that Michael and Rose had thought so far ahead about starting such an organization."

Rebecca and Tim glanced at each other. Tim spoke up. "We were surprised, too, considering Rose's research—on cultural and social capitalism and abuses of modern charity. She was not keen on charities as a mechanism for funding education, health, and other needed programs."

Lydia studied Rose's parents. "But I thought the foundation must have been her idea."

"Not at all," Tim said, with a rueful laugh. "That would have been a sudden turnaround from her graduate work." Rose had studied philosophy and economics, he explained, and that involved a cross-country comparison of charitable giving versus government spending and efficiency. The origin of the word *forgiving* was *giving*, and she traced how charitable practices over the years implied that recipients were wrongdoers who were weak and deserved no control. "She was adamant that basic obligations like education and health belonged to the government."

"We did not want to interfere," Rebecca interrupted. "We read that the foundation was Michael and Rose's idea, but often wondered just how and when the idea started."

Lydia ran her hand along the edge of a photo—Michael standing alongside his old car with his best friend and waving to the camera. She regretted not including Rose's parents in the planning for the foundation, not asking them about what they knew. "I would have agreed with her." She sighed. "The two of them handed over a mission statement for a foundation to Michael's attorney a few days before the wedding. The paperwork was not finalized, but the attorney said it was clearly their intention."

She paused. "Henry said I didn't have to go through with it. I didn't want to run a foundation, but I had to respect their intentions."

Tim closed his eyes, and Rebecca reached for Lydia's hand. "It was Michael's fortune, and we had assumed that the foundation was Michael's idea or yours. But then we found a letter among Rose's belongings only a few weeks ago."

Lydia was curious. Her investigators had been on site when the couple's belongings were separated, packed, and sent to each set of parents—along with a thorough inventory of all belongings. The investigators had examined computers, clothing, jewelry, books, kitchen equipment, furniture, and more.

"I couldn't bear to go through the boxes for months," Lydia admitted. "It was too painful."

"But we didn't find the note there." Rebecca offered an understanding smile. "It was in a pocket of a jacket that Rose left at our house just before the wedding. We left that jacket in the front closet." Her voice broke. "As if she were still at home."

"For months, we didn't think to go through the pockets." Tim pulled out a folder from the stack of albums, extracted a letter on notebook paper, and handed it over to Lydia.

> Darling,
>
> I'm sorry we quarreled. I appreciate that you keep saying it's our money not yours. I have no reservations about signing a prenuptial agreement and still want to, especially after seeing P last night. He certainly thinks the pre-nup is a good idea and I do, too. I know he thinks that we haven't been together for very long and I understand. He has good ideas. Lord! what he must think of us—you resisting the pre-nup and my telling him it was much too early to think about establishing a foundation. My reasons for rejecting his ideas were trivial—and if you feel ready, we can surprise him.
>
> I don't want to be old and set in my ways, and that could never happen with you.
>
> Love, R

Tim shook his head. "We almost didn't show you. Didn't want to think about the two of them quarreling before the wedding."

The writing was tiny and neat. The lines of the notebook paper were narrowly spaced. Lydia was sure the page matched the notebook paper that Michael had used for the mission statement. According to the attorney and the staff at Photizonet, the paper had not come from company office supplies. But a few coworkers pointed out that Michael often carried around his own personal notebook, jotting down ideas or working out problems.

The investigators had gone through the couple's belongings so carefully and specifically searched for such a notebook, but the one with narrow lines was not found. The investigators suggested that Michael had used scrap paper. Or the notebook had been tossed in a cleaning frenzy before the wedding.

Lydia wondered what else had not been found.

She couldn't speak, and Rose's parents shifted, uncomfortable over Lydia's long silence. "The note probably does not mean much," Rebecca offered. "They were happy, wonderful together, and neither one knew what real quarreling meant."

Tim asked if Lydia had ideas about who the P in the note might be. "I'm guessing it might be Michael's best man at the wedding. Paul Reichart?"

"Maybe," Lydia murmured. "I don't know. It's a lovely note."

Tim put his hand out, and she returned the note reluctantly. Lydia wondered if Rose's parents had ever suspected that something other than random terrorism had been behind the deaths, if they had organized their own investigation.

They asked no more questions about Paul and continued turning the loosened, yellowed pages of old photo albums. Lydia could not stop thinking about the note—it was more distracting than suspicious. Yet she no longer felt like talking and wanted to be alone.

Not long afterward, Rose's parents bid farewell, ready to leave together for their hotel room and an early start back to Toronto. Another get-together was promised.

Alone, Lydia could not sleep. Sitting in the darkness of her living room, she reflected on her detailed conversations with Paul before and after the memorial service. She had wanted to hear everything Michael had said to his friend during those final weeks. Paul never mentioned conversations about a prenuptial agreement or plans for a foundation. He certainly did not mention the couple quarreling.

She still remembered the call from Paul after he had heard television reports about plans for the foundation. He asked if the reports were true. By then, she had memorized her son's scrawled mission statement, framed and hanging on her office wall:

Alleviate poverty. Respect nature. Relish peace. With efficiency.

What you see in yourself, you see in the world.

Paul had been quiet. If anything, he seemed stunned that the couple had bequeathed most of their fortune to a foundation—the most generous and active venture-philanthropy group in the world. He pointed out the last phrase was an Afghan proverb.

Lydia had repeated Henry's admonitions to Paul, that the statement was bare-bones, the goals could be achieved in any number of ways—education, economic development, small-business support, family planning, all sorts of environmental programs, job creation. It had not dawned on politicians that there were simply not enough decent jobs or resources for the world's seven billion people—as many as ten billion before the end of the century—and Michael apparently wanted to do his part.

Paul had offered complete support for the foundation and offered to resign his company position. Lydia probably shouldn't trust her memory, but she remembered sensing a quiver in his voice as if he had been about to cry. And she had hired him on the spot. Paul and Michael had been childhood friends, a friendship she had encouraged. The two went on to be college roommates, and Paul was one of the company's earliest hires. He was not a software engineer but a sociol-

ogist, and Michael had insisted that introducing revolutionary technology required cultural sensitivity.

At one of the foundation's early planning meetings, Paul volunteered to also serve on the board, but Henry had shot that down as
impossible. The great sum of money, a deluge of applications, and scru-
tiny by government officials and media required professionals with
track records in philanthropy. Lydia had already selected the board and
wanted to keep it as small as legally possible. She reassured Paul that,
with experience, he would gain more responsibility and get his turn.
He volunteered to work overseas, and it had been easy for her to forget
his initial surprise and keen interest in running the foundation.

Henry had been adamant about keeping the board small, too, so
that Lydia could add her own imprint to the organization early on.
He urged her to decide on policies quickly, and put the foundation
on a steady path. Compensation was fair, but capped. GlobalConnect employees were prohibited from self-promotion or investments
that could present conflicts of interest. Grant recipients were forced to
work in teams including members with opposing political views.

Early on, Paul had chafed at such suggestions. He explained that
joint grants resulted in unnecessary struggles and inefficiency. "Best
standards are well known," he insisted. "You could point recipients in
the right direction from the very start."

She thanked him for his candor but also reminded him that
Michael was known in the tech field for bringing opponents together
for creative solutions.

Lydia turned on the computer, kept off during the Thanksgiving
celebration. She checked her e-mail and then searched through old
conversations with Paul, especially those shortly before and after the
bombing. The e-mails still suggested that Paul Reichart had no clue
about GlobalConnect before Michael's death, and she had long associated that with innocence. Michael's wealth was not new and he was not
arrogant. His company's management had changed little over its few
years in operation. The only new events in Michael's life were marriage
and the plan to start a foundation.

Authorities in India and with the US State Department insisted the death was a random act of violence. But Rose's note suggested Paul had known more than anyone had realized—that perhaps the idea for a foundation had been his all along. Rose initially resisted, but the couple had listened to an old friend and eventually agreed.

It wasn't much of a motive. Paul got his way. The foundation was launched, though he did not play a major role as he once might have hoped. If anything, he had more reason to resent Henry and Lydia.

She turned off the computer, but could not stop thinking. Instead, she wandered through the quiet house and sat on a window seat, staring out at the familiar shapes of her fence and maple trees against a starry sky. She couldn't remember when Paul had last tried calling with a suggestion. Maybe she and Henry had rejected too many of his ideas.

No one knew that Lydia had planned on naming her son's friend as her replacement.

It bothered her that Paul had not mentioned his role as a mediator in the couple's quarrel about a foundation. An imagination could run wild at night, especially after a day of indulging in memories. Perhaps Paul owed Lydia an explanation, but he was more than six thousand miles away, and she wasn't sure what questions to ask.

CHAPTER 6

The villagers were eager to rid themselves of Najwa before the day began. It was still dark as Sofi helped tie Najwa's few belongings, mostly worn clothes discarded by the women of Laashekoh, into a bundle, and the boys readied the donkey that would take her away.

The hum of a distant engine, an ATV, interrupted from the valley below. A visitor had arrived, and delivering Najwa to the compound would have to wait.

By the time the visitor arrived, the sky was mottled blue with streaks of rose clouds near the rising sun. Paul Reichart entered the gate, embraced Parsaa in the Afghan way, and explained he was on his way to another village. "It's good to be back," he said.

Parsaa chided Paul for traveling alone at night. Travel in the remote areas around Laashekoh could have treacherous moments. The nearest roads were desolate and rough. Parsaa did not mention he had seen the man camping out the night before.

"More people, more problems." Paul smiled and, noticing the donkeys with packs, asked if Parsaa was about to leave.

Parsaa explained that the errand could wait and directed the guest toward the courtyard. Ahmed shouted for older children to bring breakfast for the visitor—mashed fruit and yogurt, naan, a large glass of warm milk.

Parsaa was pleased. Paul had been immensely helpful with returning orphans to their home villages and listened to suggestions from the villagers. He had provided supplies and encouraged the families to welcome the returning children.

But many parents took the news hard. Parsaa, Paul, and the American soldiers had to explain repeatedly that the children had not missed out on a grand opportunity. Instead, villagers had been tricked into thinking their children would train as apprentices and save. The parents would have received no payments by post. Instead, the children would have been sep-arated, to work long hours at dangerous or humiliating tasks—and pun-ished if they even mentioned their parents or home villages. Eventually, the young laborers would have forgotten details about their old life, and the parents would never have heard from the children again.

A few families had danced about, hugging their children, over-joyed about a rescue from a life of unending work, abuse, and misery. Others wailed, berating Parsaa, Paul, and the soldiers, demanding to know how families would handle another mouth to feed.

Parsaa trusted Paul after such an experience, and hoped that the man could eventually answer his questions about the foreign women who claimed to represent an orphanage.

Parsaa didn't have to wait long. A younger boy carried hot water for tea. The boy's stuffed animal dangled from a thin rope looped around his waist, and Paul's eyes locked onto the toy. "You had visitors?"

"A group from an orphanage in Kabul," Parsaa said. "A day ago."

Paul seemed to know about the women yet asked Parsaa to describe the visit.

"They are seeking Afghan partners," Parsaa said. He noted the women were controlling, yet not as prepared as Paul to work in Afghanistan.

The assessment pleased Paul. "They are new to the country," he said. "Do not worry about them."

Paul bent over the dish, scraping the plate with the bread and downing the milk as if he had not eaten in two days, and Parsaa nodded for the boys to bring more food. "The women asked about orphans and wanted to help. But of course they were too late."

"Did they mention me?" Paul asked.

"They knew of you. One spoke Dari, though we did not under-stand everything she asked."

Paul asked how long the women stayed, and Parsaa explained it was not long because they arrived by helicopter. Paul said a word to himself. It sounded like *dama*, fog, or perhaps it was an English word.

"Their priority is not Afghans," Paul said. "They're trying to make a name for themselves and push their way into my work in this area. They won't last long."

Parsaa explained how the women were keen to find young children so he did not mention Najwa, and Paul said that was wise. Parsaa then asked if Paul had heard any word on Najwa's parents.

"Nothing," Paul said. "I checked online and made calls to Helmand, Kandahar, and other provinces on the off chance she did not come from Ghōr. So many children are not registered, and thousands go missing. All ages."

Parsaa did not want the other villagers to hear talk about the Internet with its stories about Laashekoh and asked if Paul had told other charities about Laashekoh, the trafficking arrests, and the orphans.

"No." Paul was adamant. "But more representatives of charities will travel here. Some will be helpful, and some will interfere." Leaning back, he asked what Parsaa thought of the two women and if he would consider partnering with such groups.

Parsaa thought a moment and was careful with his response. "They think they have a better way. We don't need such partners."

Paul laughed. "You are not alone."

Parsaa asked how many foreign charities were in the country and Paul explained there were more than fifteen hundred organizations. "We call them nonprofits or nongovernmental organizations. Some provide food, education, or healthcare. Some want to build schools and hospitals. Others train lawyers or businesspeople. Others want to preserve antiquities or protect wildlife. The list is long—more than the rocks in the walls around this village."

Parsaa worried. *Zakat* was an obligation for his community—to help those in need. The village enjoyed excess harvests and was generous, distributing a larger share of the harvest than required to other villages less fortunate. Parsaa had never imagined that others might see his community deserving of *zakat*.

The foreigners could not understand which villages were in need and most deserving. Even Paul did not know the full extent of Laashekoh's resources.

Parsaa asked why the women and other workers traveled to Afghanistan. "Why don't they stay and help their own country?"

Paul sighed before explaining how some felt guilt about the war and the disruptions. Others wanted stability in Afghanistan, and many accompanied the soldiers to promote education, health, and systems of justice. "For others, it's just a job or even a way to become famous in their fields."

Parsaa frowned. He asked who paid for the costly programs and travel. During the war's early years, other countries provided the money for Afghanistan, Paul said. Later, corporations and other private sources sent donations.

The man paused and then explained that about 90 percent of Afghanistan's government budget was funded by foreign sources. Parsaa was stunned and asked about Paul's organization. How did he get his money?

"It's from a wealthy woman in the United States," the aid worker said shortly. "Her son invented a product and started a big company, which earned him more money than one person could ever need."

"The parents control that money and give it away?" Parsaa asked politely. "*Zakat?*"

Paul shook his head. "He died young. He was in the wrong place at the wrong time."

"But how does this woman know what is needed here?" Parsaa pressed.

"People like me," Paul said. "We visit, ask questions, identify problems . . ." His voice drifted off.

"Is she a Muslim?" Paul shook his head slowly.

The funding and the sources bothered Parsaa. The warlords once distributed money, too, but villagers understood the reasons. "These groups—we need to know their plans in advance."

"Most of the charities mean well. They seek local partners and they listen."

But that's what the women wanted from Laashekoh, Parsaa countered.

"Be careful what you sign," Paul advised. He offered to look over any paperwork. The groups were supposed to register with the government, describing purposes and funding sources.

"Villages should take care of their own problems," Parsaa said. "If outsiders come in, we lose control."

"Government officials like nonprofits. In my country and Afghanistan, too. They bring in money, they spend money locally. The good groups hire Afghans—more than seventy thousand are working for nonprofits."

Parsaa asked if the governments had control of the nonprofits.

"They pay little attention," Paul said. "Unless there are complaints. But it's too early . . ." Parsaa waited, sensing that Paul did not trust the women from the orphanage. "Besides, I doubt they will return."

Parsaa hoped Paul was right. "Allah rewards those who give, if their motives are good. Otherwise, giving can divide villages, and cooperation vanishes. Charities can look for problems that do not exist, and villages learn to claim problems they do not have. Laashekoh does not need such help."

Paul turned to Parsaa. "You understand why I want to escape my office and visit a village that is self-reliant."

Parsaa was direct. Laashekoh was grateful for Paul's help in returning children to their villages. The village welcomed him, but not funds from a foreign charity.

The two men sat quietly and avoided looking at one another. Parsaa poked at the fire's smoldering embers with a stick. The morning sun was full and golden. Conversations about good and evil were better suited for the nighttime when opinions could be expressed around a dying fire and reactions went unseen.

"Charity is not enough or too much. It seemed so simple when I started. Now I wish that I had never heard of GlobalConnect."

Paul then asked Parsaa if he ever thought about the children they had returned to the villages in the north. "Did we do what was best for them?" he pressed.

"Parents do the best they can," Parsaa said. The men had little choice but to walk away from the worried eyes. Despite the mixed reactions from parents, Parsaa had felt only relief when Paul had distributed food and other supplies to each family. That helped ease the anger, but for how long? Parsaa was ashamed he had not thought to question the source of such supplies. "The families will be more careful in the future." Paul did not answer. "We must trust them. The matter is in Allah's hands."

Paul slapped his knees and stood. "That's a problem for people in my line of work—it's tough to prove what might have been."

The man was ready to leave, and Parsaa mentioned the plans to send Najwa away from Laashekoh. Paul asked if the girl had shared more details about her village or family. Parsaa shook his head, but then mentioned the *peshkabz*, adding that she must have been hiding the weapon since her arrival. Paul asked to see the blade, and Parsaa retrieved it, showing the other man once they were walking down the hill, out of sight of the other villagers.

"It's unusual," Paul said, suggesting the handle could be tied with a region. He asked to borrow the weapon, and Parsaa happily agreed.

"She is not happy here. The women suspect that she doesn't want to locate her family." Parsaa shook his head. "It's a mystery that we may never solve."

Paul asked about her next home, and Parsaa explained it was isolated.

"Keep her busy," Paul warned. "Boredom is the road to trouble."

Parsaa asked if the girl might be better off in the city at an orphanage.

"Probably not," Paul said. "Children who head to the orphanages tend not to return home. And if she is not being truthful, it would be even easier for her to lie to foreign aid workers than to you."

"If she does not work out at her next home, could you take her to one of the orphanages in Kabul or Kandahar?"

Paul was nervous. "I'll admit—if I were to bring her back, that could start a round of questions about the other children," he said. "It's not a good time to reveal that one did not make it home. I'm sorry, friend."

It was as Parsaa had suspected. The man had his own problems. "She is our responsibility and we will handle her."

"You are fortunate not to have to deal with bureaucracy," Paul said.

The men were far enough from the village, but thick brush could hide curious ears, so Parsaa lowered his voice to ask why Paul seemed anxious. "Is there trouble you have not told us about?"

"No worries for you," Paul said. "But there were questions about how I handled that group of orphans. There is no shortage of people who want to criticize our work, like those women, so they can step in to secure funding. They complain that our office is not doing enough research, not identifying atrocities, not supplying enough services, not following procedures. Those two from the orphanage? I must deal with people like that every day."

"What would they have us do?" Parsaa was puzzled.

The laugh from Paul was short and embarrassed. "We did the right thing, returning the children to their parents quickly. Transferring them to the city for screenings would have meant long delays—that didn't seem right, not when thousands of children are going without education or healthcare." He sighed again. "Procedures may be more rigid in the future."

"Surely, you can explain?" Parsaa questioned.

"You flatter me to suggest that I have control."

Parsaa didn't understand American ways. He would dislike working with others when obedience was not automatic and rules were unclear. "I thought you were the supervisor of many. They don't obey?"

Paul described large networks of donors and charitable organizations, with hundreds of workers and millions in funds. "Many who work for me or others in the country are ambitious, and some want to get ahead by proving that I'm not doing a good job. Too many compete to find trouble here."

He explained how so much charity was based on whims. "I sometimes feel as if all that matters is an administrator's last conversation with a donor. A donor hears a report that children are going without shoes and soon we're unloading crates of shoes, every size and style imaginable, most of them inappropriate for this terrain. So we look for storage, often paying to lease the space."

"Surely you can explain what is not needed here," Parsaa pressed.

"Maybe someday," Paul replied. "I never dreamed that so much money could be a curse. I did the hard work, building trust, before GlobalConnect, before there was so much money. But other groups are rushing in. People who know nothing about the place! One celebrity wants to open a girls' school, another wants to renovate mosques, another sends thousands of copies of a children's book—signed. And any who ask questions or offer suggestions are tagged as troublemakers."

He was tired of aid workers who thought they knew better than the people they purported to help. "I love this country, but I work for people who don't even try to understand. Laashekoh is fortunate that it can keep to itself."

Paul paused. "So you understand why I cannot tell anyone that Najwa is still in the area."

"Of course," he murmured. It was shameful when a community could not care for its children properly, and Parsaa wished Najwa could stay in Laashekoh. The women would have accepted her if she had been more agreeable, but older children struggled to fit in. It was easy for others to provoke them into misbehaving.

Parsaa worried about the sudden interest of charities and wondered if the villagers could handle the changes destined to come their way. Tempers would flare if aid groups helped the wrong people. "There are charities that are helping Leila?"

Paul admitted that the young woman was winning sympathy. "They could not determine her exact age and tried her as an adolescent. She is young, disfigured, uneducated, and has little trouble convincing others that her husband and father coerced her. She could be a gold mine for a charity that publicizes her plight." He apologized for speaking crassly about a young woman's injuries.

"She is devious, and the charities should know about her crimes." Parsaa was bitter. In anger, Leila had confessed to killing Ali, but was not formally charged. Her prison sentence was for her role in the trafficking ring, and Parsaa asked how anyone with integrity could pay attention to a woman in prison. "Her punishment does not cover the extent of her guilt. She murdered my son, and she cannot blame her husband or parents for that."

Paul pointed out that Parsaa could do little without proof. He promised to check on Leila's status when he returned to the city. "Leila has a child, and that may be why the women visited your village—to gather information."

"The women also asked questions about who owns the surrounding property." He gestured to the valley below, so much green and gold nearby, gray and lavender in the distance. "Why would they care?"

Paul explained that the area offered potential for mining, but Parsaa shook his head. The area around Laashekoh had no history of major finds of gold or gems.

"They could be looking for something better than gold, and they could pursue leases." Paul talked about a group of minerals called rare earths. Old Soviet maps suggested large reserves of the minerals, and the United States Geological Survey had confirmed those holdings. "Some are in Helmand. Not far from here."

Paul continued. "They don't look like anything special. Some are gray, others are shiny. But they're essential for cell phones, computers, modern electronics."

Another worry for the village, Parsaa thought to himself and frowned. "Mining is not compatible with farming."

Paul asked if the village's ownership was secure.

"What is ever secure, friend?" Parsaa repeated the sentiment from Zahira, and Paul gave him a strange look. He asked if the village was in a position to reject offers, and Parsaa nodded. "If the village can avoid the temptation, they cannot bother you."

The two men reached the part of the path blocked years earlier with an avalanche, deliberately triggered to keep outside influences at bay, and Paul paused to scan the valley in the morning light. "This view makes all problems seem so distant," Paul said.

Parsaa emphasized that the village appreciated Paul's ways and would not want to work with others. Paul thanked the Afghan warmly but did not look happy. "And that could be part of the problem."

Then he asked Parsaa to do him a favor. "I doubt if others will make it out this way, but don't mention that I traveled out here alone. Best if you deny that I was here at all. The organization has strict rules, and I could be in trouble."

Parsaa waved a hand to dismiss his friend's concern. "Their rules are not our rules. Your secret is safe with me."

CHAPTER 7

Parsaa returned to the task of delivering Najwa to the compound. Saddiq saddled the donkey, and Parsaa asked Ahmed to keep the courtyard clear until he left the village. He did not want other villagers gawking while he unlocked the shed, removed Najwa, and transported her away from the village.

Then Parsaa hurried to his home and advised his wife not to expect him until after darkness fell. Sofi asked her husband if he should bring Saddiq along.

Tradition required that women be accompanied by male relatives during lengthy travel. If Parsaa left quickly, they would arrive before sunset. "It's not a good idea to involve him with the compound."

He was impatient to leave and remove Najwa. But his wife was troubled.

"You must talk with the boy," Sofi whispered. She explained how Saddiq had once enjoyed reading but had stopped abruptly. "He is acting odd and searches for excuses not to attend lessons."

Parsaa repeated advice he had given before. "Boys enjoy outdoor activities. Do not pressure him or he will resent reading the rest of his life."

She urged her husband to talk with Saddiq soon. "As the weather turns cold, he should enjoy sitting on the rug and adding logs to the fire. But no, he's upset." She hesitated, and Parsaa prompted her. "It only happened once, but he asked if Thara and the other sisters could also attend the lessons."

Leila's sisters. The two families had once lived next to each other and the children had grown up together—until their mother and sister were arrested.

"That is not a decision for us to make. Thara and the others must be punished for crimes committed by Mari and Leila."

"I did explain." Sofi was nervous. "He does not see how the girls did wrong. . . ."

"He argued with you?" Parsaa was annoyed. Every village family had a reputation. A son's view should not deviate from that of his parents.

Sofi shook her head quickly. "No, he did not argue. It was one comment. But there was a look in his eye when I told him the other parents would not allow their children to be near Leila's sisters. He's so strong-willed, and after what happened with Ali . . ."

Her worries were left unspoken. Grief swept through Parsaa and he leaned against the wall. It had been more than a year since the death of their oldest son, and memories of Ali's smile were fading in Laashekoh.

Grief should add clarity to memories.

The family could not bear the loss of another child.

"It only happened once," she repeated. "And as you say, we cannot anger him. He did not argue, but we must watch him, talk with him, protect him against these urges to defend Leila's sisters."

Saddiq was intelligent. The boy would avoid wasting words on useless arguments and alarming his parents. Parsaa placed both hands on his wife's shoulders.

"Do not make Thara an object of pity for him," he whispered. "We cannot speak cruelly of her or forbid Saddiq to talk of her, or it's all he'll think about. He will crave her."

Sofi nodded, and Parsaa wondered how long his wife had been holding on to her fears. "Have Karimah or the other women noticed?" he asked. He was relieved when she shook her head.

"Not yet," Sofi said. "I will ask Karimah to keep a close eye on Thara, give her work, or even keep her indoors for the next few weeks."

"No!" He was firm. "Do not talk to the other women about this, and let me know immediately if anyone mentions Saddiq and Thara in the same breath. Scolding will drive them together."

Perhaps he should take Saddiq with him to Zahira's, but he did not want his son locked to such visits. Once he brought one of his sons to the compound, his relationship with Zahira would change forever.

Sofi asked what she should say to Saddiq.

"Do not talk about Thara or her sisters. If the topic comes up, be kind. Remind him that the sisters no longer have parents. If they work hard, they will enjoy a better marriage and life. If he cares for them, as a good friend should, then he and the other children must leave them to their work."

He took her hands and she leaned against his shoulder. "Can we keep our sons safe?" she asked.

"Has he tried to spend time with her?" Parsaa murmured.

Sofi's worry was limited to the classes. "No, Saddiq works too hard. He spoke of her only once and mostly talks of Komal and how I will teach her someday. And yes, that is what I will probably do."

It was not reassuring that the boy avoided talking about Thara. But Parsaa would not worry his wife. "Perhaps he cares for his friends. That is all."

She took in air as if in deep water and ready to drown. "Ali spent time alone with Leila and we never knew it."

"And Saddiq knows what happened," Parsaa said. "We will give him more work and watch him. If we don't pressure him, he will forget Thara." Parsaa wished that he felt that reassurance inside, especially as he planned to visit the compound. His only tie with Zahira was friend-ship, but that did not lessen his guilt.

~~~~~~

Saddiq hurried with his assigned tasks—helping other young men in tying and moving bundles of late-harvest grain for winter storage—and waited for his father to leave the village. He had his own plans for later, to find Thara and remind her that she was not despised by all.

The children in Laashekoh had played with the sisters all their lives. Leila, as the oldest, had watched Saddiq and his younger brothers for years. Overnight, the villagers suddenly despised the girls as if their parents and sister were the only influences, and evil was more powerful than goodness.

Saddiq thought about the many influences over his life—his parents, his brothers, the men of the village, the vendors at the market in the city, especially the ones who were generous in handing out samples or telling stories about distant places. He wondered how good transformed into evil and couldn't think of many points of disagreement with Leila over the years, no sign that her father or mother or the sisters might be dangerous. All he knew was that he missed the gatherings in the girls' home and long talks with friends. The family had to bear Leila's shame, but Saddiq couldn't overlook his own shame for ignoring his friends. Maybe the evil influence of Leila was stronger than he realized. Maybe that was behind the urge to disregard his parents' dictates.

He couldn't ask his parents about his feelings. They would take more steps to separate Thara and the other girls.

And so he kept his many questions to himself. Could dear friends turn into evildoers overnight—and could the same happen to any member of his family?

It was painful to think of Thara watching the children enter his mother's small library, imagining them by the fire, listening to the stories. He no longer attended his mother's reading program and tried to convince other children not to go, too.

If he and others stayed away, then maybe Thara would feel less hurt.

Herding goats and sheep were no longer part of his duties. Early on, while his mother was reading, he found excuses to climb the hills and offer reminders to his brothers who took over the task, or to search for new stands of dry wood. He returned only after the sessions had ended as his mother hurried about the kitchen, preparing the evening meal. She tried questioning him about his absences, but his father interrupted. "Let the boy take the lessons at his own pace."

Saddiq liked the sound of that—taking lessons at one's own pace. He did not have to hurry with an activity from which dear friends were excluded, and there was less pressure to sort out why he disagreed so vehemently with his parents on what was moral and good. It was terrifying to think that his parents could be so wrong.

Not that he always agreed with them, and this was especially true with his mother. Both parents monitored his tasks and those of his brothers. His mother could be fierce about working hard and driving her children to do the same.

He could not argue with his parents, though. His father would lose all respect for Saddiq and that would be unbearable. His parents were raising the youngest of the four ostracized sisters in their home and might eventually agree with Saddiq someday. His mother adored the baby, holding and playing with Komal, talking with her throughout the day, yet she was careful not to let anyone outside the family witness her fondness for the child. Sofi had already warned her sons to hide the family's joy in caring for Komal, insisting that a life of shame in Laashekoh was better than an early marriage with a terrible man.

If his mother could break rules and be kind to Komal, then he would do the same. His parents acted as if shedding a friendship was easy, part of being an adult. True friendships could not vanish overnight. Komal would have questions in only a few years, and Saddiq wondered if his parents sensed the discrepancy in what they asked their sons to do.

If his parents had secrets, so could he.

Saddiq no longer had to make excuses to miss the lessons, and he bided his time trying to meet Thara. He spent long hours outside with his father and the other men, ensuring that others saw him tending the fields, collecting firewood, reinforcing the rock walls that surrounded the village. And all the while he watched for a girl working alone.

Over time, Saddiq detected patterns.

He would find her once his father left the village with Najwa. He had no idea when his father might return, but asked no questions. As Saddiq watched the donkey plod away, he realized that no one in the village had asked questions. They didn't care where Najwa was going.

He hiked a distance away from the village toward a stand of black locust trees battered by a violent windstorm. The wind had taken care of so much work, with the ruined trees and broken limbs. He had scouted the site earlier in a hunt for an easy source of wood and then applied extra work to the stand each day, trimming away branches and preparing the logs for transport.

He dragged a stripped log toward the village. His mother would ask no questions about how Saddiq had spent time that day.

Passing along the edge of a nearby meadow, he heard eerie moaning and stopped to listen. He determined the direction but couldn't make out the words or the voice. He stepped among the soft grasses and paused behind each tree to conceal his approach.

Even as he advanced, the chanting faded. The girl's voice had become softer, less frantic, and he could almost make out the words. A painful recitation from the Koran, one verse, over and over: "... and I turned to him soon. Repentance is for those who do evil in ignorance, and I turned to him soon. Repentance is for those who do evil in ignorance and . . ."

Holding his breath, Saddiq waited.

He had to move gently, not frighten her. He had not spoken with Thara in months and couldn't bear the thought of her running away before he had a chance to assure her that their friendship was still strong. The entire village had not abandoned her.

At last, the girl was in his sight, the voice dropping to a whisper as she methodically circled a tree, gently tugging at a clinging vine and letting it fall into a neat coil on the ground. Eventually, the vine caught against the tree's ragged bark. Lifting her arms, the girl jumped and hefted herself onto a lower branch to climb among the branches. She wanted to preserve the wild grapevine in one long and unbroken piece.

From behind his tree, Saddiq watched Thara climb higher and stretch out along one limb to release the snag. As she descended, her headscarf slipped away. Thara's gray eyes and soft lips looked so serious, as if she had forgotten how to smile.

Leila's sister had once been his closest friend. But since her mother and oldest sister were sent away to prison, the family's home was quiet and empty, used for storage of belongings no longer wanted. The villagers prohibited contact with other children, and assigned them lonely tasks. The sisters worked nonstop every day, taking their meals alone, sleeping in corners of back rooms, kept away from other family members. The other children of Laashekoh whispered about the sisters. The gossip was cruel, and he listened because it was the only way he heard about Thara. He understood why his mother had cautioned him and his brothers not to tell anyone that Komal slept in their parents' bedroom.

Saddiq studied Thara's face, searching for evil intent. But then he had not observed evil in the oldest sister. He wondered if Thara had known about Leila's crimes beforehand. That question should wait.

He edged closer, whispering her name. She did not turn, and he called out louder. Thara jerked with fear, before scrambling down and reaching for her scarf, ready to run. "I'm not allowed to talk with others," she cried.

Holding out his hands, Saddiq tried to explain he meant no harm. He waited for her response, but she stared like a wild animal. He pulled her underneath a canopy of low-hanging branches, out of sight from anyone passing through the meadow, and then he stood back.

The sun was going down, and a night chill took over the meadow. Every breath they exhaled was visible. Thara was wary, studying his face, before releasing a happy smile.

Saddiq had so much to say, but did not rush. Like a hunted animal, she might dart away. "You are working so hard."

She proudly explained how she collected reeds, vines, bark, and other materials to soak, dye, beat, and shape before weaving them along with cloth and wires into baskets that would be sold at the market. "The baskets pay my way to live with Ahmed and Karimah, and I also save for my dowry," Thara pointed out. "If I weave more, Karimah says that I'll have a better marriage." She looked down with embarrassment. "I'm the oldest and don't have as much time to work as my sisters. Karimah warns if I don't work hard, then the best I can hope for is to be third or fourth wife to a very old man."

The thought made Saddiq feel sick. That couldn't happen to Thara, he thought to himself. He wouldn't let it happen. He tried guiding her to a nearby fallen tree, but she reached for the strand still connected to the branches overhead. "I cannot sit," she protested. "Karimah checks how much I collect every day."

"Just a moment," he pleaded. "Then I'll help you retrieve the vines." She glanced around the meadow before retrieving her bundle of vines and sitting beside him. Even as they talked, she stripped the leaves away from a long strand.

He picked up the other end to help.

"How is baby Komal?" she asked.

Her first thoughts were of her youngest sister, and the question made him sad. Saddiq couldn't imagine having to ask others for news about his brothers. His parents refused to talk about the sisters, and he had not realized how intent the village women would be on segregating the sisters.

"Komal is healthy. She loves my mother, and my mother is kind." He hoped she didn't think of his family as cruel like the others, but he couldn't tell. Thara kept her head down.

"You don't see your sisters at all?" he questioned.

Thara shook her head. A tear fell down her cheek. "Our parents brought shame to this village. The others want to forget us as quickly as they can. We are fortunate that we can still live here. Karimah says that other villages would banish us to the city and force us to fend on our own."

He nodded, but was less sure that she was fortunate—not if she couldn't see her sisters.

She pinched away leaves with her fingernails, and wrapped the strand into a tight coil around her arm. "Have you heard anyone speak of my sister and mother?" Thara asked.

"Nothing," he admitted. It was as if the family had never existed. "What Leila did was wrong. I can never forgive her for pushing my brother from a cliff. But it doesn't explain why they are so angry with you."

She was skeptical. "Don't you know?" He shook his head slowly.

"You know why they are angry," she retorted, cringing. "You can't fool me, and you are here for the same reason Ali met Leila."

But Saddiq didn't know and demanded to know what she meant. She ordered him to leave her alone.

"If we are caught, I will be punished," Thara scolded as she stood. "It's painful to have you near."

Saddiq was crushed. "I don't understand," he pleaded.

"You really don't know," she mused. "If I tell you, you must promise not to be angry."

The promise was easy. What could have been worse than Leila murdering his brother or helping her father and mother in luring children away from their homes with false promises of jobs? "Tell me," he urged.

"You cannot tell anyone." She held her arms out as if to hold him back and refused to look into his eyes. Her voice dropped to a whisper, as though she feared a pummeling. "Leila was with child when she left Laashekoh."

Saddiq tried to think. Leila was arrested the night of her marriage. "Her husband's?" he asked.

Thara shook her head. "Then whose?" he pressed.

Ashamed, she tugged at her headscarf and hid her mouth. "Leila said it belonged to your brother. She told my mother that his fall was an accident as they argued. She was upset about Ali leaving for school, and he was upset, too. That is why my parents hurried to marry her to Jahangir."

Saddiq was still. The explanation hit his brain as if he had fallen into an icy river. He should have been angry, but his heart ached for his brother. He missed Ali, but he missed Thara, too. "Do my parents know?" he asked.

"About the pregnancy? Perhaps. I've heard Karimah whispering with others." She took a deep breath. "But about the child belonging to Ali, I do not think so. The adults do not speak about this." She reached for another vine to strip. "Then, I am alone and do not hear much. I'm not like my oldest sister. Do you understand that?"

He nodded slowly.

"So you should leave if that is why you are here." Thara took a dignified pose, and pressed. "Did you plan on using me as Ali used Leila?"

"No," he said softly. So much more made sense, especially why the adults kept Thara and the other girls away from the other children. Why his brother had crept away from the bedroom in the middle of the night. He could not understand why Ali was at fault or why Thara thought he was ready to use her.

Leila had somehow tricked his brother. He was sure, but to say as much would anger Thara, so he kept quiet. He had to pose careful questions rather than accusations. He asked when Thara learned of Leila's predicament.

"Only a few nights before Ali's death," she explained. "Leila was terrified. Can you imagine how alone she felt? Our mother had warned us that it was our duty to avoid tempting others, and Leila worried my parents would never speak to her again. But my mother kept her secret and arranged her marriage quickly."

She paused. "You know the village would have killed them both. Leila was furious that all Ali cared about was going to school. She could not understand why he wouldn't help when she was so desperate."

Saddiq could not understand such angry hatred for Ali. Village girls knew more than the boys did about such matters. Many mothers told their daughters about marriage well in advance rather than leaving it to the new husband or his mother. Fathers in Laashekoh told boys about their duties a few nights before the wedding contract was signed.

"Maybe he didn't believe her," Thara admitted, retying her headscarf as if to protect herself. "Our mother was so eager about Leila staying in Laashekoh. She often talked about how wonderful it would be if Leila married Ali and stayed."

Saddiq could not imagine his brother convincing his parents about such a marriage. He also could not imagine his brother keeping such a secret and told Thara as much.

"Perhaps she lied," Thara mused. "We will never know. What would your brother have done had he known?"

Saddiq couldn't answer and didn't know which was sadder—his brother keeping a secret before his death or dying without knowing about the child. Regardless, the child's mother despised his family.

"There was little they could do," Thara noted, adding that her sister and mother had reached the same conclusion. "Karimah blames my parents because they waited too long to plan Leila's marriage, so she wants no delay in marriages for me and my sisters. They want to get rid of us soon, and that is probably for the best."

Dipping her head, she stared into his eyes. "If anyone saw us talking now, they would blame me."

And the adults would be angry because she knew so many details about others in Laashekoh. Adults did not like thinking about what they did not know. He plucked a tall strand of grass apart and split it into thin threads. He did not want to leave for school. He did not blame Thara or her sisters for his brother's death. He was grateful for Thara's honesty and wanted to protect her. He wondered why he was so different than his parents.

"Perhaps it is better we do not know," he said.

"Perhaps." They were quiet for a few moments, and she sat next to him again. "Or people of Laashekoh don't know because they don't want to know. Why didn't your parents pursue murder charges against Leila?"

Saddiq couldn't answer. There was too much to think about, but he was in no hurry. He offered to help with the vines and pointed toward the sky. "I'll climb the tree?"

Thara laughed and told him getting outside was the best part of her day. "Collecting material for the baskets is an escape from cleaning the kitchen and Karimah's sharp tongue." She leaned close and thanked him. "It's a joy being treated as a friend again."

"You have talked with no one else?"

"Everyone is afraid, as if my family is tainted with evil." Her laugh was sad. "And maybe it is."

"You could never be evil. We were good friends, and that's all I want."

Tears came to her eyes again. "I am working for a good marriage. I only hope they don't send me to someone awful because of what Leila did."

Saddiq suggested that he try talking with his father. "My family should be more forgiving."

Thara panicked. "You must not! He would punish both of us!"

He soothed her by explaining that he would talk about Komal. "My mother loves her, and that may make her realize that others are being cruel to you." He asked if she would be collecting grass from the slope soon.

"It is dangerous to plan meetings." Thara was adamant. "We should not take the risk."

Saddiq vowed to do everything in his power to help Thara and made her promise to meet again.

~~~~~

That night, Saddiq returned home and watched his mother in the kitchen. She smiled without breaking her rhythm while mashing pumpkin, onion, and chickpeas together, shaping them into small balls and then flattening them for frying. The oil sizzled in the pan.

Saddiq offered to help, and she told him to play with the younger children. Saddiq approached Komal, who played quietly in the corner, and she looked up with a joyful smile, forgetting her arrangement of old sticks and carved blocks that had belonged to him and his brothers. Crouching down to her level, he saw that she had built a tiny shelter for her rag doll, the only possession the child had been allowed to keep. Komal clung to the doll day and night—and sobbed if anyone tried to move it from her sight.

He stretched out along the floor, adding another circle of blocks to protect the doll's shelter. His mother paused in her work and smiled.

"Komal—surely you will read to her someday?" Saddiq questioned.

Worry instantly replaced happiness on his mother's face. Pausing before placing a flattened cake into the pan, she studied her son's face. "Only if the others have forgotten about her sister and mother by then," she said. "But that is not likely. We must get along with others in this village, and you will understand someday."

CHAPTER 8

Over the years, Parsaa had gradually allowed more months to pass in between each visit to the compound, and Zahira was amazed to see him again so quickly. Once inside the small clinic, he bowed his head, closed his eyes, and took in the fresh scent of orange blossoms and mint that followed her.

She leaned close, and his embrace was polite, stiff. Annoyed, Zahira stepped back and waited for him to speak.

"I need a favor." He was earnest.

Zahira turned her back to him and wondered why the words seemed like an insult. Parsaa didn't notice and talked about a girl rescued from traffickers. He asked if Zahira might have use for a young servant.

Surely the villagers could have found some use for an orphan girl. The girl was an excuse for another visit. "Is she disagreeable?"

Parsaa thought and shook his head. "Just odd."

She couldn't help giving him a hard smile. "And so you thought of me." The story wasn't unusual. An orphan girl with an unknown background would not be trusted, and of course, the women in the small, close community of Laashekoh banished her quickly. Zahira leaned against the counter as he talked on about the girl and the village. Despite her fury, all she cared about was the sound of his voice. He needed her for something, and she liked the idea that she could say no to him and send him on his way.

When he paused, she asked questions about the efforts that went into locating the girl's parents. She could not agree to his request too quickly and let Parsaa take her for granted. If she said no, he might not return for months.

"We tried," Parsaa said. "We found the other children's parents quickly. But not hers."

She waved her hand. "You are wasting your time searching for parents who don't want to be found." She then asked why he didn't send the girl to an orphanage in the city.

He was stubborn. Leila and her parents had made promises and helped remove children from their homes. "The village is responsible for providing a home until her family can be found."

"But I'm not of Laashekoh," she said pointedly.

Zahira understood Laashekoh better than the villagers themselves, he suggested. "And you are a suitable guardian. Better than most women in Laashekoh."

His assessment flattered her, but she did not respond. Instead, she went to her desk, and did not invite him to sit. Parsaa rarely stayed long unless a computer search caught his attention. He continued, almost as if he spoke to himself. "We give you privacy. A stable village is in your interest."

"Tell me the truth about the girl." Zahira was blunt. "Is she disruptive?"

"She is not happy." He chose his words carefully, and Zahira wondered if the challenge was the girl or a village that disliked willful women. "She does not do well with many people, and I thought this could be a good home."

The compound could be lonely, Zahira warned. She rifled through a drawer, pretending to search for a notepad and pen. She was torn about taking in a stranger, though the compound could use more help. She asked if the girl was intelligent, but he did not know. "Do you think she will like it here?"

Parsaa nodded. "You are a good influence."

More flattery. The offer was tempting. The girl could do chores and help with Arhaan and his birds, giving Aza and Zahira more time with the child.

If the girl did not work well, she could return to Laashekoh, though that could be a problem. Zahira did not want the girl gossiping about the compound with the villagers. But Zahira could hide her secrets, and Aza and Mohan would do the same. Her husband, engrossed with his mynas, would pay no attention.

The villagers already resented the girl and would not listen to the ramblings of an orphan.

Parsaa pressed her. "So what do you think?"

"You are in a rush to leave this girl. Be truthful, Parsaa. How big of a problem is she?"

He did not avoid her stare. "She is rough and strange. She keeps secrets. But she is not dangerous."

He was in a hurry, and Zahira shrugged. "We all have secrets. Bring her by and I will decide."

Heading for the door, he replied that the girl was ready to work that night.

"So presumptuous!" Zahira protested. She asked what he would have done had she said no. "We are busy here, and need time to prepare!"

He was embarrassed, and Zahira checked her anger, silently tapping her finger on a counter. The girl could work out, especially if she was not close with other villagers. There were so many tasks associated with the infant, more than Zahira had anticipated. She wondered if the girl would think it odd that Parsaa had not mentioned the child. Zahira could lie and state that she was caring for a friend's daughter.

Better to give no details at all. The girl was a servant. Zahira did not have to explain. She followed Parsaa to the door. "So you trust me with a child?"

"Of course," Parsaa replied. "Najwa is not so young. The older ones can be difficult to train."

She asked if he would trust leaving one of his own children at the compound. He nodded quickly enough.

"If I take this orphan, you must return in two weeks. If the arrangement does not work, you must take her away."

He protested that two weeks was not long. "It's the best I can offer," Zahira said coolly. "I do not understand why she is a problem there, but helpful here?"

He reminded her that the village was still caring for Leila's sisters. "Their father made no plans for them, and people are uncomfortable about so many girls in the village."

She wondered how much he knew about the girl in prison. "Have you heard news of Leila?"

"The two foreign women know of her." He bitterly described Leila waiting out her time in the Kandahar prison with support from foreign charities. He opened the door to the dark night sky full of stars, and Zahira stood with him in the cool air.

"The authorities may trust a woman," he mused. "You could tell them she does not deserve support."

She denied that the foreigners would listen and advised that he not worry. "The charities do what they want. Let Leila get a taste of their foreign ways. Once she wrongs them, the foreign charities will snatch it away. If we antagonize her, she will return for vengeance."

He asked if Zahira thought some illness caused Leila and her parents to act as they did.

"Greed is not an illness." Dwelling on Leila's character made her uncomfortable. "It is taught by parents."

"If that is her only flaw," Parsaa said. Parents could suggest their children were better than others and deserved more from life. Parents could complain and blame others, sowing discontent that lasted a lifetime.

Zahira asked if Parsaa had ever suspected that Leila had criminal tendencies. He leaned against the door and shook his head.

"Could her sisters repeat her ways?" she pressed.

He did not know.

"Think hard," Zahira urged.

The sisters were close, he explained. Leila was good to her parents and sisters. "I have tried to remember every conversation, every glance. We missed something. She was her father's treasure."

"So that shaped her character?" Zahira questioned.

Parsaa thought. "Perhaps. That and how much others admired her beauty. But how does it matter? What could we have done differently?" He admitted to having never imagined that Leila could hurt his oldest son.

He paused again. "The other girls have done no wrong so far. They are quiet, sad, and seem to understand that their parents brought their troubles on themselves."

So far ... A parent never knew how much could go wrong with a child's life. Zahira tightened her headscarf and crossed her arms to shield against the chilly night breeze.

"People like you are unusual." Parsaa smiled.

She looked at him with surprise.

"For staying here. For caring and not wanting more. It's a good way."

"You don't know what I want." But she returned his smile. "And it's not wrong to want more knowledge or family or love or comforts like electricity or water. It's not the same as wanting money or control."

He did not respond. Shivering, she suggested that he bring Najwa inside.

Parsaa tried to reassure her, suggesting if a problem developed, Zahira should send the caretaker to Laashekoh. His unflustered attitude added to her exasperation. "It is late." She waved him off. "Bring her to the house."

Reaching for her hand, he thanked her. "Your household has fewer people. That means fewer complications."

"Never forget that it's complicated here, too, Parsaa. Two weeks may be too long. . . ."

He slipped away, and she almost thought about calling him back and telling him that she needed more time to think. She should warn her husband.

But Parsaa would think of her as flighty, and instead she ran across the courtyard to her home.

Zahira would listen to the girl's observations about Parsaa, his wife, his children. Najwa was a reminder of days that the people of Laashekoh wanted to forget, and that could be useful.

CHAPTER 9

Parsaa climbed the hill and returned to the small clearing where he had left Najwa. The girl waited among the shadows of the tall pines, out of reach from the lights of the compound. She sat on a large rock, her back hunched forward, hands folded and head down as if in prayer. As he approached, she lifted her head, a quick flash of defiance accompanied by a meek voice. "Am I staying here?"

He was curt. "For a short while." If the length of her stay was uncertain, Najwa might behave.

Najwa reached for the small bag containing her meager belongings. "Did you bring my blade?" she asked. Parsaa scolded her, explaining that a sharp weapon was not necessary in the tiny compound, and she murmured that the tool was all she had left from home.

"You will be safe here," he said. He promised to bring the *peshkabz* during another visit.

Guilt lingered. He had not been forthright with Zahira. Najwa was not dull or dangerous, he was sure. Yet she was more than odd, irritating others by staring, eavesdropping on conversations for no good reason, and balking at answering questions about her family. She seemed older than her years and manipulative. Najwa had displayed few opinions since her arrival and was unusually stoic. Parsaa could not deny that he was abandoning a responsibility and toyed briefly with the idea of bringing her back to the village. Both Zahira and Sofi would think he was foolish.

Zahira should form her own judgment. She would put Najwa to work, and the two weeks would pass quickly. That could help determine where the girl belonged. The pair approached the main house with smooth walls of yellow clay. The structure resembled a golden shrine in the night except for the noisy cackling of birds. They sensed a newcomer.

Najwa asked if more than one family lived in the compound.

"No, just one," he said softly. Then he spoke loudly so others would hear. "Zahira is a capable woman, and this is her childhood home. You must do whatever she asks."

A silhouette waited in the doorway—still and nothing like the memories of his youth.

~~~~~

Blacker invited the strongest and smartest boys from nearby villages to train at the compound. When the selected boys were not tending herds or helping their parents in the fields, they headed to the busy compound for training in tracking, climbing, weapons, and hand-to-hand combat. The man observed the boys, testing them on strategy puzzles, strength, and endurance.

When not studying with her tutors, his daughter sat underneath a canopy of trees on a slope overlooking Blacker's playing field. As the boys clashed and tumbled on the field, she read from a schoolbook, occasionally lifting her head at a sudden outburst. She was Blacker's only child, a few years younger than Parsaa. The warlord treasured his daughter, trusting her as an adviser. He purchased furs, embroidered silk clothes, jewelry, horses, and whips with trailing silk cords for her— but more than anything else, she longed for books and an education. She left the compound for long periods to attend a school in the city, already showing a talent for reading, math, history, and three languages.

Families in nearby villages regarded the girl as odd and warned their sons against whispers or stares cast in her direction. The games and lessons were more relaxed when the girl was not around.

At night, after the boys returned to their homes, Zahira answered her father's questions about which ones were intelligent, loyal, and trustworthy. The bond was strong between Blacker and his only child, and the boys had no idea about how much their benefactor relied on the young girl's assessments.

During the few occasions when she was not attending school or studying for tests, Zahira helped the house servants prepare and distribute lunch to the group of boys—thick stews along with an unending supply of naan, fresh fruit, and milk. She was aloof, like a mother or an older sister, and once the meal was served, Zahira sat near the boys, nibbling fruit while listening to the boasts and complaints of fatigue. She was quiet—an observer rather than a participant—and for the most part, the boys ignored her. Then one day a boy teased Zahira for serving Parsaa the largest portion of stew. That was the boy's last day at the compound.

Zahira took pains to show no preference for Parsaa, but the servants and older boys already noticed her keen interest. Eventually Blacker recognized his daughter's fascination, too. The man turned his intense gaze on Parsaa, observing and waiting with neither approval nor disapproval. As his daughter so often noted, the boy was quiet, loyal, and kind.

A few months later, Blacker visited the boy's parents with a proposition. He saw potential in their son and offered to pay tuition and board at a *maktab*, or school. Parsaa's parents were excited, and Blacker gave them fair warning about the long-term nature of the duties. Blacker expected Parsaa, when finished, to return to Laashekoh and help manage and secure the properties.

The parents had no qualms about entering their son into a lifelong commitment. Young Parsaa enjoyed spending time at the compound, and an education and a guaranteed position meant their son could return to the fields of Laashekoh rather than leave for fighting. After tea, Parsaa's father accompanied Blacker to the horses. "He should leave immediately." Blacker issued the quiet order. "Your job is to instill loyalty and gratitude in your son."

Parsaa's father gave his promise. "With Allah as my witness, you have my word."

Summer days passed, and Parsaa no longer showed up for training at the compound. Zahira could not bear it any longer. As the boys paired up to practice with swords, she tugged at her father's sleeve and asked about the boy's whereabouts. Her father explained that Parsaa had left for school early, and Zahira was furious.

"You attend school," Blacker countered. "Why don't you want the same for him?"

Fury turned to tears, and her father was stern. "You say you want to become a doctor, and if you're serious, that means leaving this place." Later, he suggested that her goals and Parsaa's duties did not combine for a suitable marriage. Zahira blushed, refusing to respond to the bold suggestion. She had imagined friendship, not marriage, and she wondered which her father detested more—her love for Parsaa or her dream to become a doctor and work outside of Afghanistan.

Parsaa's parents had already planned his marriage, her father explained. Besides, he warned that she would not be happy with Parsaa as a husband. "He is a servant, nothing more," Blacker cautioned his daughter. "If you study medicine, I doubt that you will return to this part of Afghanistan. Parsaa has no reason to leave. But should you return, he will remember our kindness and keep you safe."

He took his daughter into his arms. "This land and home will be safe. No one can touch you."

Her father was intense, describing every detail of the transaction, as though he suspected that his daughter might not leave Afghanistan.

~~~~~

Najwa stepped inside the home and Zahira—tall, commanding, beautiful in a deep-blue *perahaan tunbaan*, a loose tunic and pants in soft, brushed cotton—waited for a reaction. Three yellow kittens tumbled behind her.

Parsaa hung back, ready to speak—though that may have been wishful thinking on Zahira's part—when a sudden gust of wind slammed the door on him. Parsaa did not knock, and Zahira was tempted to fling open the door and call out. At least wish him a safe journey back to Laashekoh.

That was unwise in front of the girl. Every gesture could be misconstrued.

Zahira could wait for Parsaa to return in two weeks. She turned and assessed the girl. Oversized clothes did not hide Najwa's large bones and awkwardness. Her cheekbones, wide and flat, pressed her eyes into a squint. Her plain brown hair was dry and dull. Her skin had dry patches.

Najwa stared at the surrounding walls that rose toward a painted arch, detailed in gold and red paint, bathed in light so late at night, as if she had stepped into a world of magic. The home was grand, its ceilings higher than any in Laashekoh. Zahira expected a stronger reaction. After all, the compound—the large home surrounded by nearly twenty other structures of varying sizes—had been built for the region's toughest warlord and the top deputies of his militia.

That was years ago. Zahira had since updated the home and renovated the armory as a small clinic. The barn that once sheltered Blacker's horses served as her husband's workshop, with cages for his mynas.

Other than a small home in the center of the compound for the caretakers, Aza and Mohan, the other structures were closed or used for storage.

The main home was warm, spacious, and modern. Perhaps the comfortable furniture, ruby-red Afghan rugs, and golden light from lamps intimidated Najwa, and Zahira took that as a good sign. Though the compound was lonely, the girl might want to work hard and stay.

Zahira was not friendly, though. Blacker had trained his daughter how to manage household staff and newcomers: Never trust them. Offer scant attention, especially in front of others, and make them nervous and unsure, ready to please.

She barely acknowledged Najwa. Zahira called for the woman who ran the household and curtly ordered Aza to prepare a space for Najwa: "We'll decide what to do with her in the morning."

Aza suggested putting Najwa in one of the smallest huts once used by seasonal help. Zahira was cold. "She may not stay long. Show her the kitchen. She can heat what's left of the carrot soup and take it back to her quarters."

Aza ordered Najwa to pick up her own belongings.

Zahira turned her back, dismissing them. She hoped that Aza would think up enough tasks for Najwa to do. The girl was probably not capable of cooking fine meals or handling expensive belongings.

Guests were rare, and Zahira still enjoyed being useful around the house, preparing meals for the small group, helping Aza with the laundry, reviewing the accounts, not to mention feeding, cleaning, and comforting the child.

If anything, Aza set the agenda for the compound and supervised Zahira. The younger woman trusted Aza as if she were an older sister.

Arhaan did not lift a hand to help poor Mohan.

Aza ordered the girl to wait outside. Once alone with Zahira, Aza asked if Parsaa knew about the child yet. Zahira shook her head, and the older woman frowned. "Once he knows about the child, he'll be more willing to secure this compound."

Zahira did not agree and shook her head.

"He is still outside. You can tell him tonight."

"I'm not ready," Zahira said.

"Mohan and I can tell him?" Aza questioned.

"Not yet." Zahira was stubborn.

"The baby will wake soon," Aza reminded. "Be prepared to quiet her quickly."

Zahira hurried toward her bedroom to check on the sleeping child. Her rosy pout and lashes like tiny fans were set against creamy, white skin. Zahira tried, but she still couldn't think of the child as her daughter.

The baby was renamed Shareen, after the woman who had died giving birth to Zahira. The name, rarely mentioned when Zahira was a child, should not prompt so many memories, and she hoped those would fade as the child exerted her own personality. One day Zahira might tell Parsaa about the baby. Only if she could be sure that the knowledge would draw him closer to her and the compound.

Bending over, Zahira picked up the baby. Shareen whimpered but remained asleep as Zahira left the house and moved slowly among the shadows to observe the compound. Privacy was the ultimate luxury at the compound, but so easy to steal.

Aza was preoccupied with settling Najwa in a squat building with no windows and summarizing the routines that had not changed in years. Breakfast was served just after sunrise and dinner at sunset. Both were served in the kitchen. "For now, this is your space, and you must take care of it. If compound guests arrive, you must give up the space."

Najwa stood in the doorway as the older woman lit a lantern with a warning that the hut did not have electricity. "But there's a fireplace and small stove and wood here. There's a cistern, so you don't have to collect your own water. Use it sparingly. The rain is not as plentiful as it used to be." She handed Najwa a key. "I have the other copy."

Picking up her parcel, Najwa seemed nervous about stepping inside. "I don't share with other servants?"

"More servants make for more work," Aza snapped. She brushed past Najwa in the doorway.

"Is there a master of this house?" Najwa asked.

The question could be viewed as bold, suggesting that Zahira might struggle to control the compound. Aza was calm. "Master Arhaan is here. But he is busy, and you won't see much of him."

The woman paused. "Three warnings. Never disturb the master and mistress while they are at work. Lock your door at night, and I will check. And do not utter a word about what you see or hear in this compound. Or I will cut your tongue out."

Najwa showed no fear and closed the door slowly. Aza, bent with age, faced the closed door for a long moment, before walking away.

The strange girl could not go near the infant. Zahira should have asked Parsaa more questions. Still, Zahira liked the idea of another person at the compound more awkward with children than herself.

Stepping back inside her home, Zahira returned the sleeping infant to the bedroom and smoothed the girl's fine hair. The child would not grow up in a backward place like Laashekoh. Zahira was relieved her husband showed no interest and preferred his mynas. Shareen would be beautiful, but no one at the compound would take notice. Zahira was determined to raise the child and eliminate the traits associated with her biological mother.

The child could not know her mother's identity, and Zahira and the child would leave the compound soon. Zahira leaned over and rubbed her cheek against the child's cheek. So soft.

Aza would return soon to feed and change the child.

Zahira slipped back outside, heading for a group of stone huts not used in years. The interiors were musty and dark, and she checked that no one else wandered outside before opening one door. Her eyes needed a moment to adjust and spot the figure waiting in the corner. She moved closer, and Paul Reichart wrapped his arms around her, stroking her hair.

"Is he gone yet?" he whispered.

She shook her head, grateful Paul did not say the name aloud. She loved Parsaa, but she needed Paul. "He will be here a while longer. Are you warm enough?"

He pulled her down to the floor strewn with carpets. "I am now," he whispered. "You sure no one will come back here?"

"No one has used these places for years." The thought of when the rugs had last been beaten made her uncomfortable, and she pulled away to sit up.

She was nervous with no lock on the door and Parsaa so close.

Paul wanted to know the reason for Parsaa's visit. "Did he ask about the charity workers?"

"Not this time," she murmured. "He would be thrilled to know they won't return."

"I doubt anyone will find the crash site," Paul went on as though using a checklist. "The helicopter didn't burn. It was easy to push boulders and branches from the cliff above. With winter coming..."

As he spoke, Zahira traced a dark leaf, part of the carpet's design, with her finger. She should ask if Paul had checked the helicopter for survivors. He placed his fingers under her chin and tipped her head back.

"You don't trust me," he commented.

She didn't respond.

"No one knows that they stopped here." He leaned over to kiss her, and she turned her head. "It's far enough away from the compound."

"People won't ask questions?"

"The two women annoyed everyone they met." He gave a short laugh. "They hurried to purchase a helicopter and didn't buy proper insurance. They couldn't wait to meet with me for advice. They'll be forgotten soon enough. You are fine."

"I had nothing to do with them!" Zahira insisted. To scoff about others' death was wrong and reflected on his own weakness. She gave him a sidelong glance, but his face was in the shadows. The two dared not use a lantern.

Paul had warned her about the women's search for Afghan partners, how they were intrigued by healthcare workers who might know about unwanted children. They relied on a list of Paul's contacts in Afghanistan. The helicopter landed out of sight in the canyon, far enough away from the compound, and the three occupants hiked to Zahira's clinic. She responded coolly to their nervous questions.

At the time, she had not realized that she would be the last one to see the group alive. Mohan, Aza, and even Arhaan had heard the exchange, but not the crash. They did not know Paul had been nearby.

No one had to know about the visit, Paul promised. Tightening his grip on her, he placed his other hand under her chin and forced Zahira to face him. "The helicopter had a heavy load that was improperly secured. It's a pilot's responsibility to check loads along with the fuel and other gauges before takeoff."

The crash site was rough terrain, and Zahira didn't want to check the scene herself or know details. "They will ask why we didn't report it."

"If you didn't hear it . . ." He was calm. "Do you want investigators and questions?"

But investigators would arrive. She wished that the accident had happened far from her home. "Did you see them take off?" she asked.

"I was nowhere near the place." He sat up. "I saw the wreck on my way here, and it was too late to help. But the problem is evident enough."

He paused. "The pilot probably had no problem moving upward or forward, but once he turned to exit the canyon . . . the load shifted, probably a broken strap. He lost control. An accident. End of story."

She should not know such details, especially if the crash went unreported. The timing for a broken strap was off. The helicopter added no new load from the compound and had taken many turns during the journey from Laashekoh. She was nervous. Three foreigners were missing. Search crews would be dispatched. Investigators would focus on the last stop and the last person who saw the group.

Zahira didn't like the uncertainty. But she needed Paul's help to leave Afghanistan and escape constant reminders of a life she didn't share with Parsaa.

Paul grasped her shoulders and pulled her close. "They were a nuisance. It's a sensitive time, and we don't need more questions." He kissed her and she closed her eyes, forgetting about the women, the helicopter, the compound. Zahira could only think of Parsaa and how much he didn't know.

CHAPTER 10

Before departing for Laashekoh, Parsaa met with Aza's husband. Mohan was a trusted aide to Zahira's father and more than a servant. His age of more than seven decades was unusual in the area, and the man was more cautious than ever. The village had celebrated *norooz*, the start of spring, more than twenty times since Blacker's death. Although many years had passed with no disturbance, the old man still worried about the compound's security.

Mohan was intent on collecting details about the newcomer.

He directed Parsaa to take a seat among the pillows and lit a lantern, casting a gold glow on the tiny space. Zahira had wanted to connect the caretaker's home to a generator, but Mohan refused. His house, a haven of simplicity, had not changed in years.

Mohan did not speak as he poured hot chai, thickened with yogurt, into two bowls. He placed the bowls on the stone slab in the middle of the rug and then stared at Parsaa. "You bring a stranger here. What do you know about her? And why can't you find her village?"

Parsaa pointed out that an aid worker was still searching for the girl's village, but Mohan dismissed the search. "The girl does not want her family to be found! She committed a crime against her community or ran away from a marriage. That puts the compound in danger."

"We searched. She is unwanted, probably an orphan."

Mohan grunted and suggested that Parsaa was naive. "She has her reasons for this secret. How do you know she did not collude with the traffickers?"

Parsaa had not considered the possibility and was mortified. The children, including Najwa, had been tied together. Arriving in

Laashekoh, the girl wore shabby clothing and showed bruising. The American soldiers had believed her story.

Collusion didn't seem possible. But children could be wily, taking advantage of adult assumptions. Parsaa tried to remember the villagers' complaints about Najwa—how she refused to answer questions, stared at others, and crept about for no obvious reason. The girl's curiosity seemed random, focusing on ordinary conversations and relationships rather than specifics of village politics or finances. If Najwa was a spy, she had gained little useful information while in Laashekoh, unless village routines revealed more secrets than he realized. Worrying was foolish. The village had nothing to hide, and Najwa had expressed no interest in leaving, rushing to meet with traffickers and tell them what she learned.

He was convinced. A stay at the compound would be good for Najwa. The place had four adults. Fewer people meant fewer secrets. And Zahira knew how to keep secrets.

Mohan had more questions about Najwa. Did she try to run away from Laashekoh? Did she steal? Did she avoid work? The answers were no, no, no. Mohan did not ask if the girl stared in a quiet way, showed a hint of smile as she refused to answer questions, feigned puzzlement over specific directions, or wandered into other people's homes late at night to toss a book into the fire. Mohan did not ask if she was too attached to a possession like a knife. The complaints about her were vague, irrational. Perhaps that was why they were so unsettling.

Mohan then reviewed compound security. The man repeated himself every time Parsaa visited. The compound was located in a canyon with steep walls. Anyone who tried to reach the place had to pass near Laashekoh with its young guards on constant watch. Or the intruders had to be extraordinary climbers, with the ability to evade the odd traps and alarms that Mohan had set along the canyon edges, though those were deactivated when Zahira traveled or visitors were expected.

"Did the girl see the traps?" the old man asked.

"I was careful," Parsaa promised.

Mohan dismissed such assurance. "I will relocate them. If she gets ideas or doesn't like the work here, she won't escape easily enough."

Parsaa was quiet, wishing that Najwa would wander away. He wouldn't mind never seeing her again. In a flash, he rejected the thought as wrong and despised himself. In truth, he wanted Mohan's precautions to go untested. As years passed, few ventured near the compound, except those driving delivery wagons with supplies and messages for the small group. Friends of Blacker and Mohan had moved away or died. The paths leading to the compound were overgrown and treacherous. Even in Laashekoh, most young villagers, including Saddiq and his brothers, had no idea of the compound's existence.

The compound was too large for a couple without children—a worry that nagged Mohan for years. The size, isolation, security, and deliveries signaled unusual wealth and invited resentment. From the start, Parsaa had insisted that the best security was keeping people away—a condition over which they had little control unless Zahira and Arhaan cooperated.

Zahira and Arhaan did not get along, but the two were of one mind in refusing to relocate, change their routines, or embrace a modest lifestyle. They indulged in expensive hobbies that required steady deliveries. Only Mohan worried when a new driver was assigned.

The old man grumbled that neither Zahira nor Arhaan planned far into the future. They expected Mohan and Aza to live forever. As years passed, Mohan, gray and stooped, grudgingly acknowledged that more responsibility for security had shifted toward Parsaa. Yet the younger man's sense of loyalty for the compound had faded from honor to habit. So much that Parsaa often wondered if he didn't have more concern for Mohan and Aza than for Zahira or her husband. That might be why Mohan refused to relinquish control or hire other help. He expected one of Parsaa's sons and a wife to make a home in the compound and work for Zahira and Arhaan.

Yet Parsaa could not envision such an isolated life for any of his sons and delayed discussing such an option with his family. Mohan and Aza were elderly and would not live much longer. They eventually would have little choice but to move to the city, close to their son. Parsaa hoped that Zahira and Arhaan had the good sense to move away from the compound, too. Otherwise, they would be forced to accept help from others. Parsaa struggled to keep such thoughts to himself.

He wanted to take off into the night, but that would be selfish. Instead, he finished his tea and listened to Mohan's nostalgic musings. The gruff old man had no visitors and looked forward to long conversations with Parsaa about farming, village arguments, provincial politics, markets, and security. Mohan rarely asked about Parsaa's family. At first that bothered Parsaa, but he had since become grateful.

Mohan noticed that Parsaa was quiet. The conversation turned back to Najwa. "If I had my way, I would send her back with you," Mohan admitted. "Zahira won't admit it, but she wants the extra help."

The comment caught Parsaa by surprise, and Mohan continued. "She does not want to show weakness in front of you. She always wanted to keep up with you and the other boys. But I worry about her. Arhaan is taunting her. She is afraid and keeps too many secrets even from me."

Parsaa shared the man's misgivings. He had never understood Zahira's choices—agreeing to marry Arhaan, staying at the lonely compound, not having children. She had traveled far for an education that went unfinished and had been torn between two worlds since.

He hoped the couple was getting along, but the opposite could be true. It didn't matter what Parsaa thought. He could not fix Zahira's problems.

So much of the dark compound had not changed in years, and Parsaa wondered if Blacker still watched.

"We cannot control her," Parsaa said, lightly. "You cannot help unless she asks, and too much time has passed."

"She is older and more stubborn," Mohan said. "She must worry about what will happen to this place when we are gone."

"Laashekoh is nearby." Parsaa was firm.

The old man was cagey. "Your commitment could last longer than you planned."

"As long as Zahira lives." Parsaa responded automatically.

The old man smiled and poured more chai that Parsaa no longer wanted. "Do you think you are as observant as you were a few years ago?" Mohan queried.

It was the kind of question that Blacker once asked. "What have I missed?" Parsaa countered.

Mohan chuckled. "That is for you to find out."

"I observe you need more help." Parsaa kept his voice gentle. "It's one reason I brought the girl here. My sons are too young, but we could hire another couple. Good people would be grateful for this work . . ."

"They were not trained by Blacker," Mohan chided. "He chose you for a reason."

"Something could happen to me—any of us—any time." He looked away from the lantern into the dark shadows of the room. "It is hard to explain to others what this place was once like."

Mohan stressed how it was Parsaa's duty to make his sons understand. Parsaa did not argue, and the two men sat quietly, thinking of another day when the compound was alive with activity, young voices, and one commanding voice that had inspired immediate obedience and loyalty.

"There are secrets here you don't know."

"Zahira and her husband are not getting along?" Parsaa shrugged, pretending not to care. "That is not new."

"There are complications. A servant girl adds more."

The old man tended to exaggerate the compound's difficulties, and Parsaa refused to plead for details. "The girl may only be temporary. I'll return in two weeks."

"Zahira's request?" Mohan guessed.

Parsaa nodded.

"This is not a good time for us to trust a stranger," the old man fretted. "I must start training one of your sons soon. Better to start young."

"Not yet." Parsaa was firm and drained the warm tea quickly, grateful for the last sip. "They have not learned to protect Laashekoh."

Mohan asked about others. "Is there no gratitude for what Blacker did for the village?"

"They would be grateful if they knew." Parsaa was stern. "But we kept the arrangement a secret, as requested by Blacker."

"And there is safety in that secret," Mohan admitted. "How Blacker and Zahira enjoyed their secrets."

"Secrets turn into lies," Parsaa stood. "As long as Zahira does not keep secrets from you or Aza."

Mohan did not respond, and Parsaa readied to leave. The old man was stiff, and there was an air of sadness. Too much talk about age and a need to choose their replacements.

Parsaa warned, "Keep a close eye on the orphan—and bring her back to Laashekoh if she is any trouble at all."

~~~~~~

Parsaa set off in the darkness along the compound's old, familiar paths. Relief mixed with guilt over leaving so much work for the old lieutenant still loyal to Zahira and the memory of her father.

Before long, Parsaa heard a rustling noise and soft tapping against the dirt. Parsaa took a few steps away from the path and waited. The man following paused, cocking his head as if puzzled over how the quarry had vanished. One only had to freeze in place to elude a blind man.

"Salaam," Parsaa spoke softly so as not to alarm Zahira's husband or the myna clinging to his shoulder.

"Sal-aaam." The bird's tone was like a shrill order. "Sal-aaam."

"Ah, so it is you." Zahira's husband was pleased with himself, and then the odd smile vanished. "Why not stop by my workshop?"

"It's late." Parsaa kept his voice flat, prepared for a difficult exchange. Arhaan took pride in his keen hearing. He was sensitive to tone and rhythm and regarded any shift as evidence of deceit. Zahira snapped at him in a monotone. Mohan and Aza spoke with him as little as possible. Parsaa had little sympathy for the man.

"This is a lonely place. Like my wife, I welcome company any time of night."

"A quick errand—an orphan needs a place to stay for a short while and can help Aza and Mohan."

The man stepped closer. Blank eyes aimed at Parsaa's neck. "I assume you saw my wife."

"Briefly." Parsaa did not want to talk about Zahira.

"Yes, she has time for all but her husband." The bitter man's head bobbed with every sarcastic word. He resented his wife's control over the compound. Arhaan had supplies for his birds, books, computers, his own workshop—but Zahira handled the funds that ran the place. The compound could never truly belong to Arhaan. His wife and the servants kept too many secrets.

Closing his eyes, Parsaa tried to think of something to say, anything, to move the conversation away from another man's wife—but the mind was tricky that way. In trying to avoid the one topic, all he could do was think about Zahira. Men should not talk loosely about their wives around other men. Arhaan's distrust was constant, a character flaw that invited others to keep secrets.

Encounters with Arhaan added to Parsaa's determination to prohibit his sons from living at the compound. Arhaan regarded Mohan and Parsaa as servants, replaceable, and he would be just as haughty with the next set. Arhaan assumed that he owned great tracts of land, and Blacker had urged allowing that misunderstanding to continue as long as possible. Such secrets protected Zahira, but not Parsaa or his sons.

Parsaa thought about telling the man that it wasn't safe to wander about at night, even at the compound, but he stopped himself. Arhaan regarded advice as threats or insults. Every topic was off-limits with the man.

At last Arhaan broke the silence. "Is the orphan a girl or a boy?" Arhaan queried.

"A girl," Parsaa replied.

"*Dokh-tar, dokh-tar*," the bird screamed, lifting its wings.

Arhaan chuckled as he gently stroked the myna's head. "So Zahira asked for help?"

"The possibility was raised, and she agreed." He once knew more about Zahira's life than Arhaan did, but that was no longer the case.

"Zahira will tire of her before long." Arhaan leaned too close toward Parsaa. "No one can measure up to her standards. You know it. Perhaps I'll find use for the girl with the birds."

The myna lifted its head, letting loose with a string of unintelligible phrases.

"And Parsaa, the next time you visit, be sure to see me first." The tone was imperious, dismissive. "I do not want another man sneaking about my home."

Tapping his cane, the blind man hobbled away. Parsaa was weary and not for the first time worried about Zahira. The match approved by Blacker had not led to love or acceptance, and Parsaa could not protect a woman from a husband. He glanced back toward the compound where one lonely light glowed from Zahira's bedroom. The other buildings and canyon walls were cloaked in darkness. Parsaa could not detect the outlines and felt almost as blind as Arhaan.

Parsaa headed for the narrow trail. So many times he had raced down the hillside, eager to reach the compound, but now he only looked forward to the steep climb and journey home. He had so many jumbled memories of a bustling place, huge meals and games among loyal friends, the hearty bursts of laughter. Zahira never talked about the boisterous gatherings and her father's many friends. She rarely talked about her father at all.

The attention from Blacker once made Parsaa feel superior, a feeling that had vanished long ago, replaced by regret for not spending more hours with his parents and brother. Parsaa wondered if too many secrets were attached to the place, if the secrets really protected the compound.

Moving with care, he stepped carefully along the narrow ledge etched into the canyon wall, and as he walked, he could still remember his shock at hearing that Zahira and Arhaan would become man and wife.

~~~~~~

Blacker made the announcement after Parsaa had returned home from a school break to a cold and empty home, shortly after the death of his parents. His father had been the victim of a shooting accident—a young hunter chasing down a duck for his family's dinner—and his mother had died from grief soon afterward. Fortunately, his sisters, all older, had already left for marriages. With his parents dead, Parsaa's younger brother had decided he didn't need school. Long envious of his older brother's ties with Blacker, the brother traveled to join a distant militia and never returned to claim his share of his father's property.

His parents had already been buried, and Blacker took care of punishing the hunter. As with all his breaks from school, Parsaa immediately rushed for the compound to thank his benefactor and tussle with old friends.

His life changed that day. Zahira rushed to greet him, but Aza scolded. "He is a man now, and you are a woman."

Normally, Zahira would have ignored Aza. This time, she walked away.

Blacker was impatient that day, his greeting truncated. He directed Parsaa to enter a match with other young men who had been practicing daily. After a few rounds, Blacker embraced Parsaa, announcing that school had not diminished the young man's skills, and Parsaa remembered the hard punch of pride coming from inside.

Then Blacker had moved on to introduce a young man waiting at the edge of the field. The man was detached, in fine clothes that made his nervous ways more pronounced. He gripped a thin walking stick and listened intently to avoid the rowdiness. Blacker explained the newcomer was well educated, with an advanced degree in ornithology, and from that day onward, he would make his home at the compound.

"Arhaan is one of us," Blacker pronounced. "And he will marry my only daughter before the year is through!"

The crowd went silent, as if in a stupor, before a few older men realized that Blacker was serious and let loose with a belated cheer. Blacker and Zahira were such vibrant personalities, too extraordinary for conventional marriage. So attentive to her father, Zahira had gradually taken on duties as mistress of the compound. At times, the man and daughter often seemed more like husband and young wife, though no one dared suggest as much.

Parsaa had the good sense to hide his resentment and raise a fist in the air in support. Amid the cheering, jealousy coursed like hot blood through every part of his body. He could not be certain whether he was more upset about Blacker bringing another man into the family or Zahira taking a husband. He stared at the newcomer and only then realized that the man was blind. Then Parsaa glanced at Zahira, who returned a cool stare that suggested she knew exactly how he felt.

Later that night, the contract was signed in a ceremony. From threads of gossip winding through the compound, Parsaa learned that Arhaan was a distant cousin whose parents had died and left him and another brother property in the city. He had studied at the university in Kabul and was known for his ability in training songbirds.

Just before the contract was signed, Blacker whispered something to Arhaan, and the young man's face went pale. Then, after the ceremony, as the guests relished a huge meal, Blacker asked Parsaa to step inside his private chamber, separated by a rare interior door.

Blacker closed the door and invited the young man to sit among the fine silk pillows.

"I saw your reaction," Blacker said. "Yes, you are like a son to me. But she is not the right woman for you, and it is wrong for a brother to marry his sister." The man lit a pipe and passed it to Parsaa. "Not tonight, but someday you will realize this is best for the both of you."

Parsaa inhaled and watched the smoke drift around the room, irritated that Blacker thought he could read his feelings.

"Sit back and listen, there is something much more important to discuss regarding your father's death." Blacker then explained that he had secretly borrowed from Parsaa's father and repaid the man before his death. He extracted a document from a chest and handed it over to Parsaa. "Here are the forms, signed by your father."

Parsaa unfolded the papers and studied the scratchy line that served as his father's signature. His father could not read or write, and Parsaa had never seen his father sign anything. "Your father agreed to payment made in property." Blacker explained that the transaction had already been registered with the proper office in the provincial capital. "The government is unstable," he added with a sigh. "The payment does not include this compound, only the surrounding land including Laashekoh and the fields. He cocked his head toward the door. "No one else knows. Only your father, and I will soon tell Zahira and Mohan. But not Arhaan, he doesn't need to know."

Parsaa was unaccustomed to smoking. The expensive tobacco made his head swim, and the details from Blacker came too quickly.

"The two of them won't be here long. Both of them prefer the city, and my daughter wants to finish her studies." The man had shrugged, but his voice was firm. "I want this property secured. And you have no plans to leave."

It was not a question, yet Parsaa offered a short nod so typical of his conversations with Blacker.

"Your father said as much. It is why the property is in your name."

"I would not have known about this debt." Parsaa stared at the papers. "You did not have to tell me. We owe you so much. More than what you could have possibly owed my father."

"What do you know?" Blacker snapped, suggesting the comment showed a lack of respect for Parsaa's father. "No one needs to know the circumstances."

Debt severed all love. Parsaa's throat was tight, and he wished he could talk with his father. He wondered if the debt was real or if his father had signed an agreement that he did not understand.

Parsaa stubbornly asked about Arhaan. The marriage contract was brief, and Blacker's sole heir was Zahira. Her property transferred to Arhaan by rite of marriage. Only later Parsaa understood how Blacker chafed under Afghan dictates on inheritance. He could not favor friends or distant relatives or protégés over his only child. Arhaan, blind and forced to trust others to read the documents, made assumptions about Blacker's holdings, and Blacker let those assumptions go uncorrected.

Blacker did not trust Arhaan. "He knows there will be consequences should Zahira suffer from abuse or untimely death," Blacker said. "I trust you and Mohan to handle those."

Blacker spoke not with the relief of making final payment on a debt, but with intent to control the land beyond the grave. He issued his orders.

"I expect you to protect the compound in all ways. Be an advisor to Zahira. Provide security. An attack here is a threat for Laashekoh." He tapped the papers on his desk. "The two of them think of themselves as wise, much more intelligent than you or me. My daughter is resourceful, but she is not prepared for the coming changes. And both of them are foolish enough to think that money and property give them power or control." He shook his head and explained that new forces were determined to take over Afghanistan. The zealots wanted more than money and would not question Parsaa's control. "Turbulent years are ahead."

Blacker went on to explain that Parsaa could share benefits with Zahira or not as he wished. "Should she give birth to a child and decide to stay at the compound, should you feel uncomfortable with this arrangement, you may organize a similar debt to transfer the land."

He glanced at Parsaa. "I trust you to do right by her."

Again, he urged secrecy. "You will find it easier if others do not know the details. The passing years will secure this arrangement."

Parsaa was too troubled to be grateful. He had long imagined his life stretching out peacefully, marked only by marriage, children, harvests, and the passing years. The villagers lived in Laashekoh only because of Blacker. Most trusted the man and did not expect a sudden change. Most counted on him giving his daughter away in a marriage to a strongman like himself.

Instead, Blacker had approved of a weak husband for his only daughter, hoping to control his world long after death. That required help from loyal men like Mohan and Parsaa. The night was a turning point for Laashekoh, yet only Parsaa knew. The village, once linked so tightly with Blacker, could protect the land in its own way.

Blacker chose the right man. "My father, did he understand?" Parsaa's voice broke.

"You are a good son to think about your parents. I hope Zahira feels the same for me someday. And I promise, the story behind the debt does not sully your parents. Your father provided fighters over the years and other favors. Trust me, he was grateful for this transaction. He trusted that you more than anyone else could protect the land from parasites."

The warlord suddenly seemed haggard. Blacker embraced Parsaa and waved him away. "This is our secret. Now enjoy yourself and do not hurry. There is no need for you to head back to school."

~~~~~

Arhaan still assumed that he owned the property surrounding the compound since his marriage to Zahira. He certainly played the role of wealthy manager, expecting deference from Mohan, Aza, Parsaa, and Zahira. As Blacker had advised, keeping the secret was easier than not.

The man was slightly younger than Zahira, and before their marriage, she was sure that she could control the blind man. Blacker had understood that no man put up with such nonsense for long, and the most insecure were among the worst.

Over the years, Arhaan posed no challenges about the property. The couple talked about relocation but made no real plans. If they remained in Afghanistan and didn't try to sell the land, there was no reason for Arhaan to learn the truth. The couple had no children or close family members who would try to make claims. All Arhaan cared about was ample space for his birds, books, and equipment.

Zahira had spoken with Parsaa about the land exchange not long after her father's death. She expressed relief for the arrangement and gratitude for his complicity. Already, the marriage was strained, and there was always the possibility of her lashing out at her husband during an argument, revealing the true owner of the land. Zahira taunted her husband but held off revealing the secret, even as Arhaan tried to humiliate her, Parsaa, and the others. Instead, she smiled, enjoying a secret shared with Parsaa.

Mohan and Parsaa were cool with Arhaan, never letting on that they possessed greater understanding about the property and the intricacies of the couple's life. After so many years, Arhaan would be furious to learn that Parsaa owned the land, knew more than he did, and patronized him like an ignorant child. The two men let Arhaan think that he wielded power over them, and that made him less dangerous.

Mohan had once confided in Parsaa that Aza, though she loved Zahira as a daughter, detested the bickering and wanted no part of it. Only loyalty to Blacker kept them at the compound to care for the ornery couple. Aza often expressed disappointment in Zahira and berated her husband. "They take us for granted. Blacker did not expect her to stay behind in this desolate place. If we left, that might motivate Zahira to leave, too. I think that is what Blacker really wanted."

Aza, arthritic and tired, often avoided contact with Parsaa. The couple should have left long ago, and perhaps the woman blamed him.

But Mohan found it hard to leave. Yes, Blacker had rewarded his trusted lieutenant with an ample trust fund, and Aza missed their only son, who worked in the provincial capital. The young man didn't like witnessing his parents working so hard at their age. He had reserved ample space for them in his home and urged them to move to the city. For Mohan, it was hard to walk away from so many memories or admit that he was no longer useful. The man assured Parsaa that he was firm with his wife. "I owe Blacker much and won't abandon his daughter. We leave only after Zahira decides to leave."

After such conversations, Aza would not speak to her husband for days.

Parsaa pitied the compound's unhappy occupants, but he could not interfere with a husband and wife. So it wasn't hard for Parsaa to turn his back on the dark compound. He took long strides in climbing and aimed for the stars overhead—*Aaronj, Oqaab, Almesian*, the elbow, the eagle, and the shining light. Memories of the compound no longer brought joy, and walking away was a release. The small group focused on old worries. New ideas were rare. Perhaps Najwa would invigorate the compound, but he doubted it.

Parsaa would be ashamed to trap one of his sons into working for the compound. Sofi would never forgive him. With every step away from the compound, Parsaa felt younger, freer, thrilled to escape his past and return to the comfort of the present and his family.

CHAPTER 11

Zahira left the small hut and watched Parsaa walk away into the darkness. She dismissed Aza and took the infant into her own bed.

She could not sleep. Men knew so little about women and didn't care. They also didn't understand how a woman might react if held back from pursuing what she wanted.

Parsaa would not dispose of his orphan and other problems so easily. He and the other villagers made the mistake of thinking that Zahira depended on him. Laashekoh was linked to the compound. The village would not exist without the approval of Blacker and his daughter.

Parsaa suggested she was a good influence but would not recommend others to seek out her assistance for medical treatments. He claimed that he could not control the women who whispered together when they gathered to wash clothes, work the fields, or cook communal meals. He did not expect the villagers to invite Zahira and her husband to their gatherings.

Not that Zahira would have attended.

Women of Laashekoh thought of her as arrogant. They resented her. All Parsaa had said to other villagers was that the families could stay on and live at Laashekoh. The villagers assumed that Blacker's heirs owned the land, but they assumed that Parsaa had some control over her. They did not want to know more.

Time and time again, Zahira imagined the nearby villagers coming to her in desperation. She especially longed for Sofi to appear in her doorway, pleading to end a pregnancy. Zahira imagined her own loftiness in considering the request, asking many questions before proceeding, then insisting on securing Parsaa's permission. He would admire Zahira and thank her.

But Sofi never knocked at the door, and Zahira never met the woman.

Most villagers thought of Zahira as inept. She had returned home before completing her medical studies. Whispers swirled about her skills. Early on, a few young wives from nearby villages had sought care for a difficult pregnancy or a child's illness. But older women from nearby villages discouraged the visits and chided the young mothers for a lack of faith. No person should be so curious about another woman's body, the women whispered. Better to trust prayers over cures recommended by a woman who studied in foreign lands. Visits dwindled, and so did Zahira's confidence.

Alone in the darkness, Zahira had to satisfy herself with visions of desperate women waiting outside, afraid to knock. One woman had trusted Zahira's care, but she no longer lived in Laashekoh.

~~~~~

As a young mother, Mari had ventured into the canyon during the coldest month of winter, an infant strapped to her back. The baby took ragged breaths, punctuated by sharp coughs. The mother handed the infant over to Zahira and wept. "She is my first. I tried everything."

Zahira's gratitude for a patient was mixed with annoyance over being regarded as a caregiver of last resort. She loosened the child's covering and listened to the baby's chest, then asked what the others had advised. The woman wailed, and Zahira understood. The villagers had urged the woman to take the child far from the village and walk away. They didn't want the baby near their children.

The baby let loose with a ragged cough and then tensed, her sweet eyes widening over the struggle to suck in air. Zahira asked if the child had lost much weight and Mari shook her head. The baby had *siyah solfa* but showed no signs of dehydration. Zahira placed the child on the scale, documented the weight, and bundled her tightly. Handing the child back, Zahira told the woman to hold the baby upright against her chest, head against her shoulder.

"Rub her back firmly," she ordered. Zahira then filled her largest pot with water and placed it on a stovetop. She covered the pot, turned a switch. After waiting for propane to drip into the line, she lit a match. A flame flared on the stovetop, and Mari jumped backward.

"Hug her tight." Zahira pointed toward the stove. "Move close to the stove, and let her breathe. The idea is to get her to take in warm, moist air."

Clutching the infant, Mari ventured close to the stove. Zahira opened a drawer and grabbed a thick towel. She had to convince the woman to drape the towel over the child's head and trap the steamy air. If not, Zahira would take the child and do it herself. She went to a large walk-in closet filled with boxes and jars of medications. The labels were in English, French, Dutch, and more. Directions in those languages were crossed out by aid agencies overseas and replaced with names and brief directions in Dari or Russian. Zahira studied the rows before removing a large jar of off-white powder.

"*Aard*?" the mother asked.

"Not flour. Medicine." Zahira did not want to confuse the woman by explaining an antibiotic. As the water neared a boil, Zahira turned the flame down and explained how the steam would help the baby breathe easier. She held out the towel and asked to cover the child's head to capture the steam.

Mari complied, bending close to the pot. Zahira draped the towel over them both, hiding the fearful eyes of mother and child. Then Zahira stood back and waited, feeling protective of the young mother and child. She wanted to start the child on erythromycin, but dispensing the antibiotic would be easier once the mother saw a hint of improvement.

That didn't take long. Moments later, the mother's muffled, excited voice called out: "Her breathing is better! She is calming down."

Relieved, Zahira leaned against the counter and advised them to stay under the towel. "As long as you can stand it," she said.

Mari stood still over the steaming water until the exhausted baby fell asleep. Only then she stepped away, her face red and sweating. She thanked Zahira, who warned that the child was not out of danger. "Can you leave the child here for ten days so I can give her complete treatment?" Zahira asked.

Mari thought a moment and gave a quick nod. Zahira asked for the child's name, and Mari said Leila. Zahira measured powder and placed it into a container and added water halfway. She applied the lid and shook well before extracting 2.5 milliliters with a syringe. Zahira gently lifted the baby's head from her mother's shoulder. Her dark hair framed skin that was like the freshest milk, and the sparkling eyes locked onto Zahira's.

"She is precious," Zahira murmured. Using one hand, Zahira pinched the rosebud mouth, and with the other hand, aimed the syringe toward the back of the baby's throat and squeezed. The baby swallowed and then wailed. A harsh cough interrupted. "Keep holding her tight," Zahira advised. She added more water to the pot and turned up the heat. "It won't be long before the coughing subsides."

"I can wait and take her home?"

Zahira shook her head. She did not trust anyone in Laashekoh and would not risk a lapse in a full course of antibiotics for the child. Otherwise, the coughing would return with renewed force.

Mari reluctantly left the child behind, and the girl's health improved steadily over the next few days. Mari visited almost daily and asked how she could repay Zahira. But Zahira advised that there was no need for payment.

Mari was grateful, and Zahira had expected more patients to arrive after hearing about the successful treatment. But no one came. Later, Zahira learned the other villagers did not ask where the child had stayed for the ten days, and Mari kept her visit a secret. Zahira wondered if Mari resented others in Laashekoh, too, refusing to share a resource—or did she fear being ridiculed for panicking and seeking help from an outsider?

Zahira did not mind. If swelling numbers of patients arrived, many would have been less fortunate than baby Leila. She did not have to please the villagers. One difficult case, one setback, and the families would have despised Zahira even more.

~~~~~~

Mari had visited sporadically over the next few years, seeking treatment for her children when they were younger for ailments less serious than the whooping cough. They didn't have to stay overnight, and Zahira handled the cases quickly. Several years went by without Zahira seeing Mari. Until one night when there was desperate knocking and cry from outside. Aza opened the door. Panicked, the rain mixing with her tears, Mari asked to speak with Zahira alone.

Zahira wrapped a wool shawl around her shoulders and advised the woman to follow her to the clinic. Mari promised to return, but first hurried toward the path. Moments later, Mari and an older girl entered the room, removing their shoes at the doorway, Zahira handed over warm towels so they could dry themselves, and Mari introduced her oldest daughter, Leila. Near adulthood, the girl was stunningly beautiful, poised, and healthy. Zahira was struck by how much time had passed since the infant had been treated for whooping cough.

Zahira suddenly felt old. She had accomplished so little as a health provider since the girl had been born. She blamed the villagers and their ignorance. She was still disappointed that Mari did not talk about the treatments.

Embarrassed, the mother explained. Her daughter had conceived a child. She was not married and needed help. Zahira asked how many menstrual cycles had been missed. "Just one," Mari responded for the girl. Zahira handed over a cotton sheet and pointed to a small room, advising Leila to undress for an examination.

Once the girl left the room, Zahira sternly asked what Mari expected.

"She is not married," Mari whispered. "You know Laashekoh. They will ostracize our entire family!"

"I do not know Laashekoh," Zahira retorted coolly, directing Mari to wait in another room. By then, Leila had returned to sit on the edge of the examining table. She did not keep her veil on or hold the cover close to her chin, trying to hide her nakedness. Instead, the white sheet stretched tight across her breasts, twisted into a knot at the center.

Zahira directed the girl to lie back and lifted the sheet. Hovering over her, Leila asked questions about activities, eating habits, and daily routines. The responses were curt, with no hesitation. The girl's abdomen was lean and firm, suggesting she probably was truthful about how far the pregnancy had progressed.

Finally, Zahira asked about the father of the child. The girl drew back. "Why do you want to know?" she asked flatly.

Zahira was not surprised. The village women considered basic care as prying. "You came to me for help," she said. "The detail should influence your decision and could influence mine, too." She waited a moment and then turned for the door.

"Wait!" Leila shouted. Zahira paused. "There is no convincing the father to help me. He is dead."

"So it shouldn't be a problem to tell me who he is." Zahira stood tall, in no mood for nonsense.

At last moved by some feeling, Leila turned her head away. "Ali, the oldest son of Parsaa and Sofi. He was leaving for school, and I didn't want him to go." She covered her face with her hands. Her voice was bitter. "We were together that way only once. He refused to touch me after that."

Zahira quickly turned, facing the counter and pretending to look for an instrument. She did not want the girl to see the reaction. Thoughts about what she might do next pierced her mind like slivers of glass.

Returning to her patient's side, Zahira was gentle. She lifted the sheet and examined the girl's pelvis once again. Leila would not show for another three, maybe four months, depending on what she wore and how she carried herself. "You are sure about the father?" Zahira questioned.

"There was no other man," the girl insisted.

Zahira kept her voice soft. "And what do you want me to do?"

Leila was upset. "You must know! The women have talked about you. They say you can remove the baby. That no one needs to know."

Zahira wanted to know what else the women said, and the girl bit her lip before replying. "That you are lonely and angry. They think you have ended pregnancies for women in nearby villages, but no one knows who the women are. They say you charge high fees for this service, but that you keep our secrets."

"What has your mother said about me?" Zahira asked.

"My mother said you provide good care." Leila had no idea that Zahira had treated her before. "Nothing more."

"Don't believe all that you hear," Zahira said sharply. She waited until she had the girl's full attention. "What else have you tried before coming to see me? And do not lie."

Leila was embarrassed and explained how her mother had forced her to chew on fistfuls of cumin and wild sage, as much as they could find, until she became sick to her stomach. Later, she had tried punching herself in the stomach and asked her younger sisters to help. "None of it worked," Leila admitted.

The rest of the examination did not take long. Zahira told the girl to dress. Plenty of mifepristone and misoprostol waited in the storage area. The pregnancy could be easily ended.

Instead, Zahira went into the next room and advised Mari that there were complications. She could not take steps to end the pregnancy. "It would be dangerous, and you could lose your daughter."

Mari moaned. As soon as Leila entered the room, her mother took her by the arm. "I must think of something else," Mari said softly.

"I will leave Laashekoh." Leila was flippant. "I do not want to stay."

Furious, Mari struck the girl, and Zahira stepped between the two.

"You must accept this," Zahira noted. "Give up trying to swallow herbs or striking yourself. The baby is strong, tightly attached, and you will only hurt yourself. You need care and may have missed more menstrual cycles than you think."

Mari frowned as the girl protested.

Zahira apologized. "I cannot help you, and it's best that you marry quickly."

"I told you the father is dead!" Leila snapped.

"Find someone else, his brother or another man, and soon," Zahira pressed.

Blushing, the girl howled. "The father was younger than me. And it's not Laashekoh's way for the women to marry village men."

Mari agreed. "Such arrangements take time."

Zahira wondered if Parsaa knew about the relationship, if that was why he had not visited in a while. She spoke kindly. "Perhaps your mother can help find a willing man." She paused. "Or you could return in another month or two, before you show. You could stay and I could care for you. No one needs to know."

"I do not want this child." Leila moaned, turning away from the two women. "I thought Ali would change his mind about leaving. I hate him and want nothing to do with this child!"

Mari and Zahira glanced at one another. "The months will pass quickly," Mari promised.

"It's safer for you to give birth and keep the baby healthy." Zahira was direct, even offering to let the girl stay at the compound after the birth. "Can you do that?"

The girl did not answer, but stared at Zahira, deeply skeptical.

"Other villagers would ask too many questions." Mari prepared to leave. "I will handle the child," she said in parting.

Zahira was not sure whether Mari meant her daughter or Leila's child. The mother and daughter walked away, shoulder to shoulder, and Zahira felt lonely.

Zahira sat at her desk and studied the calendar, counting days and recounting them to estimate when Leila might give birth, and she anticipated Leila's return to the compound.

~~~~~~

Leila did not seek refuge in the compound. A few weeks later, her father arranged a fast marriage with a man who did not care about a wife carrying a child that belonged to another man. The night of the wedding, the couple and Mari were sent away to prison.

The week after Leila's estimated due date, Zahira traveled to Kandahar. The prison building was large and new, with thick, concrete-block walls painted pale blue and lots of windows covered with screens of thick wire. The place was surrounded by tall chain-link fences topped with curled razor wire. Inside the prison yard, children ran and played.

One entrance was marked for visitors. A plaque over the door read: "In the Name of Allah, the most merciful and the most compassionate." Zahira stopped at the office, introducing herself as an aunt before dropping coins into an empty box labeled *sadaqa*. She needed both forgiveness and protection against evil. A guard guided her through a maze until they reached a series of large cells shared by women and their children.

"How is the baby?" Zahira whispered. The guard unlocked a door and shrugged. The door slammed, and Zahira searched for Leila.

Bunk beds lined the walls on either side, and colorful sheets shielded each space. The crowded room was lively with chatter. Women sat on the edges of the beds, holding and feeding infants. Toddlers crawled and tumbled on a carpet in the center of the room.

The women were accustomed to strangers coming and going, and offered no greetings. Instead, they stared, as if waiting for Zahira to tell them what to do next. Zahira scanned the group a few times before eyeing Leila crouched in a corner, leaning against a wall and trying to quiet a wailing infant. Using her thumb and finger, the young mother tried to stretch the infant's mouth open while using her other hand to guide the baby's head close to her chest. But the infant was red-faced, letting loose tiny, sharp cries, as furious as the baby Zahira had soothed so many years ago.

Hurrying over, Zahira crouched next to Leila. She hesitated to reach for the squalling child. "Babies want so much," she said in a matter-of-fact way.

Only then Leila looked up. Shiny patches of ruined skin stretched along one side of Leila's face—the scar was long healed, the damage from before Leila's prison stay. Zahira was surprised that Parsaa had not mentioned such an event, but then he had suppressed many negative details about his precious village. Zahira tried not to react, but Leila was keen. "They are going to fix my face," she retorted. "My attorney is collecting money. They will schedule the operation now that she has been born."

A little girl—that pleased Zahira. She asked if the infant had taken the breast.

"A few times," Leila said. "But she fusses."

"Let her calm down before you try again," Zahira advised. "And in the meantime, lay her on your thighs and rock your legs side to side. Gently."

Leila followed the instructions, and the infant stopped crying and locked her unblinking eyes onto her mother's face.

"At last, peace." Leaning back, Leila closed her eyes. "If I could move back to the other cell."

Zahira faced the girl and sat, trying to ignore the worn carpet with splotches of dried food and stains of unknown origins. She asked about the other space.

"The noise here is driving me mad," Leila explained, dropping her voice to a whisper. "Women with children must stay together, and I miss being with the women without children."

Sighing, she looked around the room. "The other cell block was pleasant. Here, women only talk about their children. They don't like me. Most are older, and they're jealous because the foreign NGOs are interested in my case. So they ignore me but help one another with their children and washing so they can nap or go to classes." Leila glared at her child. "I'm only in here because of Hasti. She is never satisfied. She doesn't let me sleep, and the other children are tiresome, too. I can't bear it much longer!"

"She will become more accustomed to feedings and your schedule." Zahira tried to soothe the young mother.

"Hah!" Leila was ready to cry. "She cries more than she sleeps! One woman claims Hasti is terrified of my face! Do you think that is true?"

"No," Zahira spoke firmly and took the girl's hand. "The baby is not crying now. And you are right. The others envy the attention directed your way."

The baby's eyes were wide open, her breathing was shallow, and Zahira wondered if the child was getting enough liquid nourishment. She asked how old the baby was, and Leila said five days. Zahira suggested that she try giving the infant another chance to feed. Sighing, Leila leaned forward and exposed a full breast. Shifting her own position to block the curious stares from others in the room, Zahira directed Leila to sit up straight and then helped lift the infant, gently arranging her in Leila's arms.

A mother should not hurry. Zahira cupped her hand around the full breast and squeezed with the other, using her fingers like scissors. Milk leaked out and Zahira suggested directing the baby's mouth closer to the damp nipple. The baby latched on, sucked a few times, before pausing to stare up at Leila with beautiful eyes. Leila leaned over the baby, using her right hand to shove the breast back into the mouth.

As the baby turned, Zahira noticed the top of her head was slightly sunken.

Leila was frustrated. "They're right. She doesn't like looking at me." Moving the baby to the floor, Leila let the blanket lay loose. "Let her go hungry and cold!"

Then she quickly relented, swaddling the baby tightly and roughly plopping her down on a nearby cushion.

"She may not be hungry," offered Zahira. She was amazed the baby did not fuss more, but had to show she did not care. She wanted to ask about the color of the baby's urine, but too many questions would put Leila on the defensive. Instead, Zahira pointed out that a baby that young could not possibly care about her mother's face. The girl did not respond.

Zahira sat back and waited patiently. Leila's stare hardened through the long spell of silence. "Why are you here?" she asked.

Leaning back so Leila could not check her face, Zahira explained she was in town for other business. Then Zahira pointedly asked about other visitors from Laashekoh. The girl shook her head. "Will you tell Parsaa that you have seen me?" Leila asked bitterly.

"Not at all," Zahira said.

"You know he is why I am here?" Leila was nervous. "A good man would have understood that I had to follow orders from my father and my husband. Parsaa could have simply punished us and allowed us to remain at Laashekoh. He did not have to involve the foreign soldiers. That is what my attorney says."

Zahira asked the length of her sentence.

"Six years." Leila's laugh was short. "It's strange. This is supposed to be punishment, but I like it better here than living in Laashekoh. I would never go back. If only I didn't have the child."

The mother was eager to rid herself of Hasti, and the infant sensed the resentment. But Zahira could not plead for the child. The idea had to come from Leila.

"Could a relative care for her?" Zahira questioned in a cool tone.

"My mother is in another prison," Leila snapped. "And my sisters are stuck in Laashekoh and would be fools to ruin their marriage chances by caring for my child." Leila suddenly twisted her head sideways. "Is that why you came here?"

Zahira was silent and resisted glancing toward the infant. She could not show Leila how much she cared.

But Leila saw.

"This is why you refused to give me the abortion?" Leila charged. "You care more about her than me. And now you want me to hand her over to you?" She demanded that Zahira look her in the eye.

Zahira faced Leila with a set expression and kept her voice steady. "I told you then. Too much time had passed. Only so much is possible in an area as remote as ours. It's not my fault you did not come to me earlier."

"That is not what others tell me here!" Leila snarled with fury. "Why do you want her?"

Other prisoners went silent and stared, and Leila sat up, resuming a polite demeanor.

"She is not the only infant in Afghanistan," Zahira tried well-practiced disdain before softening her voice. "My husband and I have no children and a large compound. It's a good home with many resources." She paused. "We could explain that I'm an aunt, and I could take her away today."

Leila was thoughtful. "My father said your father owned all the property around Laashekoh. That he allowed the villagers to farm and live in Laashekoh."

Zahira stiffened. "We have property, and I can also provide her with an education, a dowry."

Leila scoffed at the offer. "My attorneys are promising me great wealth."

Irritated, Zahira stood and prepared to leave. She would not let a girl in prison push her around. "Your daughter won't live long enough to see your wealth. She is dehydrated and needs a doctor. Not an attorney. I am trying to help. What more could you want?"

The inmate stood, too, placed both hands on Zahira's shoulders, and whispered in her ear. The older woman stood still, absorbing the impossible request. "That would not be easy," she finally responded.

"If you really own the land, you decide who lives there, no?" Leila asked. "And he is nothing to you." She smiled, somehow knowing that was not true.

Leila did not wait for an answer. Regal and impulsive, she dismissed Zahira. "Go ahead, be my aunt. Take the child with you today. Do with her as you please. As long as you find a way to take care of Parsaa."

And Leila ordered Zahira not to return because she didn't want to think of Laashekoh again.

~~~~~

Zahira did not argue. Taking the child was easy after meeting with the prison warden and explaining she was a relative who lived near Leila's village. The man made a notation and waved her away.

But Zahira could not force Parsaa's family to leave Laashekoh because she no longer owned the land.

There was time. Leila could appeal her sentence but would be in prison at least a few more months. Besides, Leila had not set a deadline. The girl despised Laashekoh and would not want to return after her release. She talked about money and plans to travel. So Zahira convinced herself. She could move away before Leila returned for the child. She did not want Shareen to know the identity and cruel detachment of her birth mother.

Turning slowly back and forth, Zahira cooed to the baby—Parsaa's first grandchild. Zahira was proud about nurturing the infant back to health so quickly. The little girl was plump, content, alert. Before finding Shareen, Zahira had once believed that abortion was kinder than adoption. A mother could never trust a stranger with her child, and thoughts of Shareen with another woman were abhorrent.

Zahira had rescued the child not once, but twice. Their relationship was exceptional, though it was ironic how much Zahira sounded like the women who opposed abortions for others but vehemently justified their own.

Studying the baby's face, Zahira thought she could see Parsaa in her eyes and definitely Leila in the outline of her jaw and mouth. Zahira did not want Parsaa to know of the child's existence, not yet, and certainly not the identity of her parents. Otherwise, Parsaa and Sofi might try to claim the child, insisting on raising her in the intolerant village where the girl would never be treated as equal. Zahira might eventually tell Parsaa about the child, but only after leaving Afghanistan.

She needed more money to leave and buy citizenship in another land, as advised by Paul—the $750,000 that would take her to Spain or Greece and all she had to do was purchase property. Or, $1 million would take her to the United States if she could create ten jobs. Canada and England were too cold.

The United States was the safest destination. American soldiers had arrested the traffickers, and Leila would be regarded a security risk. Zahira needed Paul's sponsorship and more money. Perhaps she could convince Parsaa to sell some of the land and share the proceeds. Or she could convince the western charities, so free with funds, that she needed more.

"I rescued you before you were born and afterward, and I will rescue again," she cooed to the child. Shareen belonged to her, and that made Zahira determined to restore her inheritance and pass along a new life, much more than a compound hidden away in a desolate canyon, to her baby girl.

~~~~~~

The conversation with Mohan meant that Parsaa returned to Laashekoh much later than he had intended. He slipped underneath the layers of blankets and, once still, could hear his heart pound. His mind played games at night, mixing past and present fears. He couldn't stop thinking about the compound and how Blacker presided over his staff and the group of boys as if he were a king, training them to regard his dangers as threats for them. He remembered his own foolish, youthful pride as Zahira's dark eyes constantly followed him.

Such foolishness locked him into a secret, lifelong obligation. Yet the land around Laashekoh meant everything to him. No one knew who controlled the land, not even his wife. Blacker had claimed the transaction was registered in government offices, but the man was wily. The papers could have been forged, a ruse to convince Parsaa to do his bidding.

Parsaa came to the same conclusion as always. He was afraid to travel to the provincial capital to verify the deed. He didn't want to know. His life depended on everything staying the same—and that meant not asking questions or revealing his own secrets. And the old and never-changing decision pushed him into a fitful sleep.

CHAPTER 12

The leaves were long off the trees, but the day was unseasonably warm. Lydia wished she could take a walk in the nearby meadows protected by the city. Instead, she waited for two consultants. Henry didn't want her dwelling on Michael's death, though he did recommend trying a new strategy to collect information.

Thus, the meeting with the consultants. Lydia waited alone, rocking slowly on her porch, with a cup of tea and a good mystery.

The consultants had called to let her know that they were en route from the Lansing Airport. Less than fifteen minutes later, a rented Passat pulled in to her driveway. The loose-weave linen curtains moved with the breeze, blocked their view of the porch interior. The two did not hurry from the car. Instead, the young man looked down, probably studying a set of directions. The young woman behind the wheel was on the phone, gesturing toward the house.

Lydia smiled. The two should have been warned that the woman who controlled a multibillion foundation lived frugally, keeping a low profile in mid-Michigan, far from the New York offices of GlobalConnect. She couldn't blame them yet hoped they could provide state-of-the-art research and handle unexpected results.

After a few minutes, the couple stepped out of the car, both dressed in neat, casual business attire well suited for the Lansing area, no expensive jewelry or shoes. As they walked up the driveway, Lydia opened the porch door and welcomed them.

~~~~~

The young pair, Cara Rodriguez and Lawrence Walker, surprised her by accepting her offer of tea. Lydia set the water on the stove, found a tin of tea in the pantry, and arranged cream, sugar, and cups on a platter—while stealing glances from the window overlooking the porch. The pair set up two laptops and arranged papers on the table for Lydia to examine.

She quickly delivered the hot water and tea to the table along with oatmeal cookies. For herself, she poured boiled water with no tea. The consultants looked surprised. "A habit learned from a dear friend in China," Lydia explained. "Her family could not afford tea during the Cultural Revolution. The habit stuck, and she insists it helps digestion and circulation."

The two nodded and began their presentation. Based in Los Angeles, the former journalists had started their consulting firm, the Rodriguez-Walker Group, and quickly became known for matching charities with celebrities in need of redemption. Because of their meticulous research, the matchmaking worked well, and clients reported record donations. Nonprofits clamored to work with the firm, but the consultants were selective, searching for worthy causes and serious voices to ensure their own reputation for success.

The firm eventually turned its efforts toward transforming recipients of charity into celebrities to draw attention to hard-to-solve problems. Once again, nonprofits, corporations, and government agencies eagerly sought these services.

Rodriguez and Walker were skilled at evaluating foundations, improving performance, and crafting publicity that went viral overnight on social media. Lydia had already decided to hire the consulting firm. The problem was convincing them to work for GlobalConnect. The pair thrived on discovering obscure individuals and building global stories, and rumors abounded about the firm rejecting work from philanthropy's most prominent players. Lydia could not appear too eager.

Cara was up-front with her reservations. "Mrs. Sendry, the foundation's figures on administrative costs are already quite strong. We don't have to tell you that GlobalConnect is already a leader in the field."

"But shouldn't we all strive to do better?" Lydia relied on her friendliest business tone.

"Of course," Cara agreed. "Our firm specializes in developing narratives for fundraising. We have a proven track record in that area. But..." She took a deep breath. "Because your foundation does not actively raise funds..."

Lydia interrupted gently. "My son's foundation."

Lawrence took over. "Yes. Please realize that the use of narratives for purposes other than fundraising would be new territory. We'll be frank. We wouldn't mind applying this approach to new areas."

"GlobalConnect would be a guinea pig in this new area you propose," Cara added. "Our goal is to promote best practices for philanthropy. Many projects are started, but as a result of our research, some are left unfinished."

Pleased by the candor, Lydia tried not to smile. She followed closely as they reviewed the contents of a binder packed with graphs, photograph, and data—prepared specifically for the foundation. She also kept an eye on the window overlooking her front garden, annoyed by a group of small wrens chasing off a cardinal at the birdfeeder just outside. The cardinal flew off to a nearby maple, waiting for the feeder to clear.

One possible way to increase motivation among employees and clients would be to highlight strong narratives with personal appeal, Lawrence explained. "Improved employee morale can increase trust and reduce administrative costs. We would conduct thorough research to identify specific employees and aid recipients with the approval of GlobalConnect's board. We would use these stories to publicize the good work and connections."

Lydia offered more tea. Both nudged their cups forward for her to pour. Cara asked to try hot water.

"We specialize in international investigations," she continued. "For us, a story that relays international challenges and connections, through equal partnerships, is everything. We find the stories, fact-check them, shape them, and train the people to do the telling. You'd be surprised how many people don't realize the opportunity of turning every day into a story. They don't realize their level of control. We could develop training to motivate employees and select role models."

Both consultants nodded as they spoke—Cara's a gentle bobbing while Lawrence's was barely perceptible, a slight tilt of his chin. The two were so earnest, smart, and young, qualities that triggered reminders of her son.

"Have you ever not found a story?" Lydia queried.

"There are always stories," Cara promised. "What's difficult is finding appropriate themes, extracting two or more stories, and getting them to blend. And of course, ensuring there are no conflicts of interest. Solid research is essential and prevents embarrassment for everyone involved."

"But surely some stories must be flawed?" Lydia pretended to struggle to think of an example. "How often are there inaccuracies, exaggerations? Even criminal activity?"

Lawrence was confident. "It happens quite often. We vet the backgrounds and all aspects of the subjects and organization very, very carefully."

Lydia then asked if she could see an example of data for a profile subject. The partners hesitated. "No names, but I'd like to see how details are organized and how much you can collect on someone based in a developing nation," Lydia added. "A country without a lot of computers and record keeping. Say, a place as remote as Afghanistan?"

Lawrence asked if GlobalConnect supplied employees with phones and laptops, and Lydia nodded. "That gives us great leeway," Cara murmured.

Lawrence reached for his laptop. "Give me a moment," he said. "I can strip names from a data set." He typed for a few moments in silence and then handed the computer over. Lydia tapped her way through the detailed worksheet on one beneficiary that described activities, categories of annual expenditures including alcohol and food, television and computer habits, and more. Another worksheet listed travel history, credit-card expenses, telephone and Internet records, and transcripts for a worker based in Africa. "Impressive," Lydia murmured. Noting her appreciation for confidentiality, she asked how they obtained so much information.

Taking a deep breath, Lawrence resumed control of the laptop. The consultants relied on the newest data-collection software and analytic tools. "All legal surveillance," he said. "We can provide layers of privacy protection as your organization needs, though it saves time if we can review personnel and case files, even e-mails, for story ideas. We do that because organizations often don't recognize a great story developing before their very eyes. We collect a wide range of possibilities, make choices on which stories to pursue, and then conduct background checks. That process weeds many out."

"Many," Cara reiterated.

"And unlike the employee-background-check industry, we destroy data when we are done. From our point of view, it's unconscionable for businesses, nonprofits, and universities to collect data on employee applicants, not just the employees themselves, and keep that indefinitely."

Lydia was surprised, and he assured her it happened more often than most realized. "We could present the complete data set for you, so your team can review, or just summaries and our recommendations for finalists."

The service was ideal for her purposes. All that was left for her to do was point them in a direction and convince them to provide a complete data set on Paul Reichart. She wanted them to move quickly.

"Of course," Lawrence said. "We must stress again, using the data for anything other than highlighting narratives for publicity purposes is untested. We cannot guarantee to reduce costs at the foundation."

"With this uncertainty, can you bill me and not the foundation?"

He glanced at Cara. "That can be arranged." Lydia had no more questions, and Lawrence thanked her. "You have been more specific than most of our clients. That's helpful."

Lydia's nod was deliberative.

"Our top researchers are ready to work on this project." Lawrence pointed to the laptop.

Lydia smiled and commented that the male cardinal had returned to the feeder, delicately poking its head about, probably separating and selecting sunflower seeds.

There was no reason for delay. Lydia advised them Henry was waiting to review the contract, and they could start working right away.

CHAPTER 13

Saddiq was obsessed with finding scraps of time with Thara, but he was cautious. They could not get caught—he worried more about her punishment than his. So he quietly set about observing the routines of his parents and other adults, and advised Thara on when to gather grasses along uneven hillsides with clusters of trees that would shield them as they watched for passersby.

Alone with his work, Saddiq focused on speed and refused breaks, following the example of his mother, who hurried her own tasks to make extra time for reading.

Early on, Sofi had scolded Saddiq for missing lessons, but he pretended to have no interest. His mother was sharp and would have wondered why her son attended some sessions and not others. Just as suddenly, she gave up pleading and seemed content that he was willing to work long hours in the fields.

Yes, his mother seemed distracted by reading and organizing books, as well as working in the kitchen and caring for Komal and the younger brothers. Still, Saddiq sensed that he was being watched, that his parents kept tabs on his work, and so he was quiet, working steadily alongside men in the fields and, later, cutting and gathering wood into stockpiles for later retrieval.

With his parents, he was respectful. At night, he listened intently as his father read aloud.

Saddiq dared to meet Thara only when his father traveled away from the village. Often, he could not be sure how long his father would be away. Saddiq made a point of offering to accompany the man and was secretly pleased when his father declined.

On the day his father left for the market, Saddiq did not immediately rush off alone and instead helped his mother in a far field, digging for the last of the beets, potatoes, and turnips. When she was near, he took his time—lugging bundles to a cool cave, meticulously following her directions to arrange the root crops on a cloth, keep the vegetables to a single layer without letting them touch one another. At the cave's entrance, she lingered to watch.

"The others are not so careful," he noted about the work of other villagers.

"They don't remember hunger," she responded.

His parents were planners, but also flexible. They planned ahead for the fields, the markets, their children's education and marriages. For his parents, contentment meant respecting traditions and following rules, blending in and avoiding any behavior that might distinguish them among the villagers. Yet his parents were open and considered new ways. It was why his father gathered the opinions of others on how to protect the village and listened more than talked about politics. It was why his mother experimented with new techniques in the fields and why she was so excited about the occasional deliveries of books from the other side of the world.

It was why his mother cared for Komal in a loving way when they were alone.

Saddiq loved his parents. He agreed with his father that the world around them was changing rapidly, and Saddiq wished he didn't have to hide so much, especially his opinions about Thara and her sisters. He was like his parents, with the constant urge to make plans and control his own life.

Best to keep his thoughts a secret.

His mother smiled, noting that they had finished the work quickly. She thanked him for his help and giving her more time at the village's tiny library that afternoon, and Saddiq smiled, too, though for another reason. He reminded his mother that he had promised his father to start gathering goats from the higher pasture and gradually move them to the lower pastures, closer to the village center, for the winter.

The move took days because the goats could not handle an abrupt change in diet. With each gradual shift, the boys arranged rocks and branches as temporary blockades to prevent the animals from roaming.

"Your brothers should help," she chided. He shrugged, explaining he had started the project and the younger boys could attend her lessons.

With a small frown, his mother handed over a small pack that contained bread, fruit, and yogurt mixed with honey, and Saddiq waited until his mother was out of sight. She didn't know, but he had already moved the goats earlier in the morning—and so instead of climbing the hill, he dashed toward the meadows near a narrow section of the river. The banks were steep, lined with trees, and the place promised privacy.

Saddiq kept away from the path, instead walking in and out of the mottled shadows of trees and brush lining the river's edge. It didn't take long before he spotted Thara near the river. He paused, watching her kneel on the riverbank, her hands never stopping in collecting stems and organizing them in a basket.

Anyone could be watching, and he held back from calling out her name.

Their meetings could not appear planned. They had agreed on a signal so both could look around, ensuring they were alone, before speaking. She hung an empty basket among the branches if other girls worked in the area. He ducked behind a tree and gave a soft dove call. Thara looked up and down the river before heading toward the trees, too.

Then they waited, each listening for intruders as they took a slow, twisting path through a stand of noble pines.

Saddiq could not forget the news of Leila's baby. Rather than feel ashamed, he was energized and proud. He was an uncle, and his parents had no clue. That made the child his responsibility, though Saddiq didn't understand why he cared so much about an infant he had never met. Even Thara did not seem to care as much. She was puzzled by his curiosity, insisting that his parents and others in Laashekoh would be furious about the child.

For Saddiq, the village was broken if he could not care for his brother's child.

The child belonged in Laashekoh, and Saddiq wanted to plan a rescue. Thara told him the name of the prison where her sister was held, but he assumed that Leila would refuse to see him. Not that he wanted to see Leila after she had pointed a gun at his head and threatened to send him off to work in Pakistan along with other children tricked into leaving their homes. Thara agreed that Leila would still be furious with his entire family for ruining the scheme and sending her to prison.

Leila might be willing to hand the child over to her sister if she didn't know that Saddiq was behind the plan. At night, he envisioned the steps, leaving Laashekoh for Kandahar after sunset, traveling all night, inventing some errand for the next morning. Other villagers would not realize he was gone for hours.

But he needed Thara and a head start. Saddiq's father and the other men would waste no time tracking the two of them down. But surely his parents' fury would subside once they knew the baby belonged to his brother Ali. Saddiq had to elude the trackers just long enough to retrieve the baby. He needed no more than a day or two away from Laashekoh. He had saved money by helping his father sell goods at the market over the years.

Paying for a few meals was the easy part, and perhaps they could catch a ride to the city. He had to find a way to bring Thara along. Once out of Laashekoh, the two could pretend to be brother and sister and behave accordingly. Allah wouldn't mind, he convinced himself.

Sighing, Saddiq wondered if this was how his brother Ali had thought of Leila before falling to his death. He had heard his parents whispering about Ali and Leila meeting alone at night without supervision. They sounded puzzled and old.

But there was no talk about a child.

Since those events, the parents of Laashekoh had repeatedly warned the boys, even the youngest, against spending time alone with the village girls. "You can play as a group," his mother had warned. "But never alone."

He had once resented his mother for forbidding him to speak with Leila's sister. But Thara's news of a baby added to his understanding.

Secrets could be dangerous. He wanted to tell his parents about the baby, but Thara was terrified. She insisted no one in Laashekoh would want the baby, including his parents, and made him promise not to tell. Saddiq didn't argue. He could not forgive his parents if they refused to accept Ali's baby.

Saying yes would be easier once his parents held the child. Thara might accompany him, but only if he had a sensible, organized plan.

The two certainly couldn't leave the village together. That would be disastrous. He could organize supplies in a cave nearby. She could leave first and wait for him. The village would organize a search party, and Saddiq would help, accompanying his father and brother for at least a day. And then Saddiq could get separated, meet with Thara, and head to the highway that led to Kandahar. He had heard that it was easy to catch rides to the city, especially if passengers could pay or were willing to do small errands.

Thara and Saddiq were young and strong, accustomed to the outdoors. They would wear the best shoes they could find and keep a steady pace. They would stay away from open roads and villages during the daylight hours. No one had to know they left for the city together.

They could return separately. Afterward, he could explain how he had retrieved the baby on his own. Thara could claim she was lost and then hid because she was frightened. Perhaps his mother and father would be overwhelmed at meeting Ali's child for the first time, and that would reduce their questions.

It was a plan. He enjoyed daydreaming about traveling with Thara to Kandahar and thought less about returning to Laashekoh.

Saddiq mimicked the soft coo of a dove once more, and she returned the call. He hurried, taking a winding path around the trees until they met. They sat on a slope underneath the twisted branches of a wild rose tree. They would see anyone approaching from a distance, giving them enough time to separate.

"I must hurry," Thara whispered. "Karimah will scold me for not bringing back more materials for the baskets."

Saddiq asked what happened when Karimah complained about a

slow pace. "She assigns more chores and makes me work through the night," Thara said. "And I would be miserable if they did not let me out alone anymore."

She was firm. "I need the baskets for a good marriage."

"I brought you something." He placed the lunch from his mother between them, and then handed over another thick bundle. Opening it, Thara smiled at the strands of grasses in a range of pastels, perfect for fine weaving, along with a small, heart-shaped rock. Her voice broke as she thanked him. He explained how he had gathered the grass while tending the goats. "This way we have more time together and you return with plenty of material."

And then they talked about the goats, the hills, and the coming winter. Thara asked about her sisters, and he gave her the little news he knew. And then they talked about Leila. "You're sure you know where Leila is at?" he questioned.

Thara nodded and wrapped her hands around her ankles.

"And the baby is there, too?" She nodded again. "Ali would not want his child in prison."

"It's Allah's will," she said solemnly.

He shook his head stubbornly. "We must help the baby. We will go to the city and get her together. That is Allah's will."

~~~~~~

Parsaa woke up late, long after his wife had already rounded up the younger children to help carry jugs of water back from the nearby spring. In the distance, he heard a particularly shrill *akak*. The insistent call came from downhill, along the trail leading to the village: *eeee-eeee-eeee-eeee, eeee-eeee-eeee, eeee-eeue, eeue.*

Then abrupt silence.

A magpie's song was more melodic and sustained, inviting response from a nearby partner. The odd call suggested unusual activity, and unannounced visitors could be dangerous. The boys watching the village had become careless and should have signaled first.

Parsaa issued his own warning for the village—no words, just two sharp claps—a signal repeated throughout the village. Villagers stopped beating rugs, cutting vegetables, whatever work they were doing. The women gathered children, hurrying them inside the nearest homes and warning them to remain quiet. Men and older boys retrieved weapons, ensuring each was loaded.

Ahmed came running from work in the fields. "Visitors?" he asked. "Are you sure?"

"Who was on watch?" Parsaa snapped.

The younger man shook his head and mentioned that the village had been quiet for too long. Parsaa was impatient, cutting him off and watching as villagers took their assigned places. Parsaa and Ahmed prepared to face the group without weapons, and a few men and women gathered in the courtyard with them, even as a few snipers waited behind the cover of trees and walls, watching for any sudden move or fingers that strayed too close to a trigger.

~~~~~

Four Afghan soldiers entered the gate, in sunglasses and dusty camouflage, their helmets tied to their packs. Three men fanned out against the wall, facing the villagers and holding M16s with both hands. The fourth, his weapon slung across his back, strode toward Parsaa and Ahmed waiting in the center courtyard.

Ahmed offered breakfast. But the men shook their heads and, with little introduction other than to state that they were members of the Afghan Special Forces, started in with questions. The leader tried Pashtun and was annoyed that the villagers spoke only Dari. "We are investigating a missing helicopter," he said. "Three foreigners who work for an NGO."

Ahmed explained that the three had visited the village. "The foreigners were not here long. The helicopter landed by the river and left the same day."

The soldier stared at both men. Finally he spoke. "They were expected back in the city, but there's been no sign of them." He asked about the purpose of the visit.

Ahmed briefly described how the women said they ran an orphanage. "They had heard about orphans found by this village. But the women were too late. The children were not orphans and already were returned to their parents."

The man pressed. "And that was all? Did they make promises, offer money?"

The questions made Ahmed nervous, and Parsaa replied. "They provided toys for the children, and we sold potatoes and other produce to them. We explained that we take care of our own."

The soldier asked how the women responded.

Ahmed again glanced at Parsaa, who answered. "They were disappointed, but not surprised."

"Did you exchange harsh words?"

Parsaa was calm, shaking his head.

"Did you hear them quarrel?"

"No," Parsaa said, adding, "Except a scolding for their pilot."

"Ah," the man said to his colleagues. "The foreigners enjoy quarreling among themselves." He asked more questions, for descriptions of the people who entered the village, how long they stayed. Did they carry packs or arms? Did they seem in a hurry or worried? Ahmed offered brief responses.

The lead soldier then turned and headed toward the wall overlooking the road leading to Laashekoh, the lush river valley and mountains beyond. The view did not draw his gaze though, and he glanced down at the old trail leading to the village, the only access to Laashekoh.

His men kept their eyes on the villagers and their hands on the M16s.

"So empty here," the soldier concluded. He turned his back to the scene and leaned against the wall. "The reports advised this is not an easy place to reach, and they were right. Every mountain should have a road."

"We were surprised the foreign workers found us," Parsaa conceded.

"Did they talk about where they were headed next?"

The Laashekoh men shook their heads. They would not have divulged the location had they known.

The man sighed, pulled binoculars from his pack, and scanned the view quickly. "It's good that you did not try to lie to us. We saw where the helicopter landed below. Which direction did the copter head after takeoff?"

Parsaa stepped forward and brushed Ahmed's arm, before heading to the wall and standing next to the soldier. Facing the view, he pointed westward toward a tight set of mountains. "That way."

The soldier glanced at Ahmed for his reaction, but Parsaa trusted his friend and did not turn. Yes, the helicopter had initially started off in that direction, before swerving away from the mountains toward the canyon in the opposite direction. Perhaps Parsaa could eliminate a nuisance for Zahira.

The soldier aimed the binoculars in that direction and then lowered them, speaking softly so only Parsaa could hear. "These women are mischief-makers. They invent problems and claim they are here to fix them. Others have complained, and we were looking for them before they went missing." The man kicked at the dirt. "Your village could help with the search. But it could be easier for all of us if they are just found dead."

He paused. "Let me ask again, was there any trouble here?"

Parsaa stared a long moment before shaking his head.

The leader signaled for the other three men to head for the gate, and his voice took on a normal volume. "This was the last stop where people have reported seeing them. Enjoy the quiet while you can—and hope that the foreigners are found quickly."

Parsaa did not ask why. Hundreds of searchers could arrive in the area, and a hunt for missing foreign women would disturb Laashekoh for days to come.

The Afghan soldiers walked away, but tension lingered in the village. Ahmed wanted to follow, but Parsaa said no. "We should not aggravate them."

Instead, he ordered Ahmed to find out which boy had been on

watch and missed the soldiers' arrival. He also ordered a team to ruin the stretch of field where the helicopter had landed. "Add rocks, dig holes, anything," he said. "We do not need more visits from helicopters."

Not long afterward, Ahmed returned with a long face. "Who was it?" Parsaa demanded.

"Your son. Saddiq." The younger man defended the boy, suggesting that the soldiers were skilled and, if they had a vehicle, had left it far away. He didn't mind if Parsaa showed lenience. "I'm not sure any of us would have spotted them."

Parsaa cut his friend off. "Excuses are dangerous." And so were distractions, he thought to himself. He ordered Ahmed to let Saddiq rough up the smooth meadow. "Alone. He doesn't need help, and he works until it's done."

~~~~~

Saddiq was grateful to work alone on another task, though helicopters would find other landing spots in the valley. He worked tirelessly to ruin the expanse for another landing, rolling boulders and moving dirt with the help of an old rug and a few planks. As the sun fell, the task was almost done and Saddiq longed for water to clear the dust from his face and mouth. Instead, he slipped away and ran to Thara's favorite place for finding grasses, avoiding the path and twisting his way among the brush. She knelt not far from the fallen tree where they had first talked. He scanned the meadow, giving a soft bird call. She looked around, but he couldn't wait and approached along the forest's edge with the meadow.

He placed his hands on her shoulders. "I want you to leave," he explained. "The next time my father is traveling or distracted by a visitor. Just walk away."

"But I'm not ready," Thara said, alarmed. "And I cannot leave on my own."

"And we cannot leave together." He explained that she would have to hide and wait until he could safely escape, too.

She asked about the soldiers. "More may come to search for the missing women from the orphanage."

"That's why we must leave before they arrive," Saddiq said.

Thara swallowed. "If I leave, how long do you think the villagers would search?" She pointed out the search could end quickly if the others thought she had run away.

He shook his head, after already deciding that a long search could work to their advantage. "Better they assume you are lost. In the meantime, be sweet with Karimah so she does not think that you ran away."

"But what if someone follows and stops you? I cannot travel alone, and I cannot leave with you." She stepped away from him. Girls were warned all their lives about what would happen if they were caught alone with a boy. She didn't want to talk about how such a violation could bring the worst punishment for both of them.

"We won't travel together. Not exactly. We will leave separately, first you and then me. Then no one can say that we left the village together."

Thara glanced to the side, nervous. "But where will we go?"

"To Kandahar—to get the baby." Saddiq assured her that he had a plan and reviewed the steps for how they would reach the city. "And if it does not go smoothly, if we think you are in any trouble at all, we can find an orphanage, and they will take you in."

Her eyes brightened, but only briefly. "We're not orphans," she said, with doubt.

"Those women didn't seem to care." He was stubborn. "We must leave as soon as possible. Before something happens to the baby."

"Leila won't hand over her baby to us," Thara warned. "She is perverse and will want something from us."

He was pleased that Thara did not trust her sister.

"We will find a way to trick her into doing what we want." Saddiq darted away, through the trees, returning to the valley below to finish carrying out his father's order—making it impossible for another helicopter to land near Laashekoh.

CHAPTER 14

Once Leila had dispensed with the child, she returned to another section of the prison reserved for single women, young and old. She shared a cell with six other women—and thankfully, no children.

The younger women were expected to assist the elders, but the burden often shifted the other way. Leila charmed her fellow inmates by cleaning the cell, brushing their hair, sharing small treats, and flattering them. She was popular, and the entire group, young and old, doted on her, making tea, washing her clothes, and saving morsels from their meals for her.

In turn, she listened and learned prison ways.

The judge had sentenced her to six years for her role in trafficking children from the province of Ghōr, over the border into Pakistan. The young Afghan judge had seemed more upset about the plan to cross the border illegally—calling such dealings with Pakistan an embarrassment for Afghanistan. He also pointed out that US military personnel had cited aggravating factors, describing the young woman as a high security risk. Her attorneys were livid about a lack of specific evidence, but Leila did not protest and practiced looking contrite, and that won her a place in a more comfortable prison than where her husband and mother had been sent.

Leila truly did not mind prison. She had come so close to being trapped in a rural village with a brute of a husband who would have soon tired of her. She deserved much better than a dreary life in Laashekoh. She enjoyed hearing stories of the other women, and liked the attention from attorneys and NGO staff.

She also became accustomed to the horrified reactions to her face. What startled people the most was how half of her face was left untouched by the acid attack. One side, still haunting in its beauty, was a powerful contrast to the injuries of the other side.

The guards and attorneys were surprised by how she thrived in prison. She made new friends as, twice a day, the guards escorted her and other prisoners to the outside yard, where a larger group walked and exchanged pleasantries. At first the lawyers forced her to attend classes, but after discovering that she was one of the better students, Leila began enjoying the lessons. Every morning, guards escorted her to a classroom, led by a young Afghan woman who taught reading and writing, and during the afternoon, Leila attended classes offered by NGO volunteers. One teacher praised Leila, calling her a natural story-teller, and asked if she could share one of her essays with an attorney for an international nonprofit on women's rights. Journalists, NGO representatives, researchers suddenly wanted to interview her. A medical team started planning reconstructive surgery for her ravaged face.

Before long, Leila had a team of attorneys, one for her criminal case, another to monitor and negotiate media contacts, and another to review contracts and handle her finances. The attorneys set up a fund for her legal fees and plastic surgery, and they assured her that she would not have to worry about an income after prison. They were already working on securing permission for her to leave the prison for surgery outside the country.

"You have attracted the attention of the major international charities," one attorney confided. "They will support you as long as you are a model citizen. Be yourself, and do nothing to anger them."

Leila complied. She was a model prisoner, never complaining, fighting, or defying orders from the guards. From the start she cooperated with cellmates and worked hard to get along. She volunteered for prison tasks, but since the foreign charities had taken an interest, she no longer had to do the most unpleasant prison tasks. Prison administrators wanted to avoid international condemnation for mistreating a young woman who, despite her crimes, had already suffered so much.

The lead attorney maintained that the maximum sentence for a first offense of trafficking children by a young adult, especially a woman who had no control over the operation, should have been no more than a year. "The children came to no harm," the lawyer scoffed. And he added that if her husband had not antagonized the Americans, a small bribe would have most likely resulted in the entire group winning fast release onto the streets of Kandahar.

The attorneys suggested that she not hurry to schedule surgery or file an appeal to reduce the sentence. Not yet, because the excessive sentence, the scars, the pregnancy helped generate sympathy.

Leila no longer minded the curious stares. If anything, her scars drew attention to her plight, followed by more donations. Her story prompted others to rush forward and show her another way of life for women. Smart, earnest, and generous women visited her, explaining that they were from other countries, volunteering in the prison or writing articles for newspapers and magazines. Most were fascinated by her confidence despite the scars, and most asked the same concerned questions. Her attorneys had advised her to cooperate and anticipate repeated questions, warning her to keep her answers consistent and avoid the temptation to exaggerate. She answered all the questions asked of her, but she avoided lengthy explanations.

Short answers let her control the details of her life as needed. In truth, she didn't really want others to know her entire life story. Leila still remembered her surprise when one woman asked if she was angry about the attack on her face. The question was a turning point for Leila. She considered her answer and, smiling, eventually shook her head and offered a simple reply. "It meant that someone cared deeply about losing me. Allah is forgiving. And so am I."

The woman wrote a long article in another language that attracted new attention. Leila's teacher showed her a copy on a computer and explained how thousands of readers had viewed the article and her photographs. Leila liked how others listened to her, transcribing her comments into notebooks and shepherding the words outside the prison walls. She would have never found such power in Laashekoh.

The article traveled around the world, and before long backtracked to Kandahar. Local religious authorities were troubled. "Such forgiveness is not her province," one imam scolded the prison warden. He reminded the warden of a verse from the Koran: "Whoever associates anything with Allah, he devises indeed a great sin."

The prison officials urged Leila to use more care with her words and assured the imam that they had punished her. But the meetings and interviews continued. Funding from foreign NGOs flowed into the women's section of the prison, and the warden would not risk putting a stop to that flow.

Leila did not spend much time in the cell, typically attending classes or walking outside. For interviews or meetings with her attorneys, guards escorted her to a private room. She did not boast about the classes, the visitors, the interviews, or the funding. When other inmates asked why she was whisked away from the cell so often, Leila shrugged. "Perhaps the guards want to show my face to others as a warning." She tried not to lie to her new friends and relied on words like *could* or *perhaps*.

The foreigners pitied her, and she used that compassion to her advantage. She had few regrets, and life in prison was more pleasant than dull Laashekoh. She did not miss her husband and didn't argue when the attorneys and the visitors from the NGOs blamed her predicament on him. Yes, the transport of children was his idea. No, she had not understood where the children were from or their destination. She had simply obeyed her husband. She was also quick to add that perhaps her father had not understood the exact nature of the operation. Leila missed her father and ached whenever thoughts of him came to mind, but she was not so quick to defend her mother.

Her new independence still amazed Leila—her terror about being separated from her mother and sharing a cell with strangers had soon transformed to relief. Mari would have complained and talked all day, trying to control every word, every move, every part of her existence in a space that was tighter than their home in Laashekoh. The woman would have cared only about money, not understanding the interests of the foreigners or the need for classes.

Without the classes, her attorneys would have never heard her story.

It helped immensely that her mother and husband refused to talk at all, let alone answer questions. Leila feigned fear, begging her attorneys not to let anyone know how much she had talked about the crimes. She sought assurances from the legal team that her words would not be repeated to Mari or Jahangir. "I fear for my life—even in here," she whispered, raising one hand to cover the scar.

Her lawyers warned against discussing any details of the trafficking operations or problems in Laashekoh with the other prisoners. "Talk to NGOs, the lawyers, but not the police or other prisoners," one attorney had warned. "Other prisoners could testify against you in court to get reduced sentences for themselves. And trust me, they will soon resent the attention and funding coming your way. And never lie to the foreigners. They have ways of checking these stories."

"You could get celebrity status," another attorney confided.

Leila promised great care in how she spoke. More importantly, she listened. Her success at telling stories stemmed from discerning what others wanted to hear. About her own life, she presented an alternative story, cemented by refining and retelling over and over. She also withheld enough details, sustaining suspense and luring her listeners into assumptions that she did not necessarily share. She longed to forget life in Laashekoh, and talking with strangers reinforced her version of memories.

She kept her opinions and dreams to herself. The end of some stories should not be told.

PART 3

Allah does not love the mischief-makers.

—Koran 28:77

CHAPTER 15

The board of directors met monthly. Lydia did not attend most meetings, traveling to New York no more than twice year, and instead participated via Skype. She viewed the boardroom on her screen and remained quiet, listening closely to executive staff for long periods. Colleagues who expected a disengaged participant soon discovered their error as she followed up with pointed questions. More than once, staff members wanted to sink into their chairs as she asked about specific expenditures or the methodology behind a pilot program. No one could get away with glossing over budget details or country research that relied solely on the CIA's *World Factbook*.

Lydia had dedicated an old laptop for the Skype sessions, placed slightly above her head in her office. She kept the lighting low so that slight changes in her expression were less noticeable.

Lydia was the board's chairwoman, but she let Annie, the executive director, run the meetings.

This meeting had a long agenda and included an initial survey of award candidates from the Rodriguez-Walker Group. Prepared for a lengthy meeting, Lydia had a teapot waiting nearby. Cara was in New York for the meeting, and Lydia wasn't surprised when the discussion turned hot as the consultant presented recommendations for the new award program. Lydia folded her hands and listened.

Recognition would be distributed jointly to grant recipients and GlobalConnect employees, Cara explained. The board and the executive staff would choose finalists and keep the names secret until thorough background checks were completed. She reported on the four candidates in Afghanistan, two men and two women: An entrepreneur who ran a bicycle shop and trained others to repair and distribute bikes to the community, and a teacher who organized a network of schools for several hundred boys and girls; and a young, imprisoned mother who taught other prisoners how to read and write, and an older woman who provided healthcare services to rural villages.

Paul Reichart worked with the woman providing healthcare.

Only Henry understood that Lydia wanted to put a spotlight on Paul and his connections in Afghanistan. She wanted the thorough background check. Yet Henry warned Lydia: If she was too pushy, Paul would sense a trap.

Let the program roll naturally, Henry advised.

As Lydia had expected, the board and the executive staff gravitated to the stories of the two women—and she made a note to herself to request an audit to ensure that the Afghan programs reflected the country's demographics. Favoring one gender, ethnicity, religion, or age over another was a sure way to divide communities and trigger resentment. Both women lived near the village of Laashekoh, but the similarities ended there, Cara explained. The health provider had more experience. She had no staff and started with a group from the Netherlands before meeting Paul and obtaining a steady stream of supplies and funding through GlobalConnect. The younger woman was in prison for participating in a child-trafficking ring, and wrongly so, according to her supporters. She had been the victim of an acid attack, yet she was taking classes and using her new skills to train other women in reading, writing, and activism for women's rights. The younger one had an active legal team, and NGOs were competing to represent her.

Neither woman could present much documentation to support outcomes. Neither had conducted research.

Cara summarized her report. "Birthrates are slightly below average for Afghanistan in the Laashekoh area, and the child mortality rate is low. The children are well nourished—despite a lack of nearby schools and a low literacy rate. And the family-planning candidate has been funded for years. She has provided impromptu training of other caregivers, all of this highly informal. Paul and others credit her as contributing to the area's economic security. The younger woman has tremendous support, but a short track record."

The participants in New York murmured among themselves. Annie spoke up. "Paul's woman is clearly the better candidate with the longer track record. And it would be nice to recognize someone who knew Michael." The group nodded, nervously glancing at the screen showing Lydia.

"One glitch though." Cara held up her hand. "Paul Reichart requested that his connection be withdrawn."

Everyone in the room started asking questions at once. Lydia frowned, but held off from speaking.

Cara took a deep breath. "He says the woman is shy. He's also worried that the publicity could put her life in danger."

Annie tapped the conference table for attention. "We can't force employees or recipients into this. But I must admit I'm uncomfortable with the other candidate who has a big legal team and short track record. She may be . . . too well groomed."

Another staff member recommended skipping Afghanistan. "Too much political turmoil."

But others pushed back. The country needed help. The charity had a tough time hiring experienced staff who wanted to work in the country for the right reasons.

"Could we do this by surprise?" asked another senior staffer. "Paul is too modest."

"Surprise means no background check." Cara was firm. "That's too risky." Elliot, the board member who represented Photizonet's tech side, suggested that staff send out a blanket e-mail, notifying all employees about a possible background check that required opting out. "With luck, Paul won't read the e-mail. Who does anymore?"

Henry groaned, and Annie advised such a maneuver would violate the law. The US Fair Credit Reporting Act required that employees be notified about background checks with specific notice. The correspondence could cover no other topic.

"Some employees would quit over that," Henry added.

Elliot asked if a background check was all that necessary.

"Skipping a background check?" For the first time, Cara turned to Lydia. "No way. If a candidate refuses to undergo a background check . . . if some issue is exposed later, that defeats the purpose of good publicity."

Elliot threw up his hands. "This is an award, for Pete's sake. We all know Paul." He looked around the boardroom, but found little support. Michael had always welcomed Elliot's brash ideas, but the foundation staff did not feel the same.

"He works for us, people," the director of communications said. "Can't we fire an employee for refusing a background check? The board and the foundation are liable for what they do!"

Annie shook her head. "Federal law prohibits checks on current employees without notification—unless criminal activity is suspected. I'll send you the text later."

The group was silent, absorbing the information.

Lydia kept her voice light. She could not show how much she cared about Paul keeping his name in the ring for the award. "Giving an award away may not be so easy."

CHAPTER 16

Paul arrived alone shortly after sunrise, and once again, the village of Laashekoh had little warning. The air was clear and cold as gusts whipped at trees and clothing. He explained that he had camped near the river and left his off-road vehicle far enough away before tackling an early-morning climb toward Laashekoh. Parsaa was surprised by the aid worker's prolonged stay in the area, but Paul had already traced the origin of Najwa's blade.

"If the girl and the *peshkabz* come from the same place, she is from Helmand and not Ghōr."

The detail mattered less with Najwa away from the village. Parsaa asked if Paul would help search for the foreign workers. "Did you see Afghan soldiers?"

Paul looked surprised and shook his head, and Parsaa explained how the soldiers had mentioned that the village was the last to see the women. "But I'm not so sure."

Paul stopped. "Really?"

The women had talked about another stop nearby before returning to the city, Parsaa explained. "Did they say where?" Paul asked. "Did you tell the soldiers?"

Parsaa shook his head. "A helicopter can shift direction once it moves out of sight."

The villagers were heading out for a search. Parsaa wanted to check the ridges near the canyon leading to Zahira's compound, though he couldn't imagine why a group intent on helping orphans would visit the lonely place. He invited Paul to join them.

Frowning, Paul asked if the villagers had seen or heard any sign of a crash, and Parsaa shook his head.

"Then the helicopter is not around here," Paul insisted. "There is no point in wasting your time." Instead, he advised that they wait for the Afghan military to coordinate a search.

The other villagers were pleased, easily convinced to give up on a day of searching, but not Parsaa. The women could be injured, waiting for assistance. It was better if the men of Laashekoh found the women first. Besides, he didn't want large groups of strangers arriving in Laashekoh and asking questions.

Paul pointed out that Afghan conditions, the dust and sand, were tough on helicopters. He was critical of the women's operation and suggested that they had not invested in proper maintenance. "The helicopter may have broken down. They could be anywhere between here and Kabul."

"All the more reason to find them quickly," Parsaa said. "They were not prepared for a long stay."

"Wait, friend," Paul urged. "If an air search produces no results, the army will organize a grid search, and then we can help."

Paul seemed so sure, and other villagers agreed. The men were eager to expand the fields before winter hardened the soil. Parsaa acquiesced and Ahmed signaled that the search could wait until Afghan soldiers arrived.

Once the two men were alone, Paul was blunt. He didn't trust the women. One of the missing women, the one in charge, was married to a man who headed a major mining company. "Who knows? She could be scouting this area for her husband. The charity could be a way to build connections. Or the missing helicopter could be a stunt to draw attention."

Parsaa was not worried. The government owned all underground resources. Foreigners could not take over mining operations. Paul pointed out that Afghanistan needed foreign partners to access the minerals. The big companies were good at nagging governments to change rules for jobs. "It would change the landscape around here."

"There will be no mining leases here." Parsaa was firm.

The American seemed surprised. Parsaa wasn't sure if it was because of the villagers' lack of interest in mining wealth or the confidence that Laashekoh could keep prospectors at bay.

Paul didn't argue and offered to help in the fields. "I'd rather grapple with dirt and boulders than paperwork," he said.

The frost from the night before had vanished, and men were already marking out the new edges, planning where to place walls. They divided sections and competed among themselves, using shovels and picks to loosen the dirt, clear brush, and separate rocks. Paul grabbed a shovel and tackled his section. When one of the men encountered a large boulder, a call went out and the entire group gathered, working to apply leverage and scrape soil before rolling the boulder to one side where it would serve as the base of another winding wall. Saddiq was especially industrious in rolling the massive rocks, and the other men cheered him on.

Throughout the day, children delivered water, fruit, and bread sweetened with honey. By midday, the village women joined the men, loosening and leveling the soil before covering the newly bared sections with leaves, grasses, and waste from the animals, folding the organic material into the earth before adding another layer of stalks left over from the harvest, to prevent erosion over the winter months.

As the sun moved toward the horizon, the pace of work slowed and conversations became livelier. Parsaa was quiet, thoughts of the stranded women still nagging at him. He wanted them found.

The work of expanding fields, digging and moving boulders, was tough on hands and backs. The men agreed to stop work for the day, but only after removing a massive, uneven boulder buried deep in the field. Paul joined villagers using tools to etch the soil away. The villagers worked together like a machine, without words, and Paul marveled at how the group could read one another's minds.

Shrugging, Parsaa tightened a leather strap around the boulder and then belted it around his chest, leaning forward to pull as Paul and another man pushed from behind, with others scraping away the soil underneath. The men took turns, shifting places, and sweat dampened their clothing despite the cold air. Twilight had hit by the time the group rolled the boulder out of the way. The men drained what was left of the water and drifted toward the village center.

Exhausted, Paul and Parsaa stayed behind to sit on the defeated rock, their backs to the cool breeze playing across the field, and watch the setting sun. Parsaa quietly asked the other man if he wanted to stay the night. They could head toward the ridge where the helicopter was last seen. "In the morning light we might see some sign of them."

Paul closed his eyes, nodding as if a decision had been made. "I should contact my office. For all we know, the women have already been found. You should not trouble yourself. They are not worth it."

He did not expect the Afghans to put much effort into the search. All the more reason to search, Parsaa thought to himself, and he was surprised the other man kept talking. Maybe Paul was trying to convince himself.

"The women were cocky, moving into an area researched and cultivated by others." He also complained that the women did not purchase high-risk insurance, a concept he had to explain to Parsaa. The foreigners put up large sums to pay for search-and-rescue operations by air and evacuations in the event of attack or disaster. If the group lacked insurance, the search would last but a few days.

"But we are here, ready to go," Parsaa protested.

"Don't you see? It's wrong for foreigners to expect that from villages." Paul was bitter. "People think the work is easy here. They arrive poorly prepared and disrupt the work of other groups who have been here for years. For all we know, the women changed their plans or decided to camp out."

Parsaa tried to convince the man to stay for dinner so they could talk more, but Paul declined. He had to visit other villages and expected snowfall.

"Surely not yet," Parsaa said. "The air is not that cold."

Paul smiled. "You will see over the next day. The clouds are gathering and temperatures will plunge before tomorrow evening." He didn't mention that poor weather would complicate a search for the women.

After Paul left, Parsaa joined the other men dining on a thick lamb stew, with lots of bread and goat's milk. The fire blazed and they lingered, rubbing sore arms and discussing plans for the upcoming winter. Paul had been right—once the sun fell behind the mountain, the temperatures tumbled. Any night could be the last for such easy village gatherings. The men would no longer meet around the fire once winter's harsh winds and snow blasted their way through the valley. No village home was large enough to accommodate the entire group over winter, and villagers deliberately avoided smaller gatherings that might hurt feelings and polarize the village.

Winter was a time for families.

As the group pondered winter plans, a shrill cry broke the silence, followed by a woman's voice issuing orders, sending children scurrying to other homes.

"I cannot find her!" Karimah insisted.

Ahmed hurried to his frantic wife. "It's Thara," Karimah cried out. "She is not here! The foolish girl doesn't know when to return."

Ahmed called the villagers to gather at the center courtyard, and it was determined that Thara was the only one missing. Ahmed and Karimah pointed out that the girl was well behaved and considerate. Such a late return was unusual.

The men organized groups of men and boys to search the most likely places, the meadows, the fields, even the hillsides where the goats and sheep roamed. The girl may have simply fallen asleep, but Parsaa was strict about the groups staying together rather than separating to search on their own. He watched as his own sons took off into the night. Soon the eerie sound of young voices surrounded the village, calling out the girl's name.

Ahmed and Parsaa headed toward the path leading to the stream, and once there Parsaa crossed over a shallow area. Each man followed along the banks, checking among the nearby brush and rocks, and using sticks to test the deeper pools.

The men and boys covered the immediate surrounding area that night, but there was no sign of Thara. After a few hours, Parsaa ordered the children to head home and get sleep for the next day. By sunrise, the exhausted adults sought rest, promising one another to start the search again later in the day.

Parsaa could not sleep and stood alone by the fire ring. The wind raced down from the mountains. His chest pounded with guilt. He was not superstitious and paid no heed to omens. But he was mindful of patterns. The village had refused to search for the missing women, and now Laashekoh had a missing child of its own.

~~~~~~

With the entire village worried about the missing girl, few adults slept soundly. Sofi mixed flour, water, and ghee to fry small cakes with eggs. Then she prepared lunches—slices of lamb and mashed beans spread on naan—so that the search could continue nonstop throughout the day. The smell of fresh baking bread and spicy fillings took over her home, and Sofi was surprised that her husband had to rouse their oldest son.

Groups organized once again, and Parsaa advised the villagers to be alert for signs of the missing helicopter, too. Sofi and Karimah had searched the space where Thara slept at night and found nothing missing other than the clothes she had worn the previous day. Karimah also checked the storage space where Thara's baskets were kept until Ahmed decided the time was right to carry them to market for the best prices. Karimah counted and recounted.

"None are missing." Karimah shook her head and put her hands to her mouth in anguish.

From all appearances, the girl had not run away. Worried about an unknown menace, the mothers cautioned their children to avoid stepping away from the village alone. The villagers focused on nothing else the entire day, extending the search out farther and farther, much as Saddiq had predicted to Thara. An early snow started falling in the higher elevations. The searchers examined their assigned territories with care, but the only tracks found were their own.

CHAPTER 17

After a long day of searching, the villagers returned exhausted and tumbled into beds. Saddiq had to stay quiet to hide his exhilaration. Sleep was impossible, with so many racing thoughts and his heart pounding in his chest.

The snow kept falling, sticking to the ground even in the valley, and that changed his calculations. The snow could both expose and obscure his trail. He decided to leave before the skies cleared.

Starting his journey shortly after his parents went to bed could give him a head start. And he couldn't wait to see Thara again. He was confident about reaching the city, but he had no idea what to expect afterward.

Burying his head underneath the blankets, Saddiq pretended to drift off to sleep, murmuring that he had an idea about where to find Thara, one he might try the next day. His younger brother pressed him, but Saddiq mumbled and shook his head, waiting for the whispering and squirming underneath the covers to end.

Soon, he heard the soft, easy breaths.

His parents extinguished the lantern in their room nearby.

After a long wait, he sat up, crawled to the side of the room, and donned clothes he had worn earlier that day. Retrieving two old canvas sacks from the kitchen, he slowly moved toward the main doorway, pausing and listening with every step.

Saddiq had to open the door without disturbing his father. The man was sensitive to changes in the house and would hear the door scrape against the dirt floor or feel a draft from outside.

Crouching, Saddiq rubbed his hand back and forth, smoothing

dirt near the doorway and feeling for twigs, pebbles, anything that could add noise. He reached among the pile of shoes left near the entranceway, finding his and pulling them on slowly. Then he turned full attention to the door. Using two hands, he slowly lifted the thick wooden bar and gave the slightest tug. Gripping the side of the door with both hands, Saddiq pulled steadily just enough to slip outside. The lower edge rubbed against the floor with the softest *whoosh*. Holding his breath, he stepped outside, gently closing the door.

He looked about and waited. The night was magical. Thick flakes of snow swirled, clouds smothered the starlight, and bitter cold pierced the night.

His father did not storm outside with questions. Saddiq heard no sounds from inside the house at all. He quickly added the old sacks over his shoes, tying the tops to his upper calves. Walking was awkward, but the sacks enlarged and blurred his footprints.

Avoiding a direct exit from the compound, Saddiq zigzagged around homes, circling the courtyard, then the village, before heading toward the forest beyond the fields. With Allah's blessing, more snow would fall. Other villagers would awake and head outside, covering his tracks long before his parents realized that their son had left.

Once away from the village, Saddiq proceeded carefully, studying the ground and avoiding the most traveled paths. He deliberately took a meandering route, circling back several times. Empty-handed, he used his hands to reach for trees and tried to pounce on tufts of grass or roots spreading from tree trunks to avoid leaving a trail should the snow abruptly end.

As he approached the cave, he climbed an old log and looked behind him. The snow still fell, smothering the outlines of his footprints. Allah was with him. Waiting, making sure that no one followed, he let out a birdcall, a partial chirp of the laughing dove—*ur-ur-ur, ur-ur-ur.*

A head peered from the cave and spotted him. Silent, Saddiq held up his arm and waved. Thara nodded and vanished from view. Waiting, he thought about her following his instructions inside the cave, retrieving anything she had brought with her, eliminating every sign, before slowly walking backward, sweeping the rocky floor with a handful of dried grass tied to the end of a stick.

Before long, Thara shoved two sling packs out of the cave's entrance —both made from an old wool blanket left in the rag bin that he had sliced in two—and then the small handmade broom. He studied her and decided she could pass for a boy. She wore old clothes that belonged to Saddiq's younger brother. Saddiq had given her a razor and directed her to cut her long hair as soon as she reached the cave, hanging onto the clumps, saving every strand for later disposal far, far from Laashekoh. A *pakol* was set at a jaunty angle on her cropped hair.

Again nodding toward Saddiq, she hurried off in the opposite direction. He glanced upward. The dark-gray sky was monotone, offering no hint of sunrise or an end to the steady snowfall.

They could not be too careful. Saddiq took a wide berth away from her path, hiking parallel with her for a long ways. Then he shifted direction gradually until he found her trail, placing his feet directly over her footprints.

~~~~~

Upon catching up with Thara, Saddiq passed without word and forged ahead, once again avoiding worn paths and focusing on shortening his pace so that she could follow by stepping inside his footprints.

The plan was that he would walk ahead by a hundred paces or so, close enough that she would not get lost and far enough, if either was caught, to give the other time to take cover. If Saddiq was caught close to Laashekoh, he'd explain that he had followed Thara's tracks and become lost. If she was caught, she would describe horrible traffickers who had cut her hair before she could escape. Both would vehemently deny knowing that the other one was nearby. The plan was rough, but that kept them moving, guarding against followers.

They planned to walk until the sun came up, and the two did not talk so that they would hear other passersby well in advance, separate, and move off the trail. They didn't want to run into anyone near the village of Laashekoh. The snow kept falling, the trail was empty, and Saddiq delayed signaling a stop while the weather cooperated. He moved southwest toward the highway, in a direction slightly off from their ultimate destination to keep anyone from guessing that the two were headed to Kandahar. The area was unfamiliar, and he prayed for more snow, at least until they reached the highway.

Thara seemed relieved to keep moving, and so was he. The search for her had been intense, and Saddiq didn't want to think about how his parents would panic once they discovered that he was missing. He had to keep moving and couldn't sit, sleep, or think too hard. Guilt clutched at his throat and chest, and it hurt to breathe. He wasn't sure what was worse—his parents' grief since the death of his oldest brother and their fears that Saddiq had met a similar fate, or the suspicion that he and Thara had left together.

Saddiq pushed on. Allah blessed those who moved, and they had gone too far to stop. He had brought a few rags to wrap around their hands, but cold pierced the night and his fingers.

Thara's speed and ability surprised him, and she forced him to keep a brisk pace. When he came into view, she issued a sharp call of panicked laughter, *chee-ee-ee*. The night was not anything like he had imagined early on, walking far from Laashekoh, holding Thara's hand to guide her along the rough terrain.

The two had agreed beforehand. Constant separation meant they were not traveling together.

The trail to the highway took them away from the mountains. By early morning, the snow was light, and by midday it had stopped. Wind swept across the barren landscape, pushing wisps of the dry snow around rocks and brush, weaving it with dirt and sand. The ground was hard, and Saddiq no longer worried about leaving tracks. Before long, they could hear a rumble of traffic on the highway.

Saddiq ran ahead toward a small crest overlooking the massive road, wide open with no barriers. Except for racing vehicles, no one was in sight.

Saddiq was not ready to be seen, and he directed Thara to hide in a rocky section to the east. "We must see others before they see us," he cautioned. He had heard too many stories about bandits and militants along the highway.

Worried about leaving her alone, he looked back and ensured she was out of sight. Saddiq continued southwest for a ways before shifting direction and running eastward, parallel to the highway, just out of the drivers' sight. He studied the traffic and hoped that highway patrols were irregular.

As he passed the rock outcrop, he whistled for Thara to join him.

But she did not respond. Nervous, he waited a few moments before heading up the slight incline, and there, nestled in a sandy place among the rocks, he found her fast asleep. Suddenly, he was exhausted, too.

There was time for rest. They needed to stay sharp looking for rides along the highway, and the rocks offered shelter from the biting wind, a good place to hide and rest. He doubted that a search by villagers would extend as far away as the highway, at least not for a day or two.

Long ago, his father had talked with Saddiq about travel to the cities. Many pickup trucks used the highway, and drivers often offered rides. His father warned his sons against accepting help from groups of young men. "Accept rides from families," the man advised. "But as you grow older, remember that the families will be wary of you."

Saddiq was ready for sleep. In a few hours, he would move closer to the road and observe its ways.

He emptied his pack and covered Thara with his portion of the blanket. Then he found another sandy patch, curled up tight, and pressed close to a large rock that shielded him from the wind.

CHAPTER 18

Parsaa woke up before dawn, anxious to resume searching for the missing girl. Other villagers were less eager.

Most were sure the girl had run away. Parsaa and Ahmed planned to hunt until they found a sign that that was true. Yes, the girl was unhappy, Ahmed had confided, understandable with a mother and sister in prison. Karimah was strict. Village families had hesitated to open their homes to the girls, fearing an evil influence over their own children. Karimah and Ahmed had helped immensely by taking in Thara, the oldest of the sisters, the one deemed most likely to cause trouble and follow Leila's ways.

The girl was not allowed to talk, eat, or pray with other family members. She was expected to work nonstop, making baskets and saving for her dowry. Such discipline protected the village and reminded other children to behave, though Parsaa's wife kept hoping that as years passed other villagers would soften and forget the crimes of the children's parents. Sofi could not be harsh with Komal. Parsaa had suggested the restrictions would ease once Thara left the village for marriage and discouraged criticism of anyone caring for the girls, especially Karimah. "No one can agree how to raise a difficult child," he noted. "Everyone knows best, and nobody knows. Thara is older, and Komal is the youngest. Different approaches for each can succeed."

For most villagers, the girls were a scourge. Karimah and others had tried to convince Parsaa to find marriage partners—any partners— quickly. Relatives should care for the sisters and make decisions, but in the absence of aunts and uncles, Laashekoh was responsible for the girls.

Losing Thara, failing to provide proper care for her, reflected poorly on the entire village. Parsaa was disturbed that Thara had left no hint or trail, and he wanted his sons to hurry to join the search. Entering the bedroom where the boys slept, he immediately noticed that Saddiq was up and gone. Parsaa couldn't ignore the memories of another morning, when his oldest son was supposed to leave for school.

Another son, Hassan, sat up, and Parsaa asked about Saddiq. "He didn't wait for us." The younger boy rubbed his eyes. "He had an idea about where Thara might be, and he has already dressed and left."

Annoyed, Parsaa wanted an organized search, and did not want to waste valuable time. "Did he say where? Which direction did he take?"

But Hassan didn't know and suggested his father should not be surprised. "Saddiq no longer wants to talk with me," he grumbled. "He prefers going off alone to work."

Worry swept over Parsaa. His mouth was dry, with a horrible taste, as if he had just swallowed milk before realizing it had gone sour. Saddiq likely knew where Thara went, or he helped her leave the village. Parsaa hoped it was not true, but either way, the two children could be in grave danger.

The village would not tolerate such a transgression. Young couples had been beaten and stoned for less-serious offenses. The women had warned of trouble and would demand harsh punishment.

Unless no one else in Laashekoh made the connection. Parsaa cut the boy off abruptly. "No. Saddiq is on an errand for me and will be away for a few days."

The boy gave his father a puzzled look. "You forgot this?"

Parsaa ignored the question and urged the boy to hurry for the search.

Hassan frowned. "So you know where he is at?"

"He is all right, Allah willing." Parsaa spoke softly. "He is not searching for Thara."

"But we must search for Thara, and Saddiq does not?" the boy pressed, with a hint of defiance.

Parsaa lowered his voice, giving his son a hard look that registered disappointment and a lack of trust. "Unless you want to feel my wrath, and Saddiq's, too, do not ever say his name and Thara's together with the same breath.

Parsaa was quiet and distracted as the boys prepared for the search, and Sofi worked in the kitchen, making extra meals. She asked her sons about Saddiq, and Hassan immediately spoke up: "He is away for a few days on an errand for father. I have taken over his duties."

Sofi gave her husband a worried glance but asked no more questions. As Parsaa donned his shoes, Sofi told the boys to wait outside. She clutched at her husband's wool *chapan*. "Tell me Saddiq is safe?"

Parsaa touched his chin to the top of her head, and spoke gently. "He is smart. We cannot show worry about Saddiq."

She took a sudden breath. "He cared too much about Thara and her sisters. We can't bear to lose him. Could she have . . ."

Parsaa could not lie to her. He put his hand to her mouth and whispered, "We cannot speak of them together." His wife closed her eyes at the confirmation of her worst fears.

~~~~~

The villagers widened the perimeter for their search and found no sign of the missing girl. Heavy snowfall had obliterated all signs of anyone entering or leaving the village in recent days. The only visible tracks were from the search parties.

Early in the day, the other villagers did not seem to notice Saddiq's absence. As the day dragged on with no questions, Parsaa worried that the other villagers carried their own dark ideas. He refused to raise the issue but became more uncomfortable with every encounter and no mention of Saddiq. By the day's end, as the group returned to Laashekoh, Ahmed quietly questioned where Saddiq had searched.

"He's away from the village on an errand," Parsaa replied, and Ahmed assumed the boy was at the compound.

One question. Parsaa could only hope that it was inconceivable that Saddiq, the most cautious of his sons, had left the village with Thara.

The boy was too caring. Saddiq would not leave the village and panic his parents without good reason. Parsaa refused to accept that another son would repeat the mistakes that Ali had made with Leila. Perhaps Saddiq had found the girl's trail, but the other villagers did not need to know.

He doubted that the two children had headed for neighboring villages where their parents were well known. The two wouldn't last long in the winter weather without shelter or food. Parsaa was grateful for the snowfall covering the tracks and hoped the boy had enough sense to avoid returning to the village with the girl.

Other villagers might not see it the same way. Some could look for sinful behavior and a chance to prove their own piety. If caught together, Saddiq and Thara could be banished from the village or, worse, ordered to collect the stones for others to heave as punishment. A father could not help but imagine the worst. Thara could have tricked the boy into an escape. They may have traveled to a nearby city and tried to blend in. They might pretend to be already married with their parents' blessing.

Parsaa was determined to find his son before anyone else did. He would track them down, scold them, and beat sense into them. He would hide that the two had been together.

Or, he could trust that Allah approved of whatever Saddiq had set out to do. Regardless, the family could not talk about Saddiq or ask questions.

~~~~~~

A whisper woke Saddiq. He shivered uncontrollably in the dark. He had slept much longer than intended. Thara crouched next to him and arranged the blanket over his body. "Do you know which way to go?"

That was easy. He nodded, and pointed east. "Have you heard anyone?" he whispered.

She shook her head. "We should still leave."

He agreed, although he was stiff and cold, more nervous with every step away from Laashekoh. Darkness allowed them to approach the highway's edge. He became accustomed to the roar of trucks rumbling past. Harsh headlights turned the dust into a hypnotic glow.

Thara wasn't used to the noise and speed, and at last took his hand. As they walked quickly, she asked how long it would take to reach the city. "Not long at all if we can catch a ride," he said. "But we should walk until we find a place where the vehicles pull off."

They were about a hundred kilometers away from Kandahar. She had no idea about the length of a kilometer, and that troubled her.

"How do you know such facts?" Thara asked, but he could not answer. He imagined that parents conversed more broadly with sons than with daughters.

She also fretted that someone might recognize the pair and report their whereabouts to his parents in Laashekoh. He tried to explain that Laashekoh was small. Most drivers on the highway had never heard of the village and didn't care, but she was near tears about getting caught. "Tell me we are near Kandahar," she pleaded.

He did not want to lie to her and stopped. "Are you sure that you want to leave?"

She didn't answer right away, then nodded. When she did speak, her voice was firm. "I cannot go back."

As she walked more swiftly, Thara explained that her biggest fear was getting caught. "But it's wonderful to think of living in a place where others do not know my family and I'd never have to hear another word of judgment."

"Then we must move along, one step at a time," he said.

With their sling packs secure, they walked for hours. Fast-changing clouds in shades of copper, rose, lavender, and then pure fiery gold stretched across the horizon, the colors beckoning them. The sun rose directly over where the highway met the sky, and the beauty gave Saddiq confidence.

Daylight hours were dangerous. Others could see them. Saddiq shifted direction away from the road and moved toward uneven terrain, just out of sight of the highway. The landscape was flat, dry, nothing like the fields and woods sustained by the river near Laashekoh. Rocks and lumpy sand reduced their pace and failed to provide adequate cover.

They could not get caught. Saddiq dared not bring up the possibility of gangs wandering along the highway, looking to rob him and do worse to her. He urged her to practice keeping a constant eye out for good cover in the event that they spotted someone and had to hide swiftly.

As the morning light exploded, Thara let go of his hand and fell behind. He paused so that she could catch up, but she was embarrassed, shaking her head and assuring him that she would follow. She didn't want to be seen with him.

Saddiq regretted not having brought along a rifle. But a missing weapon would have alerted his father to an unusual and lengthy absence. Saddiq shook his head, trying not to think about his family, not until he had the infant in hand.

~~~~~

Once the sun was high, the highway bustled with activity, an unending string of cars and trucks moving and passing in spurts with honking horns and smelly exhaust. Saddiq settled Thara behind a sand mound and told her to rest. Tears mixed with dust as she worried about him leaving her behind.

"You are tired," he scolded, explaining that he had to check the people gathered along the roadside. He didn't want to worry her, but she had to be prepared. "Remember, we could get separated anytime." Saddiq drilled her on what to do and say if they became separated.

If he did not return as promised? She would walk toward Kandahar during the hours of darkness. If someone asked who she was? One of two brothers. Their names? Esmat and Yar. Destination? Their father's home in Kandahar. And what did the father do? A stoneworker who helped construct homes.

"Good," he said gruffly. "Do not talk much, because you sound like a girl. Keep your answers short. Direct. And do not be afraid. I won't leave you. But we must both be prepared if that happens."

Before walking toward the highway, he studied the mound and the nearby area. The landscape was so barren compared to that surrounding

Laashekoh. Not much cover, but the best they could do. Saddiq urged Thara to rub more dirt on her face and hands and to lay low. He left his pack next to her and stripped away the clothing on the upper part of his body to reveal a folded cloth belt tied tight around his upper chest. Thara covered her eyes. He dressed, removed a few coins from the homemade belt, and directed Thara to strap it underneath her clothing.

"I have money, too." She reached deep into the layers of her clothes and extracted a thick pile of bills, both Afghan and foreign currency.

"How did you get this?" he asked, amazed.

"Leila hid her money and told me before she left." Saddiq shook his head, displeased about relying on money from Leila, which was earned by lying to children and sending them off to jobs that did not pay in Pakistan. But Thara was adamant. There was no point in throwing currency away, and someday she would help her younger sisters.

He doubted whether such money could ever be used for good. "Better you carry it all. If we're stopped, robbers will assume I'm carrying the money." Then he suggested that she sleep while he observed the traffic and stopped vehicles. He could be away for a while.

She asked how long she should wait for him, and he told her until sunrise the next day. "So long!" she protested.

He ignored the comment. "Do not approach the road or look for me. I will catch up with you." Then Saddiq took off running, climbing another crest and dropping down in the sand so that he could crawl toward the highway without being seen.

~~~~~~

Two rickety trucks pulled to the side of the road, engines running as the drivers waited in the sandy clearing. One man arranged crates of apples, grapes, and nuts to face the oncoming traffic. The other truck had a large barrel attached to the back and a scrawled sign offering water for sale.

The two men were setting up shop for the day.

Saddiq decided that the men were not dangerous. A few vehicles pulled over, and the younger man moved closer to the back of the truck where a rifle waited, ready to ward off gangs, military patrols demanding payments, or other trouble. The two men were nervous, and Saddiq waited for a lull in customers and for both men to move far enough away from the rifle.

Saddiq stood and called out, "Salaam alaikum." The men turned in alarm, and one started for the truck.

It was a new experience for Saddiq to be feared by grown men. Lifting his hands and showing a coin, he asked to purchase fruit. The two men looked at each other and demanded the boy lift the layers of clothing. "Prove you have no explosives!" one shouted.

Saddiq complied, then slowly approached to place the coin in the man's hand. The man handed over a fresh apple, and Saddiq couldn't help himself. He took huge bites, as if he had not eaten such fruit in a year or more. The memories of home were overwhelming.

The men asked his name, and without thinking, he replied, "Saddiq." The men asked why he was alone, and he stuttered a foolish explanation about walking and wanting to see the road. They scolded him, and he lowered his head, mortified that he had made Thara practice her responses so much without doing the same himself. The men introduced themselves and said they were from Kandahar. Saddiq asked if he could help them in some way.

The two men whispered, and then the younger one spoke up: "We would like to sell all the produce and leave by midday."

The older man waved his finger at Saddiq. "Do not think that you can set us up for a robbery. We're well armed." He handed over a crate with clumps of large grapes. "Hold the fruit up high," he ordered. "Let's see if you can get the drivers to stop and buy." His friend nodded.

Saddiq worked without break, and the two men focused on transactions with customers. Another vendor tried to park his truck in the area, but the younger man waved his rifle and chased the driver off.

The fruit sold quickly and the water, too. The two men were anxious to leave. Saddiq, trying to be helpful, had already loaded most of the empty crates on the truck, and the older man handed over a few coins to Saddiq.

The boy quickly thanked the man, and asked if he could instead ride with them to Kandahar in the back of their truck. The two men exchanged a glance and shrugged.

Handing the coins back, Saddiq asked if they would wait while he ran and found his brother. "A younger brother," he explained, offering a complicated tale how the two of them had walked along the highway to visit an uncle and would be in trouble for wandering so far from home, how his little brother was tired and resting nearby.

The older man did not respond. The younger one shrugged again and told him to hurry. Saddiq raced up the hill, over the crest, and shook Thara awake. "Hurry!" he shouted, grabbing both packs. "We have a ride! And you absolutely must pretend you are a boy and we are from Kandahar and we were visiting an uncle!" She sat up in alarm and Saddiq asked about the belt. She nodded and pointed to her chest. Not waiting, he pounded downhill, waving to let the drivers know that the two brothers were on their way.

The two trucks circled out of the clearing and joined the growling centipede of traffic headed for Kandahar.

~~~~~

Thara joined Saddiq at the crest of the hill, and Saddiq turned away to hide tears of frustration. Two men refused to wait and roared away in their trucks—it was Allah's will.

"We wasted a whole day," he said bitterly. "And I put us at risk by jumping out and waving to sell grapes."

She tried to comfort him, insisting that drivers probably took little notice of one boy with two vendors. She focused on their immediate concerns. It was cold, and she returned to the shelter behind the mound of sand, which she had reinforced by digging deeper along the side not hit by the wind. She was motherly. "You need sleep. We must walk tonight." She emptied their packs, and then stretched out in the new hollow she had created. Despite so much failure, she was kind.

His anger vanished as long as Thara was not upset about missing a ride to Kandahar. "I should keep watch," he said. "Those men worried about robbers."

Thara reached for his hand and pulled, urging him to sleep. "No one will see us if we stay away from the road," she promised. "If we both lie flat under this blanket, we won't be seen." He wasn't used to planning and strategizing with a girl. As he hesitated, she advised that he had to get used to new routines. Children preferred routines more than their parents did, as she had learned after her mother's arrest. She spoke sadly. "The best parents keep that a secret from their children."

There were no routines in their travels to Kandahar, he thought, and it was true he was exhausted. They were far enough from the highway. The area was quiet, and any strange noise would waken them. Saddiq stretched out in the mound, as close as possible to Thara without touching, and she arranged the blanket's two halves over both of them.

The old blanket shielded them against the cold wind and biting sand. Saddiq closed his eyes. Despite the shame over losing the ride, he tried to reassure himself. They had food and water and more than enough money to pay for a ride.

Thara suddenly rolled over and faced him. "Why are you so different from the others in Laashekoh? Why don't you blame me for what Leila did?"

He didn't know. Maybe he didn't like being thought of as so different from his parents and brothers. "One day we were all friends, and the next our parents banned us from talking with you. Maybe I'm terrified the same could happen to our family."

"The villagers don't like us. Your parents will not mind if I leave Laashekoh. But they may not be happy about you bringing a baby to the village. You could be in trouble."

He wasn't sure and didn't want to admit that his parents were unkind or unjust. Thara warned that she may know his parents better than he did. He caught his breath and wondered if the journey to Kandahar was a horrible idea. But Thara would refuse to go back, and he couldn't abandon her along the highway. He did not dare voice his worst fears aloud.

She propped herself up on one elbow. It was as if she could read his thoughts, and the fear was contagious. "You understand, Saddiq, I cannot go back," she whispered. "They would never believe that we traveled to Kandahar separately. They would punish us. Severely."

"No, not in Laashekoh . . . ," he murmured.

She sighed, and he was fascinated by the graceful curve of her neck. "Maybe not for a boy. But for a girl, one who is Leila's sister? I cannot go back. We can find the baby, but we should try to stay in Kandahar. Maybe at an orphanage. Or we could find work and care for Leila's baby ourselves."

That was not his plan. But Saddiq needed Thara to retrieve the infant and didn't argue. The baby was the only way of blunting his parents' anger. Surely, his parents could not be angry with their first and only grandson. He hoped the child looked more like Ali than Leila. How could his family blame Thara for alerting Saddiq to the child's existence?

Already Saddiq felt a connection with that child. And he missed his mother and father, but he had little doubt about how they might have responded upon hearing his plan. They would have lashed out at Thara and denied that the child belonged to Ali. Eventually his parents would listen and forgive all, but only after Saddiq returned to Laashekoh with the child.

Saddiq wanted Ali's baby. He would not allow his parents or the villagers to blame Thara. They did not trust her, and that alone would have stopped the rescue plan. It was easier to return home and explain—with an infant as proof.

CHAPTER 19

Leila's youngest attorney described himself as a victim advocate paid by a group of foreign charities reviewing her case. He had established a fund to collect donations specifically for her care. When he visited, he offered compliments and brought along soaps, creams, linens, and other gifts that made life in prison more comfortable.

He had studied in London and was an expert in international law, human rights, and gender discrimination—not that it mattered in Afghanistan courts. The country had no uniform legal system. His organization's goal was to demonstrate the inconsistencies and introduce international norms. "A *jirga* will review the appeal case and apply Islamic law as they see it. That interpretation controls your future." If the decision did not go her way, he would organize a global campaign using media contacts, Facebook, and Twitter to shame and antagonize local authorities.

In the meantime, the legal team proceeded with their claims.

He advised Leila to maintain a low profile and avoid criticism from resentful inmates or local elders. He urged her to keep sharing her gifts, distributing expensive items among the guards and the smaller items among the inmates. She continued with her classes, including study of the Koran and Sharia law, searching for examples to apply to her case—especially examples that could be supported by witnesses. "The research is tedious," he noted. "But it will bring great rewards."

Leila still could not believe that donors from other countries cared so much for her. They had never met her. "You are sure that I'm not regarded as a common criminal?"

"They are moved by your story," he insisted. "Your accusers will eventually forget, and there is plenty of money in your fund for bribes."

He negotiated all arrangements with the foreign charities. The foreign charities were generous but could also intimidate, pry, and control.

"That reminds me," the attorney interrupted. "Afghan military investigators may want to talk to you about a recent incident. A helicopter carrying staff from a Kabul orphanage went missing. The last stop was in Laashekoh."

"What can I tell them from prison?" she asked.

"They will ask if the villagers would harm such workers."

She thought about the previous advice—not to lie. But the question was too tempting. She wondered if the orphanage had checked on her sisters.

"Parsaa, the leader." She frowned and nodded slowly. "He does not appreciate outsiders. He would resent foreigners trying to remove children from the villages."

"Is he dangerous?"

"He could be." Her eyes were wide.

The attorney warned her not to answer questions without him present. Then he summarized the civil suit the legal team intended to file against Laashekoh, for her share of her father's property. He described that as a low priority, compared to the possibility of Leila working as a representative for one of the charities, earning a living, and having her own house in the city or abroad, with all the clothes and food she could ever want. "You will travel and tell your story. You could become famous."

She laughed.

"This is serious," he scolded gently. "These opportunities are not available to every woman in prison. You are fortunate in attracting their interest. Your only job is to be cooperative and friendly. But proceed with caution. You haven't told the other inmates much?"

She shook her head.

"Good. Too much talk gives the story away."

He was uptight, and she was not foolish. The attorney could not possibly trust her.

"Most important, do not lie," he ordered. "Liars are forgetful. Better to stop talking. The foreign charities prefer a neat, simple story."

Falling silent, she thought about her tale presented to him and her teachers. She had not told her entire story. In the writing class, the teacher demonstrated how to select details for essays and use only words and descriptions that contributed to the overall theme, always showing and not telling.

Leila had a theme—she had been deprived and deserved more. She had a right to discard her worst memories of Laashekoh and withhold details. The teacher praised Leila's stories and essays and distributed them to others as models.

But then the young lawyer would not let her forget her biggest mistake. "Have you had contact with those caring for your child?"

Leila shrugged and shook her head.

"Surely they will arrange visits and I can see her?"

He would not admit that he wanted the caregivers to return the child to prison, and she was annoyed.

"Travel is difficult for my family, and they cannot bring it here." Besides, she did not want to move to the section of the prison for children and mothers.

The attorney lowered his voice but did not disguise his revulsion. "Do not use the word 'it' to refer to your daughter. She is your child, your little girl, your infant, a precious treasure." He looked around to make sure no one listened. "That child is the center of your world. You are ready to risk all for her, you want a better life for her—such sentiments should be mentioned with every breath."

Leila slumped against the wall and averted her eyes. She was bored, not ashamed.

"You do feel that way about your child," he coached.

She lashed out. "You care more about her than you do about me!"

"That is not true. I represent you. Do you not realize your good fortune?"

She pressed her fingers to her forehead and wished she could erase the child from her life. "No one has asked about her. They don't need to know . . ."

"She was born in prison. The charities know about her. They will ask questions, and we must file truthful reports. The donors are not stupid. They have more money than either you and I can comprehend. But I can assure you, reactions in the United States and Britain to a mother showing no concern for her child would be similar to the reactions in Afghanistan. The foreigners can be more judgmental."

Her eyes were hard, and she questioned him gently as if he were a child. "But not about a woman in prison?"

He shook his head, incredulous. "Some of the biggest American charities are supporting your case. The NGO workers do not care about your crimes. They want to help you. But they will question why the baby is not with you. You cannot toy with them."

He expected her to lie, and she spoke the truth. "The child is noisy and needy. I prefer being alone."

He sat quietly for a few moments, and she wondered if he would give up on her. It didn't matter. She wouldn't mind staying in prison. The surgery to repair her face would be nice, but not necessary.

The attorney didn't walk away. He waved his hand. "All right. I'll avoid mentioning the child. The charities will review your case and probably still arrange the surgery and ask for early release. They will continue to take care of linens, special food, other small comforts. But the big funding could come with an official post, going on tour, giving interviews and speeches, perhaps even writing a book—and those will require the child."

She understood, but felt trapped.

"Donor interest may not last for long. The story can have no flaws."

Leila despised him when he was polite. The attorney could turn compassion on and off the way the guards controlled the prison lights, and he had once mentioned that his team had no shortage of clients. The attorneys were intelligent, and she had to be careful with her words. The men recorded the sessions and questioned any discrepancies.

He stared at her and finally asked if Leila even knew the baby's location.

"She is in good hands," she offered.

"So you know where she is at?" He was eager and pleased. "Tell me.

I can retrieve her and find a place for her in the city. Your siblings can help. We can arrange photos and visits . . ."

"No!" Leila didn't want the attorney traveling anywhere near Laashekoh and asking questions. Her sisters, already married off or in servitude, could be bitter. She had to stall the questions. Zahira was clever, too, and she would find a way to keep the baby. "I'm not ready for this."

The attorney sat back and studied Leila. "People gossip about a mother who hands her child to a community that was so cruel."

Laashekoh was cruel, and Leila impulsively decided that moment to fight for the child if Zahira had not carried out her side of their bargain. And if Zahira had evicted and ruined Parsaa, Leila would resist the attorneys and forget the child. Leila longed to know, but dared not ask questions about Parsaa. He was a petty detail in the stories of her new life.

"She is not in Laashekoh!" Leila countered. "And it won't be as easy. The woman may refuse."

His face softened. Portraying herself as victim was that easy.

"The law is on your side," he promised. Afghanistan was an Islamic republic, he explained. Parents could not lose custody rights over a child regardless of their sins. Strangers could assist orphans, but the children still should know their ancestry and the identity of their parents. "The child will help you. Hold her again. You will change your mind."

He only wanted his photographs, and Leila wanted him to forget the child. "Not yet," she pleaded. "A good mother does not want to raise her child in prison."

He nodded thoughtfully. "Westerners would understand that sentiment. If all goes well, you will have more than enough money to hire someone to care for the child." Then he pressed for the name of the woman who took the child. Leila was silent, and he asked if Leila trusted the woman.

She tilted her head, showing the unscarred side with a sweet smile. "I have lost all trust. It is better that way." She dropped her head into her hands and let tears of frustration flow. The questions ended. The lawyer patted her gently on the shoulder and prepared to leave, but did not turn off the recording device. A tiny light still glowed red. "At least give me directions how to find this woman," he said. "We should check on the child's welfare."

The baby was a minor problem, Leila thought to herself, one she could handle. Why, the lawyer himself had mentioned the new flow of donations into her fund and how she might need to pay bribes. Any baby would do for the lawyer's photos. Plenty of mothers did not want their children. Leila had to find such a woman and ensure that her attorneys did not venture near Laashekoh.

CHAPTER 20

The morning traffic was heavy again, drivers hurrying for appointments and deliveries did not want to stop, let alone risk giving rides to runaways, radicals, or criminals. The drivers were also wary of packs that could hide explosives or weapons.

So Saddiq and Thara walked until they reached the next pull-off area. They hid their sling-packs among a pile of rocks off the side of the highway, then they watched for drivers to take a break. As the morning wore on, more drivers stopped to trade goods, chat, or nap.

Taking a deep breath, Saddiq approached one driver waiting with his wife and children, while Thara followed meekly behind. He was polite, explaining that he had finished an errand with a younger brother in a nearby village and needed a ride back to his parents' home in Kandahar.

The man looked Saddiq up and down before pointing to the back of his pickup truck. Wood rails attached to each side of the back allowed the man to carry more grain into the city. The children climbed into the back of the truck, arranging themselves on top of the sacks close to the rails. Saddiq did not lend Thara assistance in climbing up and remembered to call her Yar. He told her to sit behind him so she wouldn't tumble off the back of the truck, but spoke brusquely as if she were an annoying younger brother forced to tag along.

The man's children tried to ask questions, but Saddiq's answers were curt so he did not have to think up lies. He clung onto his part of the rail with one hand and his *pakol* with the other. Thara stared out at the road and didn't talk at all.

The children fell silent too. The family had offered hospitality, and he should be more gracious. He was ashamed, but not for long. Kandahar was in sight before they were ready for the midday meal.

195

~~~~~

The highway sliced through the middle of the city, and the traffic was like a slow-moving wall. As the driver slowed, his wife called back to ask where the two boys were headed. Not knowing names of neighborhoods or streets, Saddiq insisted that the family should not go out of its way and could drop the boys off near the market area. The man drove directly to the market, and Saddiq and Thara climbed down from the truck into the startling jumble of stalls, carts, tents, and honking vehicles.

But they did not forget to thank the family profusely, and as the truck drove away, Thara and Saddiq returned the children's cheery waves.

At the market's edge, women covered completely in pale gray-blue squatted, leaning against a wall, surrounded by groups of children. He had heard about *burqas*, but had never seen the strange clothing in Laashekoh. The women pleaded for coins. "I am a widow!" cried one woman. "I cannot feed my nine children," another insisted. The younger children, thin and some deformed, were silent and held out their palms. Older ones begged alone, their eyes blank and unfocused.

Most people rushing to the market ignored the outstretched hands. It was easy for Saddiq to shake his head and deny coins to the faceless figures. But the children's faces haunted him. One vendor stopped to distribute old, wrinkled grapes, which the children immediately stuffed into their mouths. Saddiq wondered why the foreign women had traveled to Laashekoh, asking for children, when so many prospects lined the streets near the market of Kandahar. Or did the children have a reason to avoid orphanages?

Thara pulled at his sleeve. "They think you are pulling out a coin," she said under her breath. "And if you are taunting them, they will chase us down."

He jerked his head the other way and quickened his pace.

"There are many thieves here," she warned. "We must look as if we carry no money, yet know what we're doing." She was nervous.

"If anyone asks, say we are headed home," he suggested. "Our parents are waiting."

His reminder annoyed her. "You can head home, but I have no parents or home. I am no better than these children who must beg."

Exhausted, she was distraught about not having an opportunity to stop near a stream and clean the dirt away from her face and hands before entering the city. She suggested searching for the orphanage first, but Saddiq could not rest until he found the child, and he worried that Thara might not help if she found a place to stay. "We must help the orphan first," he said.

"But she's not an orphan," Thara countered. "Leila is alive!"

Refusing to argue or delay, Saddiq strode through the market as Thara trailed behind. He approached a group of vendors who were not busy with customers, and asked about the prison. One man teased Saddiq while the others eyed him with suspicion.

"Who do you know there?" asked one man, and Saddiq explained a distant relative was in the prison with an infant.

"Knowing someone there is a step to going there yourself," another vendor interrupted.

"It's not a place for children," said another man, more kindly.

"Where are your parents?" snapped another. "Street children are not good for business. Move along!"

"We are not street children!" Thara shouted. Then she amazed Saddiq by acting nothing like a girl, grabbing his arm, and charging through the crowds to another section of the market.

The place felt dangerous. Saddiq had never seen such crowds before, a group that shuffled past the colorful displays of fruit, fabrics, farm animals, and household goods. Most men ignored them and a few leered, and he was embarrassed that Thara was better at negotiating the large market. He had never felt so lost.

"Let me try," she ordered Saddiq. Plucking a few coins from her pouch, Thara purchased two sticks threaded with grilled lamb. For the benefit of older boys lingering nearby, she made a point of showing the pouch had been emptied. The seller handed over the sticks of hot meat, each wrapped in warm naan. Clutching the naan tight, she removed the stick, tossing it in a nearby bin, and took a large bite. Only then, keeping her voice gruff, she asked for directions to Samosa Prison. The man frowned but pointed back in the direction they had just traveled, explaining the prison was at the city's edge on the highway.

They had passed the prison on their way into town. "It's only three kilometers away," the man added. "You cannot miss it." He then asked if they were strangers to Kandahar.

Thara shook her head and stepped back so that Saddiq could take over. "We have family here," he said.

"Your parents are in the prison?" the man inquired.

"A cousin." Saddiq was curt, in a hurry. The vendor cautioned them. "Don't carry your valuables inside. The guards will search and make you empty your pockets. They then have trouble finding your belongings when you're ready to leave."

Thara started to ask the man a question, but Saddiq didn't wait. Moments later, she ran to catch up. "There is more than one orphanage in the city, and one is nearby!" She admitted that the city frightened her, too. "We could find a safe place to stay, and they would give us advice about the infant."

He kept walking. "We can take care of ourselves. The baby cannot."

"Wouldn't it be better to find a place to sleep before retrieving the baby?" she asked.

"The market is not the place to ask about an orphanage," he insisted.

Frustrated, Thara pointed out the vendor could tell they were not from Kandahar. She also feared the older street children searching for runaways and newcomers to rob. "We need a place to stay. The orphanage could help us collect the baby. Leila will not trust me, and if something happened to the child, she would never forgive us."

Her warnings made him nervous. Thara didn't want to see her sister. Convincing the prison guards and mother to hand the baby over might not go so well, especially if Leila learned that Saddiq wanted the child. His family had exposed her trafficking ring. Entering and leaving the prison would not be easy, and an orphanage would probably be the same. Saddiq doubted whether the directors would allow Saddiq and Thara to come and go as they pleased, and they certainly would not let him walk away with a baby.

He was torn. Thara's heart was set on finding an orphanage. Yet he needed her help. Only Thara could convince Leila to hand the child over. He wanted to reach the prison before Thara lost her nerve.

"You're right," he admitted. "Leila may ask if you have a place to stay. Tell her you have found a good home for the child. She doesn't have to know that it is Laashekoh. You were very smart with the vendors and must do the same with Leila." Thara shook her head. "You must try," he urged. "Do not mention the baby. Wait for her to talk about the child and plead for your help."

She asked what would happen if Leila refused to plead and hand over the child. Saddiq thought about pooling their money to bribe a guard, but kept the idea to himself. He urged Thara to have faith.

They walked to the prison in silence. Thara was the only person Saddiq knew in Kandahar, yet she was a stranger like the other people on the streets. He did not want to stay in Kandahar, and she would not return to Laashekoh. He had not traveled so far to return empty-handed. "Trust me," was all he could say.

~~~~~

Bicycles, cars, trucks, and a few pedestrians moved at a mix of speeds. Thara and Saddiq walked along the side of the highway, passing the prison once and then returning to pass again. The building was massive. Concrete slab walls, topped with metal fencing and razor wire, surrounded the building. Only the rooftop was visible from the street. The doors were dented and blue, and a large metal pole stretched across the front gate.

The place was designed to intimidate. Neither child was in a hurry to approach the guards. They ducked behind a building to exchange the belt containing their money. "Could they could keep me inside?" Thara murmured as she handed the belt to Saddiq.

Saddiq told her no, but he wasn't sure.

They waited for other visitors to proceed through the gates. A driver of a truck pulled close and spoke with the guards. The large metal pole lifted, and the doors opened, allowing the man to pass. A few individuals passed in and out of a smaller blue door. Some joked with the guards, and others passed by silently.

"Let us find out more." He approached a woman who had just left the prison and waited near the entrance, scanning the cars passing by on the highway. Though dressed in fine clothes, she was friendly and direct. The guards were polite to her.

Thara caught up as Saddiq explained that they were two brothers who wanted to visit a sister held in the prison. The woman's smile was gentle. "A sister? But you can't enter without your parents."

After traveling so far, he was not sure what to do next.

Thara spoke up. "Could we send a message to her?"

A large car, boxy and shiny, pulled close. The woman told the children she could help and then signaled the driver to pull over and wait. She opened a fine leather pouch to extract a pen and notebook, handing them over.

Saddiq was embarrassed. "I do not write well enough yet," he confessed. The woman looked at Thara, who admitted she could not read or write at all.

The woman understood. "Tell me what to say."

The stranger was so fast, so kind. Saddiq was flustered, but Thara dictated slowly, smiling as she admired the neat, looping strokes. "Your sibling is in Kandahar and tried to visit." Thara glanced at Saddiq. "There is nothing more to say."

"Very nice," the woman said. "How do I sign it?"

"One name is enough," Saddiq spoke up. He used Thamer, and hoped Leila would realize who tried to visit. The woman folded the note once, and then asked for the recipient's name. "Leila of Laashekoh," Thara said.

The prison guards would read the note, and the woman promised to request that it be delivered immediately.

"We could wait," Saddiq suggested, but the woman shook her head and explained that the rules were strict and there could be no response. They should return and check each day. He was crestfallen, and the woman asked if the children lived nearby.

Thara spoke up, asking where they could find an orphanage.

The woman was surprised. "Why, are you orphans?"

Thara shook her head wearily and started crying. She couldn't speak.

"No, we are not." Saddiq reached for Thara's hand. "But her . . . his mother is in jail."

Thara glared at him, and the woman looked back and forth between the two. "But you're brothers."

Saddiq was embarrassed. "Half-brothers?" he mumbled.

The woman was not angry. She placed her hand lightly on Thara's shoulder and directed Saddiq to hand the note to the guards. "My name is Fatima," she directed. "Tell them you are with me."

Worrying that the woman might walk away with Thara, Saddiq ran to the guardhouse. He already had an idea—offering to pay one of the beggars in the street to pretend to be Thara's parent. He glanced back to check on Thara. The woman crouched low and asked questions. Saddiq wanted to hurry back to listen and prompt Thara.

The guard ordered the boy to wait and picked up the telephone. Saddiq wondered if he was in trouble, but then the man gave a friendly wave to the woman. Turning to check on Thara, Saddiq was relieved to see the two approaching. Thara seemed happy, no longer anxious about finding an orphanage. "Saddiq, we have a place to stay tonight. *Madadgar* knows of a center that cares for children of women in this prison." Thara stared up at the woman, her eyes full of hope and trust.

The woman could take Thara away. He felt foolish to fail after traveling so far and finding the prison.

The guard spoke to Fatima for a few moments, and she turned to Saddiq and Thara with a puzzled smile. "Your sister. The guard has instructions to contact her attorney should any family member try to visit."

Saddiq wanted to run, but Thara hovered near Fatima and asked about the attorney. The woman explained he was an official who represented the sister in court. "I'm sure this is no problem," Fatima said. "The attorney may be willing to take you inside, perhaps even today."

Thara clung to Fatima's hand tightly. "But you need not go in if you don't want to," the woman offered. "We can wait outside for your brother."

Thara opened her mouth and glanced at Saddiq, who nodded slowly. He understood Thara's fear. The attorney could talk Leila out of handing over the infant. He could send Saddiq and Thara back to Laashekoh. Or the guard could be lying.

So close. Saddiq wanted to hide and return to Laashekoh without Thara or the baby. But he could not walk away.

The woman walked over to the waiting car and asked the driver to find cold drinks for the children. She did not seem concerned that they might run away. As soon as Fatima left, Thara whispered. "It's all right. She knows that I am a girl, and does not care."

He was astounded. "What adult does not care about a boy and a girl running away together?"

"Fatima guessed that you helped me leave. I like her and feel as if I belong here. But she suggested that we let others think that I'm a boy until we reach the orphanage."

"You didn't tell her about the plans to take the baby back to Laashekoh?"

Thara shook her head, and Saddiq refrained from pressuring her. Before long, a young man in the uncomfortable clothes favored by Westerners approached the guards. The attorney greeted Fatima, smiled at the two children, introduced himself as Abdullah, and handed the guard a small folder. "You are here to see your sister? She will be so happy, but I must accompany you."

"Thamer will go," Saddiq said. "But only if he wants . . ."

Thara smiled at Saddiq and started to follow the man. Saddiq pulled at her sleeve and asked the attorney if they could have a moment.

"Certainly," he agreed cheerfully and then turned to chat with Fatima.

Saddiq asked what Thara would say to Leila, and she sighed. "All I can do is listen to her and guess what she might want. But you were right, Saddiq. Allah is with us."

The boy was ashamed for having ever doubted her.

PART 4

Do they not know that Allah knows their hidden thoughts and their secret counsels, and that Allah is the great Knower of the unseen things?

—Koran 9:78

CHAPTER 21

Cara Rodriguez, the publicity consultant, requested a private meeting with Lydia—no staff members. Lydia asked if the matter could be discussed over Skype, but Cara was firm. She wanted to meet in person and as soon as possible. Lydia agreed, and Cara was on the next flight out to Michigan.

The two could have met at the hotel or one of the restaurants dotting the edge of campus, but that didn't promise privacy. In friendly East Lansing, too many people would stop by Lydia's table to say hello.

Lydia prepared her guest room and hoped the young woman did not mind the quirks of a home with small rooms so common in the 1930s. She set the table in the breakfast area, cozy in pale yellow with just a few touches of red—and drove to three stores to collect vegetables, bread, and cheese for a tapas-style meal and a bottle of cabernet for the evening—Caymus Special Selection. Cara was from San Francisco and would appreciate the gesture.

Lydia wanted a consultant and confidante.

The young woman arrived six hours later, dressed in beige corduroys and a hooded tweed sweater. Lydia set the table for the light meal and opened the wine. Cara noticed the label and raised her eyebrows.

"This is work, but I can't resist," Cara said.

Lydia poured, and there was no toast. Instead, she asked what Cara needed.

"Honesty," Cara said with a slight smile. "You made it clear that you preferred Paul Reichart for the award. Then he resisted the background check. Our recommendation for the board is no background check, no award."

Lydia nodded, and Cara took a deep breath. "Tell me what you really want. Is your priority giving the award to Paul or getting the background check done?"

Lydia lifted her glass and took a sip. She had to be up-front with her consultant.

"This is just about the background check," Lydia admitted.

Cara sipped her wine and closed her eyes. "Heaven ..." Returning her glass to the table, she cocked her head and studied the older woman. "That's what I guessed. But targeting one employee is a problem. It could damage the reputation of GlobalConnect. And my firm's reputation, too."

"Paul has been through background checks before."

"Still, it's his call. And this review would be more intrusive than a typical credit or criminal check." Cara took another dainty sip of wine. "Forgive me for prying into personal details. The foundation was formed after your son's death. I checked the news reports. Paul was in the United States. He had attended the wedding. All the reports suggest he was devastated by the death. He went to India and assisted in the police investigations. He represented you and the company and escorted the bodies back to California. And then he returned to Asia, helping establish foundation programs there."

She held the glass with both hands and leaned forward. "Correct me if I'm wrong. Do you want to find out who's responsible for the death of your son and his wife?"

Smoothing the top of the tablecloth with her hand, Lydia did not know how to proceed. Her grief was still surging, motivating her every day. Yet she was not so foolish to believe that exposing her son's killer would bring relief. Lydia didn't want to say much. Raw, unhindered grief frightened the uninitiated, and Cara would realize that Lydia's had not faded.

"Maybe you have ideas?" Lydia kept her voice light.

Cara put her wine to the side. "How close are you with Paul?"

He was her son's good friend. But Lydia had not met with him alone in recent years. "Not as close as we once were," she admitted.

Cara pointed out Lydia did not need permission to investigate criminal activity on the job. "You can apply computer forensics if he has used foundation resources in communications or travel planning."

Lydia's head was racing. Suspicions had crept up and multiplied, but she could be wrong. How could she explain that, until she knew, everyone was a suspect? It would be awful to destroy a relationship with one of her son's closest friends.

She had to be careful. Picking up her knife, Lydia slowly spread cheese over the warm Galician bread, indulging in a memory of Michael and Paul in kindergarten. The families were neighbors. Paul's parents were never home, and Lydia invited the boy along on playground, library, and shopping trips. She had orchestrated the friendship. As they grew older, Paul was the better student, and his parents tried to convince the boys to join soccer and other sports teams. Michael ignored the adults and set the agenda, searching for every opportunity to get outdoors, find appliances to pull apart in the garage, and practice programming on the computer. Paul adored Michael and went along. Later Michael confided that his friend had become a habit. "Like a brother?" she asked. Michael offered a slight smile. "Maybe because there was no choice."

A long spell of silence passed, and Cara was patient.

If Lydia didn't trust Paul, she couldn't trust anyone, and that made her ashamed. She couldn't let Annie or the other staff members guess the purpose behind her proposal for an award.

"This is so difficult," Lydia said. She passed the manchego cheese to Cara. "I had hoped he would replace me on the board."

"You want to clear his name." The young woman placed her hand over Lydia's. She could start by going through Lydia's e-mails for messages sent by Paul. She asked if Lydia still had her son's computers, phones, or other electronics and would go through those. "I can identify the IP addresses and check for patterns. None of this is illegal."

They could also bait Paul into cooperating with a background check. The award could lead to promotion—Paul replacing Lydia as a GlobalConnect board member. The confidential investigation would start as soon as Lydia was ready.

"Start now," Lydia whispered.

CHAPTER 22

The guard escorted the attorney, flushed with excitement, into Leila's cell. She lifted her head. "Back so soon?"

"You have a visitor—your brother!" he announced. The guard would allow a short visit if Leila agreed.

She lifted her eyebrows. She had no brothers, but she did not tell the attorney. He wanted to sit in, but Leila was stubborn about wanting to meet with her sibling alone.

"You can question him afterward," Leila assured the attorney.

He lowered his voice. "You must ask about the baby, but be careful. The walls have mice, and the mice have ears." Then he knocked for the guard to open the door and in walked Thara with cropped hair and dirty clothes. The fools! A close look at her hands, her eyes, or mouth, and they should have immediately recognized a pretty young girl from the countryside. The lawyers believed whatever lies they were told.

Leila stood and waited, her head high with the lopsided smile, and Thara hurried to hug Leila.

"It's good to see you, Brother." Leila feigned a slight catch in her voice. "The first time in months I've seen family."

The attorney pressed once more to stay, but the guard glanced toward Leila and refused. The guard might listen in, her cellmates might offer reports, but she worried most about the attorney. She waited for the door to slam.

Leila gave a happy squeal and dropped her voice to a whisper. "How did you get away? Did you run away? Is that why you're dressed like a boy?"

"It was the only way I could travel," Thara admitted.

Eager to relay her good fortunes in prison, Leila directed Thara to sit on the carpet. She talked about her classes, the charities, and hinted about a growing fund. But the girl was distracted and kept glancing around the cell. Leila asked when Thara had arrived in the city, and was pleased to hear that very day.

Leila was still a priority in her sister's life, and that meant Thara would do her bidding.

One question burned inside, and there was only one answer she wanted to hear. It would be agonizing to hear that the man who had destroyed her family still controlled Laashekoh. Even though she was in prison, hours away from Laashekoh, Leila could not let anyone, even Thara, connect her with Parsaa's demise.

"It must be horrible in Laashekoh, and I don't miss it at all."

Thara shook her head. "Not so horrible, but they do ignore us. They separated us. I was with Karimah."

"That *boz*," Leila said. "So you're not going back?"

Thara eyed the concrete-block walls and the pile of books and papers near the mat where Leila slept. "She wasn't so bad."

"But you won't go back," Leila pointed out.

Thara laughed and nodded.

"Has Laashekoh changed?" Leila had to know.

The younger girl shrugged and then shook her head. So Zahira had not kept her promise to send Parsaa and his family away. For the first time while in prison, Leila felt trapped and betrayed. Her sister looked uncomfortable, probably ashamed of a family member in prison.

"You used the money I hid." The comment was a reminder and not a question, but Thara nodded. "I'm glad because I don't need it." Leila tossed her head. "Believe it or not, I am free here. I'm alone and do as I please and don't have to work in fields." She promised that her time in prison would not last long.

Thara said she was happy that her sister was happy.

Leila babbled on with excitement. "And you will be happy in Kandahar, too. The attorneys are raising funds to repair my face, and more than enough money has already come in. There is no need for you to return to Laashekoh. The attorney can help you stay in the city. As soon as I leave prison, we can live together and even travel."

"But what about the baby, Leila?" Thara whispered.

Annoyed, Leila stood and paced in the tight space. "The attorney told you to ask? It's all he cares about!"

"He did ask, and I explained that I had to talk with you. He seemed upset that we may not know where the baby is at." Thara shrank back as if she expected her sister to have a fit, but Leila was pleased.

"That was excellent what you told him." Leila placed her hands on the girl's shoulders. "We do not want the attorneys asking questions in Laashekoh. Do not tell him any more." She spun around and resumed pacing. "Yes, Sister, you will like Kandahar. The market is huge, and the homes are comfortable and large. Wait for me until I leave here . . . and we will travel." She dropped her voice to a whisper. "But first, you must help me."

"With the baby?" Thara stared at her sister and waited.

"That is all the attorney talks about. You must go with him to retrieve your niece. She is near Laashekoh."

"I can't go back there!" Thara shook her head vehemently.

"You must tell him that and keep him away from the village. Tell him how horrible it is, how no one can be believed there." Leila moved her lips close to Thara's ear. Her words were as soft as breathing. She explained how the sisters had visited the place once or twice when they were young and reminded Thara how to find the canyon trail and reach the secluded compound. "You can do it. The attorney can force Zahira to hand the child over to its aunt. You must go and help him take the baby away from Zahira."

Thara was silent, and Leila continued. "If the woman argues, explain she did not keep her end of our bargain. She lied. That's all. No one needs to know more. Take the baby away and bring her here."

But Thara worried about the villagers and asked why the attorney could not go on his own. Leila laughed and explained how her attorneys were more powerful than anyone in Laashekoh. But he would not find Zahira's compound on his own. Thara looked unconvinced.

"And once you are outside the prison, you must explain that you are my sister, not a brother," Leila ordered. "The attorney gets very upset when I lie to him."

Thara repeated her fears. She did not want to go near Laashekoh. "They are searching for me."

Leila chided her sister about not understanding the ways of city people. The attorney had a car, and the trip would pass very quickly. "You can leave here and return in one day. Tell him how unbearable the village is, and he can protect you from Parsaa and the other fools. Bring the baby girl back here. You can be an auntie and care for her and love her and visit me."

The guard clanged on the door. The visit was over. Leila hugged her sister and whispered. "I have great wealth. Tell the attorney how much Parsaa abused our family. Help me with this matter, and once I am out of jail, I will take care of you."

"*Khoda negahdar*," Thara said softly.

The parting words sounded so final, more fearful than pleased, though her little sister would soon learn the ways of the city. Leila was relieved to have attorneys. She no longer needed her family.

~~~~~~

The attorney escorted Thara through the prison, and once again, she followed his advice, waiting to ask questions until they stepped outside. "Too many ears," he said.

After stepping beyond the prison gate, he grasped Thara's shoulder before she could run off to rejoin Saddiq and Fatima. His first question was on the whereabouts of the baby girl, and Thara admitted the child was living with a woman near Laashekoh. Crouching down, he wanted to know the woman's name, her relationship, the condition of her house. He asked how much villagers knew about the baby and if they would fight for the child.

Thara explained that the villagers had no idea the baby was living so close by, and she was not sure whether they would care. She repeated

Leila's rough directions. Locating the child would not be easy for the attorney.

"Do you think your sister is telling the truth?" he asked.

She nodded slowly. Thara had told the man enough. It was a compromise. She owed Saddiq so much, and he could reach the baby first. Saddiq no longer needed her and would leave Kandahar, and Thara could stay with Fatima, who gave her choices and would not force her to travel with the attorney to retrieve the child. Thara had her own ideas. She did not want to wander with Saddiq. She would not rely on Leila, raising the infant and waiting for her sister to leave prison. Fatima promised her shelter, school, and food. The woman asked about Thara's preferences and more than once advised that she did not have to answer questions, return to Laashekoh, or enter the prison.

Thara apologized to the attorney. "My sister is truthful, but I am not. I am a girl and must stay with Fatima."

The attorney didn't seem surprised and thanked her for extracting the baby's location from Leila. He would head to the compound the next day, and he stressed that there was no need for Thara to accompany him. He would find the place.

Thara dipped her head. The attorney and Leila did not need to know Saddiq's plans. Leila had disappointed Thara. Her sister cared little about how Thara had managed to travel to Kandahar on her own. Leila asked no questions about the other sisters living in Laashekoh. She simply expected Thara to follow her orders and be available to watch the child.

The attorney and Thara rejoined Fatima and Saddiq sitting in the shade of the large car. Saddiq sipped on a bottle of juice, and Fatima handed one to Thara. The liquid was sweet, sour, yellow, tingly. Her tongue had never swallowed a beverage so delicious.

As the two adults conversed, a hopeful Saddiq pulled Thara aside. Even once the attorney said his farewells, Fatima waited with patience.

"Did you see the baby?" Saddiq whispered.

She felt sorry for him. Placing her hand on his arm, she explained that the baby was no longer in the prison. He was devastated.

"But it may be better this way." Thara hurried to explain that the baby was not far from Laashekoh, at the compound of a reclusive woman known as Zahira. "You won't have to travel so far with the baby."

Skeptical, Saddiq asked why a woman would choose to live alone, away from Laashekoh. Perhaps Leila was lying. But Thara had no doubt that the woman cared for the child, and she pointed out that Leila's attorney also wanted the child. Thara passed along detailed directions to Saddiq for finding the canyon trail with the exact location of the entrance near the river flowing past Laashekoh. "The others don't know that you traveled here for the baby," Thara assured him. "But you must hurry. Leila is desperate. The attorney plans to leave tomorrow, and he will travel by car."

As she expected, Saddiq was nervous and ready to leave Kandahar. Thara smiled and told him not to fear. "He will struggle to find the entrance and will soon discover how difficult the trails are around there." Thara looked back at the prison and warned that retrieving the baby would not be easy. "Zahira may argue about handing the child over. Maybe you should get your father to help."

"Maybe," Saddiq said. "I'll try on my own first."

Thara told him the baby was a girl, but Saddiq did not care. "She is Ali's daughter and your niece. The baby will be loved," he said.

Feeling sorry for her old friend, Thara wondered when she might see him again. He had been so happy about arriving in Kandahar, so sure about his mission. After meeting Fatima, Thara was sure about her future, too.

"Will you miss Laashekoh?" He was resigned.

"I can't return." Thara stared at the highway and the moving cars. "Though I have learned how quickly I can change my mind. Back in Laashekoh, I missed Leila so much and felt sorry for her. And now that I'm here, I wish that I could thank Karimah for all she did. She was fair." She shook her head. "But you cannot talk to her about me, and I cannot go back."

He admitted to understanding why Thara did not want to return.

Thara tried to cheer him. "No one in Laashekoh will ever know that you brought me here, and it would have been far too difficult carrying a baby back to Laashekoh on your own. Allah is still with you, Saddiq." Taking his hands, Thara squeezed and promised she would never forget how much he had helped her. "You will always be my brother. I only want to be like you someday, ready to help another person."

Once more, Fatima invited him to stay the night at the center and leave the next morning. The woman had no idea about his mission to find the baby. Instead, he expressed gratitude for her kindness and immediately set off down the highway, back toward Laashekoh.

CHAPTER 23

A sudden shift in the weather, with warmer temperatures, allowed the men of Laashekoh to sit in a circle around the crackling flames. The ground was wet, the hour was late, and ideas and plans leaped like sparks in the fire. Muscles ached after days of hard work, soothed by the mental relief that the harvest was complete, the crops tallied and divided among households, with plenty left over for sale at the market. The women were pleased. There would be no worries over paying bills and taxes or feeding families throughout the winter.

So much work completed despite the hours spent hunting for the missing girl. Once again, most of the villagers had searched throughout the day, and still there was no clue. The consensus—the girl was no longer near Laashekoh.

Parsaa was unusually quiet, and the others didn't notice. As they talked, he kept his worries inside. He had spent the past days walking in ever-widening circles around Laashekoh, following familiar trails, hoping to find Saddiq. But there was no sign of either child. Inside, he knew the boy was capable and sensible. Like his wife, Parsaa had his suspicions, but he refused to speak of them out loud.

He would have preferred searching into the night, but that would have prompted questions. So he sat with the others and pretended to listen to banter. The man would not admit that he had no idea on the whereabouts of his oldest son or how the boy had probably helped Thara leave the village.

So far, no one connected the two children, and Parsaa was grateful. The crime was unthinkable.

Early that first day of Saddiq's absence, Parsaa had detected a few depressions in the snow, evenly spaced and rounded, but lacking the gait of a large man. The tracks circled throughout the village and also led to a nearby creek. Parsaa didn't ask Ahmed for an opinion. Snow kept falling, and searchers crossed back and forth, obliterating the soft impressions, and Parsaa kept his relief to himself.

The next day, a few villagers asked about Saddiq, and Parsaa was brief. The boy was on an errand for his father, and that ended the questions. The villagers trusted Parsaa. Such trust was why Parsaa so appreciated the village and why he felt so guilty. He wondered why Saddiq could not confide in his father.

The other men spoke about the new fields ready for spring planting. The night would be so peaceful if only Parsaa knew where his son slept. He closed his eyes with weariness and sensed an interruption only when the conversation went silent.

Opening his eyes, Parsaa glanced at the other men to follow the direction of their eyes. A shadowy figure stood by the wall. Parsaa's eyes could no longer pierce the darkness, but the figure did not seem huge. The younger men did not reach for their weapons. Parsaa waited for others to speak up.

"Salaam alaikum," Ahmed called out. "Join us, friend."

The figure slowly approached and eventually took the form of old Mohan. Mohan refused to sit, standing beyond the firelight. His eyes focused on Parsaa.

Suddenly, Parsaa remembered his promise to Zahira to return and check on Najwa. He was a day late, maybe two. But Mohan was annoyed, and Zahira was probably angry, too.

The timing could not be worse. Parsaa had led others to believe that Saddiq left the village for an errand at the compound, and he hoped other villagers did not start asking Mohan questions. Parsaa would not apologize for failing to check on Najwa, not when the village had a missing child. He approached Mohan, standing between him and the others to block their view, and held out both hands to greet him.

Mohan did not reciprocate with his usual warmth, and the two men walked away from the fire toward the wall. Mohan was curt, talking about how a broken promise could not be repaired.

"Has the girl behaved?" Parsaa questioned.

"She is a troublemaker," Mohan said. Irritated, Parsaa asked why the man had not brought Najwa back to the village. Mohan held his head high. "It is too late. Zahira's husband has taken a liking to her. You should not have brought her to the compound at all."

Parsaa pressed his fingers against his brow, and the pain cleared his head. He explained that a young girl had gone missing from the village, but the words had the sound of an empty excuse.

"Yet you have time to sit around a fire for idle conversation?" Mohan's only priority was protecting the compound and Zahira. "Zahira is worried for her life, and you no longer come around to check on her anymore? Her fool of a husband does not need sight to sense the disinterest."

More problems and guilt. "Does Zahira want me to remove Najwa?"

"She wants more than that," Mohan said.

Parsaa offered to leave for the compound immediately. "Do we need other men?" Parsaa asked.

"You could bring one of your sons. We could begin his training."

"Tonight may not be the time for training." Parsaa kept his voice low. Mohan shrugged, waved for the other man to hurry, and then climbed back over the wall to wait. Parsaa was relieved that Mohan was in no mood to socialize with the men by the fire.

The village men looked at him expectantly, but Parsaa offered the briefest explanation: "A problem at the compound."

At home, Sofi followed him as he retrieved a rifle. "What's wrong? Is this about Saddiq?"

Dishonesty is like a sedative. He wanted to say yes, but shook his head. Parsaa went to the large wooden chest where the family stored weapons and ammunition. He selected a weapon and then stared at his son's rifles. If the boy had planned to travel far, he would have taken a weapon. "This is not about Saddiq."

Sofi had heard his comments to the other men. "But perhaps Saddiq is really there . . . ?"

Parsaa glanced around the room and wondered how far the boy had gone. His toughest shoes, a knife, and his *pakol* were missing. His pack waited in the corner, though Parsaa was certain the boy was not in the vicinity of Laashekoh. No one had thought about searching for Thara near the compound, and Parsaa wondered if Saddiq had tried searching there.

"Anything is possible." Parsaa embraced his wife and told her he would return by early morning. Outside he joined Mohan, who did not speak at all, and the two began the long hike.

A sullen companion made the trip drag. Parsaa led in silence along the twisting trail. The older man could not keep up, and Parsaa tried to keep his pace in check. Before leaving with Najwa, he could not remember the last time he had traveled the path with another person— the beginning of another strange night with Zahira.

The night sounds were muffled, the air had an icy stillness.

Parsaa was not totally surprised that Arhaan befriended Najwa. Both were outcasts. Parsaa would check the compound and, whether Arhaan liked it or not, would bring Najwa back with him. She would be more difficult than before, but she would not stay in Laashekoh for long. As soon as they returned, he would leave for the provincial capital, with Najwa, to find her work. He would also ask discreet questions about the missing children. If Thara and Saddiq were not in Lashkar Gah, he would travel to Kandahar.

Parsaa thought about seeing his son. He could not bear to hear details and would order Saddiq to stay quiet. But first Parsaa had to find Saddiq—without villagers hearing about his inquiries.

Not knowing Saddiq's location was tortuous, and desperate for tranquility, Parsaa focused on a night prayer. Walking was not the preferred form for praying, and improper form could lessen the rewards unless one was confronting an enemy.

Yet there was always the enemy within, or so Parsaa had convinced himself long ago. His praying was deliberate, not mindless chanting.

Moving through the crisp night air, reciting the centuries-old words, was far more comforting than mulling over the problems of Saddiq, Zahira, or Thara.

While praying, Parsaa truly felt alone and in control. The prayers erased worries, if only temporarily, and a still mind was stronger than one pulled in many directions.

CHAPTER 24

The weather had warmed, and leaving Kandahar was easy without Thara or the packs.

Rather than walk westward, Saddiq ran in the opposite direction toward the city center, where the traffic's pace was slower than that of donkeys. The traffic on Highway A1 was heavy, as hundreds of trucks, cars, and bicycles crawled along, all trying to escape the crowded city center. Saddiq watched laborers walking away from a construction site, how they bartered for rides with drivers. He found an open area without competitors. Standing tall, he pointed west on A1 and shouted, "Lashkar Gah?"

A motorcycle soon pulled over with a loud roar.

"I'm headed that way," the man shouted. "Can you help with gas?" Saddiq showed the man a small bill.

"Hop on!" The young man pointed to grip bars beside his seat but advised Saddiq to hold onto his shoulders in traffic. "We don't want to make other drivers nervous."

Saddiq asked why the drivers were so nervous, and the man explained that Taliban gangsters traveled in pairs on the cycles, one driving and the other wielding an assault rifle. Or the extremists sent in children to rob truckloads or carry bombs when they wanted to stop a competitor's shipment. The man complained bitterly about criminals who ruined the highway and Afghanistan's reputation for hospitality.

"Good to be heading out tonight," he added. "The Afghan soldiers are running a convoy. Just keep your hands visible." The man then asked Saddiq where he was headed, and the boy described the bridge just a short ways before Lashkar Gah.

"Tap my shoulder when you want me to stop." The man then waved his hand in the air. "And get rid of the *pakol*—or prepare to give it over to the wind!"

Saddiq stuffed the hat inside his *perahan*, and they roared off, zig-zagging to pass the slow-moving trucks in the city and avoid the craters left by bombs beyond the city limits. Two hours later, Saddiq was sore after sitting so long in one position, and his cheeks felt raw, whipped by the rush of air. But the ride was exhilarating, and before long, they reached the bridge, not far from where Saddiq had left the packs. The boy tapped the man's shoulder and the motorcycle pulled neatly over to the side of the road.

Saddiq jumped off the seat and stood back, admiring the motor-cycle one last time. "It's a wonderful machine."

The driver nodded and smiled. "I hope that you own one someday, too, and give another Afghan boy a ride. *Khoda hafiz.*"

~~~~~

The sight of the lumpy packs, waiting side by side among the rocks for their two owners, made him ache. Saddiq remembered the one beautiful, peaceful night of sleeping by Thara's side, and no matter what happened to him, he would never regret helping her escape from Laashekoh.

He thought about leaving Thara's makeshift pack behind, but then he decided it might be useful for carrying the baby. He opened her pack and removed her clothes and the long, dark locks of hair. He rubbed the soft hair against his cheek, tempted to keep a few strands. Instead, he moved his pack far away before returning to empty hers. He pock-eted the heart-shaped rock. He hid her clothes and the other contents underneath some rocks. Perhaps he would return someday. With his back to the fierce wind, Saddiq shook the gray rag of a blanket and watched the hair scatter.

For the rest of the day, he walked northward. The trip went quickly without the detours and his companion, and it didn't take long to find the compound that Thara had described. The sun was almost down and he waited in a stand of trees, wondering why his father had not said much about the place.

Saddiq regretted not asking Thara about how many people lived with Zahira. The compound had more buildings than Laashekoh, most small in size. Several structures were large, modern, and well built. Other than smoke drifting from one building in the center, the compound was still—no sign of people working or children cavorting in the open areas.

With nightfall, the air again turned cold. Saddiq wished that he could find shelter from the wind and a sip of water. Yet approaching any structure without knowing what waited inside carried risk. He would have limited time to find the baby. Most buildings had windows, but all were small and high. There was no guarantee that he could overhear a baby's cry inside.

With barricades and lookout posts, the place resembled a deserted military camp—and light was plentiful in the largest building that didn't look like a home at all.

Suddenly, a man stepped away from a dark building. A dark bird rode along on his shoulder. Squawking, the bird took off for a branch high in a nearby tree and issued a call that sounded almost human. "*Door begee! Door begee!*" Keep away.

A myna. The man's movements were jerky, cautious, like those of the bird, and his smile was odd. The bird circled over the compound before swooping down to land on the man's shoulder again, pecking at a treat from his hand. They vanished into the shadows surrounding the building, though Saddiq was not sure whether they had entered. No lights went on. Silence returned, night fell, and the building remained dark.

Saddiq was anxious, ready to return to his family and sleep in his own bed. He wanted to find the baby and remove her quickly. One bad guess would ruin his chances, and Saddiq could not move until he figured out which building sheltered the child.

Exhausted, he didn't want to think about what to do next if the baby had been transferred to another location and, instead, he forced himself to study the place. The compound was deadly quiet, and the canyon walls felt like a trap. Only two buildings showed light, and the rest seemed empty. In Laashekoh, babies were demanding, crying for food or changes. Even while working, adults cooed and played with children. His parents would not want Ali's daughter to grow up in such a desolate place. He closed his eyes, willing his niece to cry out, but there was no sign of an infant.

The compound's occupants would be accustomed to silence, and any unusual noise would put them on alert. Saddiq needed a diversion, small enough to prompt the adults to check the baby, but not so unusual as to make them wary for the rest of the night. A brief disruption would allow him to search the interiors and locate the baby. He could return later to retrieve her. It wouldn't be easy. The child probably slept in the same room as her caregiver. An alarm would go up once the baby went missing, and he would not have much of a head start.

Saddiq dreaded the thought of holding a crying child while being chased.

Keeping his eyes on the compound, he hid his pack off trail and wrapped Thara's half of the old blanket around his neck.

A tapping noise began in the building where Saddiq had last seen the man and the bird. Perhaps a hammer driving a small nail into wood, as if someone was determined to work throughout the night. Yet the building remained dark.

Suddenly, footsteps came crunching along the path that wound through the canyon. A shadowy figure of a man passed close and headed toward the largest building with the light. The man tried the door, but an older woman covered in a shawl appeared and berated him about the late hour.

A visitor could work as a diversion. Bending low, Saddiq crept toward the other building with light. He glanced back to check on the woman. She opened the door to the largest building and held it open but did not follow him inside. Instead, she lingered near the doorway. Loud voices soon followed.

An argument. A better diversion. Saddiq opened the heavy door to the house and paused, waiting for a shout or question. An old yellow cat appeared from nowhere, purring and clinging to his ankles. Taking a deep breath, Saddiq slipped through the doorway, with the cat following, into the grandest home he had ever seen.

CHAPTER 25

Zahira waited behind the desk, writing in a journal. After sunset, darkness descended over the canyon. Only the desk lamp was lit, and the clinic had a warm glow. Articles, order forms, correspondence, and other papers covered the desk. From all appearances, the clinic was a busy place, and the meeting with Paul Reichart was a business meeting of sorts.

There was a soft knock, but before Zahira could stand, Aza unlocked the door and escorted Paul inside. He formally thanked the older woman and waited for an invitation to sit. Aza, still regarding Zahira as a young charge, was displeased about meetings alone with the man, but she no longer argued. There were too many reminders that a blind husband could not manage compound affairs and that Parsaa had lost interest. No one was better suited than Zahira to pay bills, collect revenue, consult on business projects, and run the place.

Zahira thanked the older woman and promised to call if help was needed, and Aza shut the door hard. "She doesn't like me," Paul commented, as he slowly drew the bolt.

"She does not like that I am alone with a foreigner." Zahira wrapped her arms around him, resting her head against his shoulder. "I told her not to interfere."

But Paul was troubled. "We must talk. About what you are storing in the huts nearby."

She tried to back away, but too late. He latched a finger on a long, dark curl and twirled. She felt the tension against her scalp.

"Why are so many supplies kept here?" He pointed out that some boxes had expiration dates more than a decade old, and he demanded to see her records.

She did not want to discuss her activities with him and, wincing, she tilted her head toward him. "I do not control what is sent here. Why does it matter? No one has ever stopped by to check."

"I received a call today. The people I work for want to give an award to an Afghan who is doing good work with the help of GlobalConnect. I had suggested you." Then the organizers mentioned background checks, and Paul tried to withdraw her name. But his employers pressed him to remain in the competition. "My future there depends on that award. On you. There will be an audit. Tell me why you have so much in storage!"

She pleaded with him to lower his voice. "No one comes here."

He yanked hard, lowering his hand and forcing her to bend sideways.

Pain seared her scalp, forcing her to move closer. "Stop!" she screeched. "You don't understand. It's complicated here."

"It's complicated everywhere, and I have time to listen." Staring, he slowly let her hair unwind.

Zahira took a deep breath. The international organizations had sent money and supplies to a woman with no patients. She had not asked for the supplies, the medications, the funding. Instead, organizers of a European NGO hunted her down soon after her father's death. The activists were intent on providing reproductive healthcare during the chaotic period of Taliban rule. The Taliban ruffians may have been few in number, not even 1 percent of the overall population, but their rules were harsh, enforcement brutal. Men carrying assault rifles closed schools, businesses, hospitals. Authorities forced farmers to grow opium and refused to distribute food donations from the international agencies. Women who tried shopping at the marketplace were pulled off the streets for beatings, rape, or even murder. Gangs visited households to collect late tax payments and had no compunction about taking their wrath out on the weakest members of the family, whether that meant stoning women and children, heaving infants to the ground, or beheading a father and ruining the lives of those who depended on his work.

The atrocities alarmed European activists who identified willing health workers of any level and organized smuggling routes for Afghanistan. Contraception supplies, pamphlets translated into Dari and Pashtun, computers, and other supplies were hidden in crates of trash with no labels or addresses, and the vile-smelling contents passed quickly through chains of underground operatives and smugglers in China, India, Tajikistan, and Pakistan.

Zahira and Arhaan were grateful for the compound's remote location. They heard the horror stories from Lashkar Gah, and lived as hermits. Mohan camouflaged and guarded the canyon against the Taliban, who would have regarded the compound's furnishings along with the music, books, wine, and birds as frivolous and sinful. The couple would have been beaten senseless, tied behind vehicles, and dragged through the nearby villages as a warning about the consequences of defying the Taliban.

Zahira agreed to serve as a willing provider, and the European group deposited funds into an overseas account for wages and bribes. Money flowed into the account, and Zahira made regular withdrawals as if she were running a clinic and counseling on the benefits of family planning. Expecting patients to arrive any day, she stored years of supplies and equipment in the compound's unused space.

She was ready, but the patients did not show up. To practice, she studied texts and prepared reports on imaginary patients, listed by imaginary initials. She kept meticulous records on imaginary expenditures. The files described the medical career to which she had once aspired—counseling patients, answering questions, tending births, passing out medication that allowed women to space pregnancies. She also reported administering the mifepristone-misoprostol regimen for terminating unwanted pregnancies, first giving the woman a dose of mifepristone, a synthetic steroid compound, followed two days later by misoprostol, a drug also used to prevent gastric ulcers.

Zahira assisted a few patients over the years, and rumors drifted about her skills. Embarrassed and then angry, she wondered how many in nearby villages had died from infections, childhood diseases, or diarrhea. How many girls had killed themselves after inopportune pregnancies? Her last patient was Leila, and Zahira had refused to provide that abortion. She didn't mind if the girl or her mother whispered complaints. Zahira had to save Parsaa's grandchild.

Paul was the first to ask questions, and she felt sick inside. She wanted no part of an award or the attention that it would bring, except that Paul had promised to take her and the baby far from Laashekoh, help her settle in places she had seen only on the Internet. She owed him the truth. Surely, he could find a way to handle the questions from GlobalConnect. "There has been a misunderstanding . . . ," she began.

~~~~~~

Blacker had asked her to return home during her last break, just before the end of her training as a physician in Russia. Not for long, he promised, and she purchased the round-trip tickets. The events of one night spiraled out of control. How often had Zahira wished that she could go back and change the past? Her shame grew over the years, and rumors expanded into outlandish lies, all made worse because the plans that night were concocted by someone she had loved and respected more than anyone else in the world.

Her father was overjoyed by her return but behaved oddly, urging her to stay close to the compound. During previous visits, he had insisted on visiting friends and attending dinners as far away as Lashkar Gah, where he bragged about her studies and plans to work as a doctor. Over time, she sensed resentment and heard the whispers. "Aren't the schools in Kabul good enough for her?"

Two days after Zahira's arrival, late in the night, she was reading in her bedroom when she heard a soft knock. She opened the door, surprised to find Blacker. He no longer trusted most servants and had reduced the household staff to two.

He asked if Zahira could do him a favor, and she agreed immediately. He looked away, admitting what he asked was not easy or fair. He whispered how war would soon come to their land. "I fought for the wrong side, and that puts us both in danger." He took her hand. "You are in danger because of your ties to Moscow."

A change in the central government was inevitable. Her father tried to restore ties with the clerics and village leaders who reserved their loyalties for Islam over government, but he wasn't sure it was enough. Zahira had never heard her father sound so distressed, and she worried her return to Moscow could be at risk. He claimed that he didn't want to involve his daughter, but he insisted that she understand the local conflicts and alliances. Blacker was among the province's wealthiest men, but most of his gains were made through connections with the Russians.

"That has lost us friends," he said.

She sighed at the word *us* and already missed Moscow. Not just because of the museums, trains, and crowds. Not the university with battered books and teachers who invited students into tiny homes for arguments about literature, philosophy, and politics over tea or vodka late into the night. Those memories were treasures. More than anything else, she missed being an individual, separate from her father. People in Moscow knew her only as a woman from Afghanistan, a quiet and polite guest, separate and alone in Russia. They didn't connect every comment, gesture, or act as an extension of her family history.

When Zahira was a child, her father often said, "Your mistakes become my mistakes." He had never mentioned that she would pay for his mistakes.

But Blacker was despondent. Her father needed her. He talked about another ambitious man who despised the Russians and envied Blacker's wealth. "I need a spy in his midst, and have a plan." She listened, and the plan seemed so easy. Zahira simply had to pretend that she was a doctor and perform a procedure. No one would get hurt.

~~~~~~

One night changed everything.

Long after sunset, stern men escorted a shivering girl into one of the compound's small huts. Carpets, pillows, and furnishings had been removed and replaced by two tables, one large and one small, both covered with clean white linen. Two would-be caregivers wore dark veils exposing only their eyes. The girl was hooded, too. The men wanted to stay and watch, but the woman posing as Zahira's unnamed assistant chased them off with a broom.

Once the door was closed, the assistant gently guided the girl to the temporary examining table. The girl clawed to remove the hood, and Zahira caught a glimpse. The child would have been pretty, if her face wasn't contorted and blotched with tears.

The assistant mouthed the words. "She cannot know who we are."

The hood should have made the task easier. The patient couldn't have been more than fourteen. Supervisors in Moscow would have scolded Zahira for not asking about age, but she didn't bother. Most Afghan women in the area didn't know their age.

Besides, Zahira wasn't doing a real procedure.

As a student at a Soviet medical school, Zahira had learned how to end unwanted pregnancies—a skill in high demand in Moscow. She had no qualms about the procedure. Spontaneous miscarriages were as common as abortions. Studies showed that as many as half of all pregnancies ended in miscarriage among women exposed to environmental hazards, substance abuse, serious infections, or severe malnutrition.

A tray waited nearby with scissors, knives, thread, aspirin, bandages, ointments, hot water—all items for show. Also waiting were tiny balls of raw opium for use after the procedure to allow easy transport of the girl away from the compound.

"Must I do this?" the girl whispered. The assistant arranged a light blanket over the patient and promised that she would feel no pain. "This will make your problem go away."

The writhing girl struggled to escape the table. Pushing Zahira aside, the assistant pressed the girl's shoulders down to the table and tightened straps across her chest to keep her there. Flat on her back, the girl clutched the blanket, moaning and twisting her head from side to side.

The assistant removed the clothing from the lower half of the girl's body and then spread the legs, tying each to either side of the narrow table. With shaking hands, Zahira tried to be gentle dabbing and cleaning, but she felt foolish. The smell of isopropyl alcohol filled the room, and the assistant smiled. Zahira wanted to knock the silly tray away, push the assistant out of the room, and admit that the ordeal was a lie.

In Afghanistan, as in Moscow, the doctor put community and

government over individual need. The Soviet oath required doctors to abide by the principles of Communist morality while medical schools in Afghanistan were influenced by Islamic ways. Most medical students, regardless of where they studied, eventually stumbled onto the Hippocratic Oath and its revisions over the centuries. The classical version, more than two thousand years old and drafted on paper long after the Greek physician's death, forbid practitioners from giving a pessary for an abortion or drugs to end life. It also assumed that only men could practice medicine, and doctors were expected to avoid "all mischief." The medical students in Moscow dismissed the oath as naive for modern medicine, so technical and complex, but Zahira was idealistic, trusting that she could become a doctor who cared for both patients and community. Blacker wielded justice in their region, as far as the eye could see and beyond. She could develop her own system of care.

Her father insisted the night's small procedure would end the fighting and save lives.

Using a metal skewer, rounded to avoid injury, Zahira tentatively poked at the girl's genital area. A choking sound came from underneath the hood. Gagging, Zahira backed away.

She could not insert the probe.

The assistant grasped the skewer. "Some people don't know about pain," the woman muttered. She followed specific instructions issued earlier by Blacker—roughly shoving the girl's legs apart, violating the girl, and then carving a small V into her upper inside leg, deep enough to leave a scar.

Once done, the assistant slammed the knife to the table.

The woman leaned over the patient, murmuring how the girl did well. Her husband need never know about her transgressions. That is, as long as she cooperated in supplying information about activities to certain messengers. "The procedure left a scar, and you do not want him to wonder how our messengers know this. Do you understand?"

The girl nodded, the hood damp with tears. The assistant shoved raw opium into the girl's mouth and joined Zahira. "She is ours now. Allah will protect us all." The woman then ordered Zahira to leave so she could clean the space. Ashamed, Zahira walked away from a patient who would haunt her memories for the rest of her life.

Zahira's father, who had given her life and education and freedom, asked for one favor and made it sound so easy—conduct a small procedure with enough blood to be messy and memorable. All Zahira had to do was go through the motions of performing an abortion the child did not need and leave a scar. Blacker counted on having an informant in the household of a rival who despised Afghans for not resisting the Russians and who questioned the wisdom of educating girls or boys in foreign ways. Blacker wanted ears inside his rival's house to learn about all visitors, purchases, documents, and plans passing through the household.

The girl would provide regular reports to a nearby vendor. Otherwise, her husband would hear the reason for the scar.

The rival's downfall was in marrying a young, uneducated girl, distraught over her own betrayal and shame. Weeping, the girl confided in her equally ignorant sisters, who had ideas about how to end the torment of guilt. During her first night of marriage, as the husband slept, the young bride wrapped a blanket over her shoulders and crept away from the bedroom into the kitchen and searched until she found a container of fuel used for cooking. Alone, in the darkness, she tipped the container, sloshing the kerosene onto the blanket, bathing herself and relishing the heady fumes.

Then she scratched a match.

The old husband was severely burned and died soon afterward. Two other wives and twelve children perished, along with a servant couple and their three children. The youngest son of the servants, Qasim, barely survived. He wasn't burned, but he suffered a head injury after his mother pushed him from a small window. Furious that a servant's son had survived flames when the household master and his children did not, the husband's extended family sent the boy to an orphanage.

The informant would have done little to help Blacker. The Soviets were already withdrawing from Afghanistan, and Afghan politics were in turmoil. With the Islamists taking control, he wanted Zahira to leave the country. But he was ailing, and Zahira comforted her father until the end.

She did not tell him that her sponsor had canceled her scholarship, prohibiting her from returning to Moscow to conclude her studies. She was a sham, not a doctor, and the conclusion of the classical Greek oath haunted her. "If I fulfill this oath and do not violate it, may it be granted to me to enjoy life and art, being honored with fame among all men for all time to come; if I transgress it and swear falsely, may the opposite of all this be my lot."

The shame of failed rationalization was more disturbing for the educated.

In embarking on a medical career, much like bearing a child, an individual must be hopeful rather than dwell on potential disaster. The hardest part about choosing whether or not to abort is that one cannot reverse the decision. A mother must live with the consequences and hope that she can survive the unending series of possibilities that tease the mind. Did the woman or her child miss a life of misery or joy? Caregivers like Zahira could not answer the question, and such is a woman's torment.

~~~~~~

Paul was livid to hear that Zahira had done no family planning. "You have not handed out the contraception or helped with childbirth?" He slammed his hand down. "I believed in you. I brought you the computer, the BGAN terminal, the GlobalConnect equipment so that you could connect with other programs for support. What the hell have you been doing?"

She waited for patients, but the rumors about a night of mischief were pervasive. Blacker's men and their wives whispered, and nearby villagers despised her, associating her with an abortion, a fire, and the destruction of a family that left a void in the region for marauders to fill.

Shame and dishonesty with one patient destroyed her confidence. The villagers did not want an abortionist or a charlatan in their midst.

"You don't understand," she said bitterly. "Abortion is evil until a woman needs one, and then her need is the exception. They pass their shame onto me."

Paul took a deep breath before swinging hard at the side of her head, knocking Zahira to the ground. "I risked my reputation on you. Damn you, I needed you."

Stunned, Zahira lay on the ground. She did not move. She deserved the blow. She loathed herself for not telling the girl the truth.

Paul crouched, and she prepared for another strike. Instead, he reached for her hands and lifted her, placing her in the chair facing the computer. "I need you." His voice was soft, resigned, and he asked if anyone had ever seen the stash of old medical supplies. She shook her head.

"Perhaps this can still work." He was anxious and prepared for the scheduled Skype call. Hurrying, he set up his laptop on her desk and explained what Zahira needed to say. He would introduce her to the woman in charge of GlobalConnect, and Zahira could describe dozens of mothers who over the years had benefited from her work delivering healthcare in the remote region. Together, Paul and Zahira would dispose of the old medicines and supplies.

"All you have to say is that family planning prevented economic disaster in this area," Paul explained. "You explain how I have supported you. You tell her about a few patients. You have records, but promised patients not to release names or other details. If you are believable, then I can promise more funding. You can leave this place to forget and atone."

Telling her story to Paul did not end the pain of years of lies—not that she had ever lied to donors. They accepted her limited skills and made assumptions, anticipating that village women would be eager for care. At least she could stop lying to herself.

Paul wanted more lies for the woman who controlled GlobalConnect. Zahira needed his help to leave Afghanistan with her daughter. Zahira worried about the questions. Her records were a product of her imagination, and a skilled physician would likely detect more hope than truth.

"You don't have to show records, and she'll expect your patients to deny receiving treatment," Paul said. "Don't worry. Caring too much makes people stupid."

CHAPTER 26

Saddiq hurried in his search, trying to ignore the plush carpets, sofas, and pillows; the sparkle of electric lanterns hanging in the air and glassware and figurines lining the shelves—all in a warm house that lacked the odors of cooking, wood smoke, or musty dirt floors.

The place was like an enchanted setting in a story, overwhelming the eye. He forced himself to ignore the trinkets—all except a tall brass vase that he could use as a weapon. His priority was to find at least one other exit, in case someone suddenly entered the home. The house was traditional, on a much larger scale than his family's home, with more rooms and intricate hallways. He had no idea how many might live in the place too silent for its size, and anyone could be waiting.

First, he checked the two massive living areas, one for men and the other for women, though he couldn't tell the two apart. He was cautious and paused at each threshold before swiftly crossing the room, keeping an eye out for possible hiding places while hoping that a guard did not wait to slice at him with a knife.

Soon after he exited the second living area, a strange and terrible shrieking started up behind him. "*Kee! Kee! Kee!*" "Who? Who? Who?"

He wanted to run, but the room's windows were high and small, designed to prevent unwanted peering yet also eliminating easy escape. Clutching the vase, ready to defend against an attack, Saddiq turned and saw nothing in the dark hallway. He dared not proceed.

Then a large black bird strutted away from the shadows. "*Kee!*"

A myna. Saddiq wasn't sure the bird understood, but he tried a friendly response. "*Kee*," he whispered. "*Khoda hafiz.*" "Allah protect you."

The bird bobbed its head, as if appreciating the response, and quietly followed Saddiq. One set of rooms led to a closed interior courtyard. A dead-end. Another doorway connected to the kitchen area, a separate building, with an exit to the rear.

The next room had an elegant carved table. Set before one of the ornate chairs was a group of small plates and elegant utensils, the kind used by foreigners for eating, or so his father had once explained. A tall rack contained numerous bottles with amber, garnet, and clear liquids gleaming in the low light. Beverages of some sort. Backing away, Saddiq searched for the sleeping areas, but the first two doors he opened were rooms used for storage, packed with boxes of all sizes.

The bird persisted in tagging along.

Another narrow hallway led to a set of narrow stairs leading to a second floor, but Saddiq decided that the woman caring for the child would prefer sleeping on the main floor and keeping her charge close. Holding the metal vase with both hands, he headed down the hall toward soft light.

The bird cackled in its happy way.

To his left, a room was lit in eerie blue, the glow coming from a box that resembled a small television. Instead of news or stories showing people, an odd pattern of squares repeatedly marched across the screen.

The house showed no signs of a child, no toys, no tiny shoes or clothes, no blankets and dishes with mashed food drying along the sides. The house was too clean.

Perhaps the infant no longer lived at the compound. Or Leila had lied.

Saddiq would have to return to Laashekoh and ask for his father's help. He headed to the end of the hallway and opened the heavy door onto a beautiful bedroom in soft golden light. Instead of a jumble of blankets on the floor, there was a raised bed with a stiff cover of rose silk and intricate embroidery in blue and moss green. Next to the bed was a table with piles of books, and on the other side was a large basket. Holding his breath, he approached the basket. Inside, a baby slept, nestled underneath another cover of embroidered silk, the rose color matching her tiny lips.

Worrying about a safe exit, Saddiq hesitated to pick up the baby. And babies could be particular. She could cry out at a strange touch.

Glancing around the room, he wondered if his niece would someday resent growing up in Laashekoh, where luxuries were few. Girls prized fine clothes, furnishings, jewelry, books, and servants. Possessions were linked with security and routines, and as Thara pointed out, that was why girls worked so hard for a good marriage.

A clanging noise came from the other side of the house. Panicked, Saddiq stretched out along the floor next to the bed. Using the brass vase, he shoved a few boxes aside and squirmed his way underneath the bed. He tugged on the bedcover with one hand, trying to smooth his entry point.

Just in time. The bird cackled, calling out "*Kee!*" Ducking its head low, the bird poked its way underneath the bed, too.

"*Kee?*" he whispered back. He could not turn his head in the tight space and had to stare at the bird and the base of the baby's basket.

Moments later, someone entered the room. Old slippers shuffled toward the child. "Ah, she left the door open, but you are still sleeping."

The soft whisper was from an old woman. Saddiq loosened his grip on the vase. The feet stepped backward, away from the baby, moving about the room before pausing again near the basket. A smaller set of feet padded behind the woman.

A yellow kitten was curious about what waited underneath the bed. The bird pecked at the intruder, and the kitten yelped.

Suddenly, the stiff cover was jerked away. Terrified, Saddiq held his breath, scrambling to think of an excuse for hiding underneath a strange woman's bed. His mind was blank.

"*Ne!*" The bird screeched and jabbed its beak toward the slippers. "*Ne!*"

Another scream, this one from the woman. Hands swooped down and latched onto the bird's neck, pulling it out from underneath the bed. Flapping its wings, the myna shrieked.

"What are you doing in this room?" The question was vicious. "Why, I should let the cats take care of you!"

A cracking noise, and the myna's wailing went silent.

Saddiq's lungs hurt, and he had to breathe, as slowly and quietly as possible. He waited, but the woman did not kneel. Only the kitten peered at Saddiq, purring and sliding against his shoulder before heading back to pounce on the slippers. "Sleep, Shareen. Sleep. You deserve better." A gnarled hand dipped down, pinching the back of the kitten's neck.

The light went out, the door closed, and the woman left the room.

Saddiq felt safe in the darkness, but that was foolish. He wanted to run, not just out of the house, but away from his stupid ideas. Thara had warned him. His plan was a disaster—entering a woman's room, picking up a baby, keeping her asleep and quiet, traveling late at night, and expecting his parents to express more joy than fury. Taking another few breaths, he tried to calm down before squirming away from the tight space. He decided to leave the brass vase behind and stood.

Amazingly, the baby still slept, and her mouth opened with each soft breath.

Saddiq could run off and leave his niece at the compound. The home wasn't terrible. He could return to Laashekoh and tell his father all he had learned—everything except the parts about entering a woman's bedroom and hiding underneath her bed. His father did not tell his family much about his activities outside of Laashekoh and might already know about the child. For all Saddiq knew, the man could already be arranging the transfer.

The baby would only hinder Saddiq's escape.

But Saddiq's arms moved faster than his reasoning. He stretched the piece of old blanket on the floor and turned to the basket. He pulled back the soft cover and gathered the baby with her blanket, placing both on top of the rag. He folded the gray blanket in half, tying the two ends around his neck and arranging the child like a pack on his back. The girl whimpered softly, but she was covered, and that muffled the noise. Before leaving the room, he bunched another one of her blankets underneath her bedcover. The lump in the basket might deceive anyone who entered the room for a quick check.

His biggest danger was leaving the house, aiming for the soft glow of the living areas at the far end of the hall, and Saddiq was at a disadvantage against any woman or man as long as he held the child. Every step took him away from the bedroom, the house, the mysterious compound—away from being challenged to give an excuse he did not have. He edged out of the room and moved swiftly along the narrow hallway. Near the living areas, Saddiq heard scratching noises on the carpet. Crouching, he slowed his pace to check. Three kittens cavorted about the space. Keeping one hand on the tie around his neck that secured the pack, Saddiq opened the door and stepped outside.

The chilly night air beckoned, offering freedom and promise. Once on the trail, Saddiq and the child would be safe.

The baby squirmed, probably because of the cold, before settling against his back—still sleeping by some miracle. Overwhelmed with relief, he reached back and gave her a reassuring pat.

No one was near. The whirling wind masked the sound of footsteps. He crept among the shadows of the dark building, scanning all directions for any sign of movement. Shouting came from nearby, and Saddiq hurried toward the stand of trees. Turning the corner, he stumbled against a person crouched low in the shadows. Gasping, he clutched the ends of the blanket and barely kept his balance.

He expected a cry of alarm and prepared for an awkward run.

Instead, a familiar voice whispered a scolding. "Be still! Or you will get us both in trouble!" Najwa, the orphan girl. "And do as I say." Saddiq complied, though he dearly wanted nothing more than to flee the compound. There would be an outcry any moment over the missing child, and Najwa would guess the culprit.

"You won't tell anyone that I was here?" he pleaded.

She pointed toward the trees. "Never. Unless you rush before prying eyes." The old woman had backed away from the large building and waited near the trailhead. In his hurry, Saddiq would have crossed her path. Najwa explained that the woman waited for her husband to return and that Zahira tolerated no interference from servants when she had visitors. "She pretends that her visitors do not exist and banishes us when they arrive. Both of them would punish us." The girl paused. "Why are you here? For your father?"

Saddiq shook his head, puzzled that she brought up his father. Then she asked if Saddiq spied on his father. Her smile was sly, and he shook his head, deciding it was better not to talk. Najwa didn't seem to notice the baby, and he wanted to get away before someone checked the basket. But Najwa wanted to talk.

"You should be careful here." Najwa tossed her head in a superior way, displaying more confidence than she had in Laashekoh. Her hair looked smooth under a headscarf, and her skin smelled clean. She kept talking about his father. "Do you realize how often your father visits this place? How Zahira looks forward to his arrival? Zahira once loved him, but now hates him, too. Her husband told me this, because he despises your father, too, but Arhaan does not hide his feelings. Maybe because Arhaan cannot see. He teases Zahira that she wants a man who does not know how she feels."

"Why do they care about my father?" Saddiq wondered aloud.

Najwa admitted she didn't know. "Arhaan says he controls all the land around here, including Laashekoh, since he married Zahira . . ." She paused. "If he hates your father and controls the land, then why does he not remove Parsaa? Yes, that is strange."

Saddiq felt uncomfortable discussing his father. So he asked if Najwa was happy, and she smiled. "Most of the time, and that is good enough for me," she said. "Zahira is unhappy, but not how other women are unhappy." Najwa pointed to the home. "She has so much but does not know how to enjoy it."

Saddiq asked about the visitor, and Najwa stared into his eyes. "You know him. Paul Reichart. The foreign man who helped your father return the orphans?"

She turned her attention back to the building. "Your father likes Paul, but your father also thinks that every village is quiet like Laashekoh. Paul Reichart knows how to find people who hate themselves and pretends he can fix their hatred."

She cocked her head toward the arguing, and they paused to listen though Saddiq still could not understand the specific words. The older woman approached the door as if to intervene. After listening a few moments, she disappeared around the corner.

Saddiq was anxious to return to Laashekoh, but not before expressing gratitude to Najwa. "Thank you for not telling my parents about me that night in our house back in Laashekoh," he murmured softly. "My parents were so rough with you."

She waved her hand to dismiss his worry. "I don't blame your parents," she said. "And I am grateful to you, too."

He didn't understand, and she explained. "You told me about the book in your house. I had to destroy it. Nothing else mattered that night."

He remembered talking with her about the large book full of photographs and maps of Afghanistan villages and countryside. He had described the book and wondered aloud if the images might help Najwa remember the location of her village. "I did not mean to upset you," he said.

She leaned back against the wall. "It was upsetting. You thought I could look at the pictures and find a familiar place?"

He nodded. Her short laugh was sharp.

"You don't understand," she said. "I know exactly where I'm from and have no desire to return. Laashekoh is far better than the place where I was raised. And I am happier here working with Arhaan and the birds." Najwa took his hand. "I will keep your secrets if you keep mine?"

She then explained how she knew Leila and Jahangir, the husband who led the trafficking ring. "Jahangir is my oldest brother. My father despised his children and complained more than once that we had ruined his life. We were under constant threat when he was near. So my brother decided to leave our village, stealing money my father had hidden away and a favorite knife he used to get his way with us. I went along. My brother had an idea for making money off of other parents who resented their children by promising to find jobs. Jahangir said it would help if I pretended to be one of the children searching for jobs."

She studied Saddiq, who could not hide his disgust. He would never forget the terrible night, the worst of his life. The traffickers had caught Saddiq, and he had seen children bound to the wagon, carted like animals, destined to work as laborers in Pakistan. Leila had tied Saddiq alongside the other children, for delivery and sale, and promised he would not see his parents again. Najwa sighed.

"Jahangir wanted me to spy on the other children, report to him if the other children were plotting against him. So, yes, I rode along in the wagon, listening to the crying and curses, their secret plotting to run away from my brother or even kill him." She looked down. "I'm ashamed. Early on, I told him about their transgressions."

She took a deep breath and looked out onto the darkness leading to the canyon wall and the start of the trail to Laashekoh. "Jahangir punished them brutally. He was like my father, cuffing them about the heads, twisting their arms, taunting and humiliating them. And I was not spared. He pinched our breasts and forced us to perform before we received our meals."

Her voice broke. Saddiq had spent only a few hours with the group. For her, such abuse was routine.

"I stopped telling him about the other children. The fool eventually realized I was holding back and took me aside to explain that he had to treat me badly or the other children would turn on me. But I no longer trusted him." Her brother was arrested with Leila and Leila's mother, neither of whom knew that Najwa was Jahangir's sister.

Jahangir said nothing about his sister, and Najwa was left behind in Laashekoh. "He had his reasons—probably to spy for him or visit him in jail," she said. "The other children never guessed that I was related to him. He didn't care for me, and I think he planned to sell me off in Pakistan, too, if it had meant more money for his pockets. But that was fine. Anyplace was better than living with him or my father. I am happy to leave Laashekoh, so Jahangir cannot find where I live, and I am happy to stay with Arhaan. I never want to see my family again."

She thanked Saddiq again. "I had to destroy the book. I was afraid your father might find my family village." Saddiq could understand her fear in admitting that she was Jahangir's sister. His parents would have turned her over to the authorities or worse. She both did wrong and was wronged. He could not despise her, and that bothered him. For too many, truth was defiance and dangerous. Lying and secrecy were a means of self-defense. He did not enjoy telling or hearing lies, but he understood the reasons. Some truths meant the loss of love and respect—with others never looking at him in the same way.

He wanted her to trust him and confided why he was at the compound. "The baby is my niece, and sleeping in my pack," he whispered. "I cannot risk that she ever goes back to Leila."

Najwa solemnly agreed and promised not to tell. "You were the only one who was good to me in Laashekoh. It may not seem like much, but you smiled. You worked when your mother taught the other children lessons." She looked up at the night sky, and it was as if she could read his uncertain mind. "Do not be angry with your parents. You learned these values from them. They may make mistakes, but they are better parents than Leila or Zahira ever could be."

So many argued over what was proper or wrong. No parent could be sure about how to shape a child's ways, and even Saddiq's own parents could be unpredictable. He placed a hand on her shoulder. "I hope you are safe."

She nodded. "Arhaan is a kind man, a smart man. Zahira and the others think that I have slept in his bed, but I have not. But is that wrong if she hates him so? Arhaan drops hints about liking me, and I do not mind. Understand that he resents that his wife meets with men alone, including Paul and your father."

He asked if she was sure about his father. But then, Saddiq knew the man had secrets.

"Your father has done nothing wrong." She was adamant. "Maybe you can convince him that Arhaan means well. The man has shown me how to care for the birds, and I do feel safe here. He is more timid than cruel and is only hurt because his wife loves another man. Your father doesn't even know . . ."

A stick cracked, and Saddiq turned.

"What foolishness is this?" the older woman scolded. "Are you spying on us for your father?" She was furious and raised her hand to confront Najwa: "Is that why he sent you here, too?"

"No ..." Saddiq sputtered, frantic that the woman might notice the child.

But she was more concerned about defending Zahira to Najwa. "Zahira is good to you. She allows you to stay here, and you gossip about her? How long have you two been meeting?"

Najwa shook her head, insisting the meeting was their first and unplanned. "I was directing him to see Mohan. Then we heard the arguing and thought he should wait ..."

The woman interrupted. "Hah! Arhaan will hear about this! He complains about his wife and won't like hearing that you sneak about at night, meeting with Parsaa's son and talking about the compound."

She turned back to Saddiq. "Such a big pack ... Does your father expect us to keep every child from Laashekoh? You look just like the Parsaa of years ago. Zahira will like that. Which of his sons are you?"

Confused, Saddiq gave his name. Brusque and efficient, the woman pointed to a group of huts and ordered Najwa to take the boy's pack to the largest one. The boy protested, but Najwa gave a slight shake of her head, and the woman explained that Najwa would be beaten if Saddiq reported the contents were disturbed. He removed the pack with care, hoping the baby would not let loose with a scream. Najwa's face was expressionless as she extended her hands.

"I'll deal with you later," the woman warned.

Najwa hurried off, cradling the bundle like the baby it was, and Saddiq observed which hut she had entered.

The old woman scolded him for dawdling and explained how Saddiq must first meet Zahira, who would then decide if the boy could stay at the compound. She rambled on about great history and important work, with words that could only describe other times and places.

"It's an honor to stay here," she said gruffly. "Plenty of work will keep you busy, but it is a good life. A quiet one, Allah willing."

The words were troubling, and Saddiq wondered what promise his father had made to the compound. What did his father owe this group of strangers? Was his father sending him to the strange place because Saddiq had refused to attend school?

The compound seemed to have some hold over his father. Najwa had mentioned that someone named Arhaan owned the land surrounding Laashekoh. Saddiq learned how little he knew about his own future—in one night and only by leaving Laashekoh.

The woman warned him not to gossip about the compound. "No one in the village needs to know what goes on here—not even your father." She asked about his father and Mohan. "What is taking them so long?"

He could not answer and did not mention that he had been away from Laashekoh. Perhaps his father had figured out why Saddiq went away, and this was his punishment. He was hurt and exhausted. Parents who practiced keeping secrets must expect their children to do the same.

The woman directed Saddiq to the largest building of the compound. The arguing had subsided. With his father expected soon, a meeting must be planned. Najwa would not want to be caught hiding the child and could return her to the basket.

He understood and didn't want the girl punished for his deed. The night was strange, and most troubling was how much he might learn about his father. The woman claimed the compound had a great history, but Saddiq wondered how that could be true in a desolate place with too many secrets.

~~~~~

Parsaa could not help it. His pace quickened as he approached the compound, an old habit developed from his eagerness long ago, and he waited for Mohan at the wooded area along the compound's edge. Impatience to conclude an unpleasant chore had since replaced his youthful anticipation.

The older man caught up, too proud to call out for Parsaa to slow down, and he struggled to control his breathing. The compound

might need more security, yet Mohan could not have it both ways—
demanding support and applying rigid controls. Parsaa could no longer
deny the need to plan for a replacement, despite his hopes that one
would not be needed. The old man was stubborn, and wresting Parsaa's
son from a lifelong obligation would be difficult.

Without a word, Mohan headed directly for the clinic and knocked.
Zahira opened the door as if she had been waiting. Her headscarf was
pulled forward, covering much of her forehead, and she was not alone.
Aza hovered behind the counter, and another man at the computer said
something in English before turning to welcome Parsaa.

Paul Reichart.

The man smiled and pointed to a computer screen—an older
woman wore no veil and appeared concerned. Paul explained that the
woman on the screen was the director of GlobalConnect and that she
was seeking advice from Afghans about how to best deliver aid. She had
questions, and he offered to translate.

Paul invited Parsaa to sit in another chair near the computer.

Parsaa declined. The Internet was another way for foreigners to
intrude. Zahira and Paul had somehow found one another, and without
understanding why, Parsaa found that disturbing.

CHAPTER 27

Lydia scheduled the Skype call with Paul, just a few hours after GlobalConnect's executive director, Annie, had advised him that he was still in the running for the award. If successful, he would replace Lydia on the board of directors and be groomed to serve as chairman.

The first step in the award process was an interview with an Afghan partner. "Lydia has full trust in you, Paul," the director had advised. "She just wants a small chat before the formal interview with the rest of the search committee and the background check. No worries—a piece of cake!"

Cara had hired a Dari translator, Kashif, a young refugee studying physics at the nearby college, due to arrive any minute. Lydia didn't want to admit it after all Cara's work, but she was uncomfortable about testing Paul and the Afghan provider. "Can we trust this translator?" Lydia asked.

Cara suggested keeping details to a minimum.

"No need for the conversation to leave here, and I doubt there will be a confrontation." Cara sat next to Lydia on the porch sofa. "For now, we are gathering information. If you need to pause, hit enter and send an empty message. I'll knock hard, and you tell him someone is at the door."

Lydia worried that the translator might have met Paul. Cara assured her that the young man had lived in a refugee camp for a decade before receiving a scholarship to attend boarding school and then college. "I checked," she said. "No connection to GlobalConnect. Don't forget, Afghanistan is big. More than thirty million people."

Cara transferred Lydia's laptop for Skype to the front porch, on a table, and set up a space for the translator and a recorder in the living room. She studied Lydia's screen view and approved. "Good. The more Paul sees of the porch, the less nervous he will be."

Not visible on the screen was a small, low table underneath the other table where a small netbook was hidden. Set for large print and muted sound, the netbook was ready for Google Chat. On the large table were papers. Lydia could sit back and pretend to examine reports while checking for messages on the netbook from Cara.

It was not yet noon in East Lansing and near 9:00 p.m. in Afghanistan.

Lydia would ask questions. Cara and the translator would test the accuracy of Paul's translation and how much he wanted the position on the board. Cara fussed over details. "Keep your handwritten questions near the keyboard and act natural. And don't worry too much about his responses. I'm recording the audio for later review."

Kashif arrived, and he admired the gardens surrounding Lydia's home. "My parents grew flowers, too," he explained. "They would have loved this home."

The two women offered him snacks, asked his preferences for a beverage during what could be a long session, and then gave him detailed instructions. Kashif grew up in a refugee camp and was perceptive. He understood immediately that another man's candor was being tested.

The translator promised to signal Cara if Paul's translation of the Dari responses was off, and Cara returned to Lydia and lowered her voice. "Forget that we're in the next room. Don't look in our direction. You must not alert him that we are listening."

She studied the screen one last time and asked if Lydia was ready. Lydia nodded and hit Paul's connection as Cara walked away. The program squawked, as if a strange box was being opened, and Paul appeared, his face close to the screen and the background blocked. He immediately noticed that she was not in her office, and she explained that she was on her porch, taking advantage of an unusually warm late autumn day.

The two exchanged pleasantries before Paul sat back and introduced Zahira. "We're in her clinic," he offered.

Paul, not Zahira, walked around the clinic with the laptop facing away from him to give Lydia a quick tour. The clinic was immaculate, modern, with stainless-steel examining tables, cabinets, sinks, and equipment. The woman was elegant in dark-violet silk, a lavender veil framing her dark hair. Her voice was quick, professional, yet uncomfortable as she directed her gaze at the keyboard rather than the screen.

Paul posed Lydia's questions to the woman, and Lydia did not need a translator to know the answers were terse. Paul did most of the talking. The woman was robotic, perhaps frightened, and Lydia found herself feeling sorry for her. Perhaps she was embarrassed about her background. She had come so close to completing medical school in Moscow, Paul explained, but did not finish.

Lydia posed typical questions about the number of patients and services provided. Paul rattled off statistics. The clinic was informal, serving a tiny population in villages that lacked schools, running water, and power. Despite the lack of a degree, Zahira was overqualified as a community health worker and had received ample funding for more than two decades to provide women's reproductive-health services—she was the only source of care for more than five hundred families spread throughout the remote area where few were literate.

The bar was set low for health providers in the poorest parts of Afghanistan.

Lydia asked about the contraception prevalence rate and sensed hesitancy from Zahira. Paul translated. "She distributes the supplies but cannot be sure how or if the women use them."

A family-planning program, while not illegal in Afghanistan, could not be publicized as pregnancy prevention. Instead, providers emphasized birth spacing that protected mothers' health. Women did not want their names revealed and preferred that records not be kept. Zahira worked alone, and Paul explained there was minimal follow-up care or counseling, before or after treatment.

Patients were also unwilling to talk with foreigners about their experiences. Paul sighed. "They would deny having asked for help or claim to have forgotten."

Lydia asked about emergency care and the location of the nearest available doctor. Zahira glanced at Paul and, again, he spoke for her. The nearest caregiver was more than forty kilometers away. "The villagers do not have vehicles," he reported. "Transferring seriously ill patients is impossible. It's a rough area, Lydia."

Lydia asked about complications around injectable contraception and implants. She didn't like to think of women handling side effects like headaches, bleeding, and more on their own. Paul translated. The response was a curt "*Ne*."

"But she is using the long-term methods?" Lydia pressed. Providers typically didn't trust rural women to manage daily pills. Paul nodded, and Lydia wondered if patients understood the trade-offs. Injectables lasted twelve weeks but could result in lasting fertility problems, weakened bones, or low birth weights for infants conceived as the medication wore off. Husbands often rejected use of implants that lasted three years.

When Lydia asked if women had to wait for approval from their husbands before using contraception, Zahira offered an earnest response, and Paul was impatient. "She rarely deals with such men. She expects the women to handle their husbands. Or lie about the care."

Zahira did not seem shy. Lydia wondered why Paul spoke so much for Zahira.

And no records. No family guidance or follow-up care. No testing or follow-up studies. No advocacy or promotion. No community committee monitoring the care. Such were the ways of healthcare associated with shame and lack of women's control over their lives. The interview was surreal.

Lydia checked her list. She was running out of questions, and there was no message from Cara over Google Chat.

The exchange with her son's childhood friend was stilted. Perhaps it was the distance or the presence of Zahira. Maybe he guessed that others listened in and Lydia did not trust him. "You are working in a tough area, Paul."

He nodded and started to talk. A knock sounded, and both Zahira and Paul turned away from the screen. An older woman pushed a disheveled teenager into the clinic with a long explanation. Shoes came off. The woman seemed pleased, but the boy was filthy and fatigued. He gazed about the clinic, and his eyes widened as he stared at the screen image of Lydia. She smiled. Boys of any age reminded Lydia of Michael.

Paul murmured something to Zahira, who snapped at the older woman. Scowling, the woman ordered the boy to sit on the floor behind the counter, out of sight of the camera. A long exchange ensued between the newcomer and Zahira, which Paul did not translate. Cara had warned in advance that the rapid back-and-forth conversation among Afghans often sounded like arguing. Longer sentences with rich descriptions did not necessarily lend themselves to exact translations in English.

The older woman alternated between scolding and cajoling, sounding like a mother giving a daughter advice.

Paul was irritated, snapping words in Dari, as Zahira returned to the chair beside him. She tried for an explanation, and he waved his hand, returning full attention to Lydia with an apology.

But there was no need for an apology, Lydia advised, pointing out how the busy clinic demonstrated support from nearby villages. As she spoke, there was another knock on the door, and Paul turned away again. Two Afghan men removed their shoes and entered, and greetings were exchanged. One was older, wiry, and short. The other man was tall, in his forties, surprised by the small gathering around the computer. He was uncomfortable, even wary, and Lydia couldn't tell if the feelings were directed at Paul or at the computer.

As Paul talked, the tall Afghan man scanned the space. The boy suddenly stood, his hands on the counter, and the expression on the man's face transformed in a matter of seconds—from weariness to amazement and pure joy, then relief and puzzlement. The boy looked nervous, as if caught in some mischief, and the man offered only a slight nod as if indicating the two would talk later.

Lydia watched as Zahira and Paul greeted the two men. Zahira gestured, offering her chair to the tall man, who declined. The older man said a few brief words, and Zahira returned a long string of sentences, as if trying to convince him of something. Paul followed with more comments. The man shrugged and leaned against the wall.

Her mind raced with thoughts of her son and his wife, his life's work, the fortune he had made. Lydia had to wait for Kashif's translation, but she could not imagine how anyone in the faraway clinic knew what happened to Michael and Rose.

Remembering Cara's advice, Lydia kept a patient smile and her eyes on the screen. She could not dwell on motives in a room thousands of miles away until later.

Paul turned back to the screen. "You can see this is a busy place." He introduced the tall man as Parsaa, a leader of a nearby village. "And one of his sons is here, too. We can ask them to wait outside until we finish . . ."

"Oh, no!" She was out of questions for Paul. "Perhaps we should ask the father's permission if the boy can stay?"

As Paul spoke to the father and son, she shifted the papers. Still no reaction from Cara. Maybe the investigators were right—Michael's death was random. Perhaps her life would never feel whole again, and it was selfish to test Michael's lifelong friend.

Paul explained that the Afghans were shy about online communications and would observe. Lydia could not resist, pointing out how such interviews would help his chances for the award.

"I can be candid with you, Paul," she said. "We don't need critics suggesting that a promotion is based on favoritism."

Paul spoke with Parsaa. After a long exchange, the Afghan man approached the computer and said a few sentences. "He lives in Laashekoh, a successful farming village near here. He understands that GlobalConnect funds my work."

"Salaam." Lydia spoke slowly. She thanked the man for guiding Paul in that part of the world and asked questions about his village. The man listened closely, and his tone was positive and thoughtful. The village was small and far from city centers. Most villagers would appreciate more contact with caregivers, schools, and services, but distance also provided a form of security. Lydia asked whether Parsaa or other villagers had a chance to meet the aid workers who had just gone missing.

Paul offered a translation, and Zahira tried to interject, but he cut her off to state that the aid workers had passed through the area quickly. Zahira, Parsaa, and other villagers had not met with them. Lydia asked how long Parsaa had known Paul. Paul did not translate but simply answered the question. The two men had met almost a year earlier.

After the attacks on Michael and Rose, she thought to herself. Lydia then asked how long Parsaa and Zahira knew one another.

Paul posed the question and seemed surprised by the answer. "Since they were children. He regards her as a sister."

A hard knock startled her—not over Skype, but from the front door. Cara waited with a small package, and she mouthed one word: "Delivery."

Hoping she appeared more confused than anxious about the interruption, Lydia apologized. "A delivery, Paul, I probably have to sign . . ." She hurried to the door, out of sight from the Skype camera, to join Cara and the student. "He's not translating your questions." Cara whispered, and Kashif nodded.

"What is he saying?" Lydia whispered.

"It's strange." Kashif was uncomfortable about his role in the middle of a disagreement. "The translations were fine until the Afghan man named Parsaa sat down. That man is very polite and wants to thank you for Paul's help in returning the orphans. The translator did not mention that. He talks about his village but insists that the place needs no help from a foreign charity—that they are in the position to provide charity to others and in fact do so. The translator repeated none of that. He also did not repeat the question about the aid workers."

Lydia asked if the missing questions could be a misunderstanding, and Kashif shook his head. "The woman wanted to make points, and the man told her you would not care for details."

Cara handed over the package, urging Lydia to get back to the Skype call. Kashif interjected. "Be careful. This man is devious, and it could be dangerous for the people in that room if he thinks you know the translations have errors."

Lydia questioned Kashif if he thought the others in the room recognized the discrepancies, and the young man shook his head. "Zahira
may know some English, but it's limited. The others do not."

Lydia returned to her seat before the computer, placing the parcel
on the desk without comment. She apologized to the group for keeping
them waiting.

"No problem, Lydia," Paul said. "We were just talking about some
other ideas for programs that could be funded." He added that the villages had responded well to family-planning and education programs.

Lydia made her move to test Paul. "Of course, it's tough to work
with extremism in that area. Two aid workers and their pilot went
missing."

Paul dismissed the concern. "They're amateurs. They didn't have
proper risk insurance, and that won't happen to GlobalConnect."

Lydia mentioned that the board had approved sending a donation
to assist with the search. "Training aid workers on proper security mea-
sures—it could be a new focus."

Paul frowned. "I'm not sure that's a good idea, Lydia."

"The training?"

"No," he snapped. "Donating to that search effort. The women
were pushy. They could be anywhere, off insulting other villages, cham-
pioning a new cause. Parsaa can tell you himself. These are sensitive
areas, and the Afghans do not like assertive approaches."

She had touched a nerve. "Are you sure Zahira or Parsaa did not
meet with them?"

His eyes locked on hers. "They did not."

"And you know this." She pressed on with patient interrogation.
"Without asking them?"

"And GlobalConnect sent money off for a search in my region
without consulting me?" He leaned forward, and she could no longer
see the others in the room. He may have raised his voice in anger, but
that also could have been the effect of his mouth taking up most of
the screen. "It's such a waste! I know this area. Annie has never been
to Afghanistan and doesn't have a clue about the cultural nuances. Yet

she micromanages and pushes us around. Even you, Lydia." He paused. "This interview. It's not about the board and giving me more responsibility. So, what is it about?"

She took a deep breath. She didn't need to defend her decisions. "We sent the donation to help colleagues on the ground. I didn't think we had to ask you of all people." She spoke carefully, keeping Kashif's warning in mind. Paul could easily lash out at others nearby.

He sat back and closed his eyes. He asked Lydia to pardon him. "It's been a long day, a rough week. Of course, I feel terrible about the two women. But it was so preventable . . ."

The women had nothing to do with Michael, and other colleagues had already suggested the two could have easily been sidetracked. Weary, Lydia asked Paul to check if Parsaa's son wanted to say hello. Paul spoke with Parsaa, and the two men waved the boy over. The boy squeezed next to Paul, directly in front of the computer, and the father frowned while eying the tangled hair and filthy clothes. The child looked as if he had not bathed in days.

Paul made the introductions, and Lydia gave Saddiq a small wave. "Be sure to show him where I live on a map."

Saddiq smiled and said a few sentences. "He's seen a television before and wanted to know how the computer was different," Paul translated. "His father says he has not seen a computer before."

Lydia asked if Saddiq attended school and listened as the boy said he would miss home too much if he left for school. He wanted to work in the village's fields. His father added that school could be helpful for that work, too.

Just as Lydia was about to ask another question, the door swung open. A man in dark glasses, wearing an embroidered vest, burst into the clinic. Waving a rifle, he tossed a black bundle onto the counter, screaming furiously.

From what Lydia could tell, he did not aim the weapon at any particular person. There was shouting, and the man fired, shattering a metal cabinet and stunning others in the clinic. They froze just a moment before scrambling for cover. At first, no one spoke. Lydia only heard the pounding of feet and slamming chairs. Paul shoved the boy to the floor, underneath the desk and out of sight from Lydia. The violent scene played out on the small laptop screen like a low-budget television show. Except the actors did not seem surprised at all.

The old man by the door tried reaching for the rifle barrel. The shooter twisted and thrust the stock, knocking him to the ground. Lydia screamed, but no one in the clinic noticed.

"Arhaan!" Zahira issued what sounded like an annoyed order.

The man aimed the weapon in her direction and fired, hitting her in the arm. Zahira screamed, and Paul moved his chair to provide more cover for the boy, also blocking Lydia's view of the clinic. She heard ranting and gunfire but only saw Paul's gray shirt.

Seconds later, Paul slumped to the side, exposing the clinic. Parsaa had crossed the room, wrapping one arm around the shooter's neck.

The gunman protested and fought as Parsaa wrestled him to the floor with the help of his son. Angry, disgusted, Parsaa seized the rifle and handed it over to the stunned old man on the floor.

Parsaa and the others in the clinic were silent.

"No, no, no." Lydia repeated the word, but she was the only one who spoke. Kashif tried to rush to her side, but Cara stopped him. Lydia stepped away from the computer and joined them near the doorway. Cara gave her an embrace, and Lydia turned to Kashif. "What can we do?" she asked.

The translator shook his head. "It's over now, and the shooting had nothing to do with your conversation," he whispered. "The man had entered the clinic, furious about an attack on his Kalila by a cat."

"Another child?" Lydia asked. But Kashif shook his head.

A bird. The translator thought Kalila was a bird.

CHAPTER 28

Arhaan stormed into the clinic and screamed, wildly swinging Blacker's old .303 British Enfield. "Who is in here? Parsaa? The foreign man? Who?" The blind man blocked the doorway and tossed a dead bird onto the nearest counter while railing about the death of Kalila, his favorite myna. Paul's online meeting turned into bedlam.

With derision, Zahira told the others in the room not to worry. "That rifle is not loaded."

Arhaan fired blindly at the cabinet, puncturing the steel. Mohan tried reaching for the gun, but Arhaan was ready and strong, easily knocking the old man to the ground. Then he slowly turned, aiming the weapon, a blind man in search of a target.

Zahira called his name, ordering her husband to leave. Arhaan fired in her direction and hit her arm. She screamed and reached for the wound in disbelief as Paul shoved Saddiq to the floor.

"Stop!" Parsaa shouted, before lunging and dropping low, edging along the wall toward the shooter.

Arhaan immediately fired in the direction of the voice and missed. Leaning against the door, he dared anyone in the room to reveal a position. "I asked one favor. To keep the cat away from Kalila. But my work doesn't matter!"

"We did listen," Zahira moaned. He fired a shot that hit her in the neck, and she fell to the floor.

Paul cried out her name, while a choking sound came from Mohan, and Aza frantically signaled her husband to keep quiet. Arhaan took a step forward.

Closing in, Parsaa held his breath, lunging for Arhaan's neck and the weapon. But not before Arhaan fired four more shots into the tight space.

The two men struggled, and Parsaa was surprised by the blind man's strength. Kicking, screaming, punching the air, Arhaan demanded to know who took his weapon away, who dared to restrain the master of the compound.

No one answered.

Parsaa managed to hold on, and Saddiq pushed his way from underneath the desk, rushing across the room to grasp the shooter's arm. Father and son shoved Arhaan to the floor, his head hitting hard against the tiles. Mohan grabbed a desk lamp, using the electric cord to bind Arhaan's hands.

Arhaan howled in protest, berating Zahira. "Only your work matters. You care nothing about mine." He fell apart, mourning a favorite bird. "Kalila . . . Kalila is dead. My beautiful Kalila is dead."

Across the room, Paul Reichart managed to sit up and survey the damage, while clutching his stomach, blood dripping through his fingers. And the only one who could possibly save his life, Zahira, lay nearby, blood streaming from the wound in her neck. Arhaan, still screaming at her, had no idea his wife was dead.

Najwa slipped into the room and sat near Mohan and Saddiq as they restrained Arhaan. She asked no questions but held Arhaan's hand and tried to calm him.

Parsaa closed his eyes, praying for forgiveness. He had promised Blacker to protect his only child. The challenge came in protecting a woman from her husband, and for that there was no sure method. He opened cabinets until he found clean linens. Kneeling next to Paul, Parsaa pressed a folded cloth to the man's wound.

"Friend," Parsaa whispered.

"Good friend." Paul gasped with pain. He moved his hand to the cloth but lacked the strength to press the layers down. The wound was in a bad place. Parsaa could use a knife to remove the bullet, but the man did not deserve more pain. Men did not survive such wounds in the isolated area around Laashekoh.

Paul was less concerned about the wound. Leaning against the desk and grunting, he pointed to the laptop and gestured for Parsaa to move it closer. Paul wanted to continue his conversation.

The old woman from another country was distressed, and Parsaa wondered how much she had seen. Countless times he had wondered how Zahira could tolerate such a machine, exposing her personal space even as she explored other places. But he shook his head. The violence had occurred on his side of the world regardless of whether a computer was in the room or not. The woman had reason to judge Arhaan and the rest of them.

The woman frantically asked questions, and Parsaa heard the word "Paul" several times. Parsaa started to explain that an accident had taken place, but then realized that she did not speak Dari. Only Paul could translate.

Parsaa wanted to urge her to stop the questions and simply offer prayers that might soothe the dying man. But Paul did not seem to mind and was comforted by the woman's image and voice. The questions stopped as Paul struggled to speak.

Parsaa was quiet. One should not interfere until one understands.

In severe pain, Paul's voice rasped in between quick and shallow breaths, and the old woman listened closely. Shivering, Paul was losing blood. His face was pale, but at one point, he turned to Parsaa, assuring his friend with a wan smile. "She is worried that you are not rushing me to a doctor. I explained the trip would be too hard. This is it."

Parsaa gave a reluctant nod.

As the two continued their conversation, Parsaa found more towels and a blanket that he wrapped around the man's shoulders. But he could find no tool to remove the bullet. Toward the end, Paul shook hard and wept. The man could hardly speak and clutched onto the machine as if it meant everything to him.

Parsaa felt sorry for his friend, the man who had pushed his son to safety. The woman was stern, as if she expressed disappointment in Paul even as he was dying. Paul muttered what sounded like prayers in another language.

Turning, Parsaa asked Saddiq to find scissors, pincers, a knife, medicines, anything to remove the bullet or stop the pain.

But it was too late. Paul closed his eyes and died.

~~~~~~

Cara placed the laptop on the table, directly in front of Lydia's chair, to narrow Paul's view of the room. He still did not know that another translator was listening nearby. Lydia pleaded with Paul to ask the Afghans to seek help, but Paul shook his head and explained that the compound was too far away from such care. Zahira, the only caregiver in the region, was dead.

Nothing could be done for him.

He wanted to confess. Thousands of miles away, Paul told his story, desperate for Lydia to understand and forgive.

"It was Rose," Paul gasped. "All Rose." Michael had refused to listen to advice not just from Paul but from other friends about convincing Rose to sign a prenuptial agreement. "Probably, you too, Lydia," Paul said slowly. Lydia would not interrupt to argue or agree. Better to let him speak freely.

Michael was stubborn, insisting that the request indicated a lack of trust. He had chosen love over money and refused to let work, wealth, any wedge, come between him and Rose.

Yes, Paul had arranged for the bombing in India. The resentful can easily detect resentment in others. While working in Afghanistan, helping tech teams on cultural issues, he had talked with many marginalized young men bitter about the unending changes in their country. The mentally ill, abandoned by their families, with no prospects for jobs or marriage, could be easily manipulated. All Paul had to do was point out that Rose was an atheist who had once desecrated a copy of the Koran—and yet the Western woman continued to enjoy the rewards of travel and vast wealth. Paul casually passed along cash and copies of a newspaper photograph of Rose to three young men. The most desperate of the three, a young man by the name of Qasim, managed to travel to India.

The bomb had been intended for Rose alone. Qasim was advised on the time and place. But Michael had skipped a scheduled conference call from the company that day and died by his wife's side.

The foundation had been proposed a week before the wedding. The three friends sat on the porch, talking late into the night, staring at the stars, and finishing a bottle of sparkling wine. Michael had mentioned that he wanted to do something useful with his share of money from Photizonet, and Paul pointed out that his friend could start a foundation and that he would donate a good portion of his stock, too.

But Rose had immediately scoffed at the idea, suggesting that Michael could be a good citizen in other ways. Private foundations were ostentatious, arrogant displays of wealth, designed for tax avoidance. Corporate executives pillaged communities, constraining government spending, wresting control over social spending, while insinuating that governments could not do good work. For her, organized charity undermined democracy and reduced a community's power over deciding wants and needs. She was so opinionated, yet Michael adored her, listening to her and treating her as his only equal. Other employees had already expressed concern, wondering if Rose might try to take an active role in Photizonet. But not Paul. Never loyal Paul.

Until that night. He had been grateful for the late hour and cover of darkness on the bungalow's tiny porch. Otherwise, Michael would not have missed the hatred in his friend's eyes. Paul wept as he explained his regret to Lydia about what he called an accident and asked if she had known about the foundation.

She just shook her head, and Paul moaned. "Why did he keep that a secret? If only he had told me his plans . . ."

Paul was fading fast. At last, Lydia knew the reason for her son's death, though it didn't help. The murders were pointless.

She remembered how much the aid workers from the orphanage had aggravated him, and she reminded him that the two women had planned to apply for GlobalConnect funding. Paul insisted the crash was an accident.

His explanation seemed simple enough. The helicopter was overloaded. The pilot did not check and double-check the straps around the load. It didn't take much shifting for the helicopter with an uneven load to lose control. Paul's breathing was rapid and shallow, his eyes bright. "They . . . took . . . shortcuts."

How did Paul know? Because the helicopter had taken off not far from the compound. As Paul spoke, his skin turned pale, shiny, and damp. His voice was rough and robotic.

She wondered why he knew so much more than the authorities about the women and why he didn't report the crash.

But she let him talk on. He begged her forgiveness and talked about wanting to protect the villages from intruders who wanted to boost their own reputations rather than abide by the wishes of ordinary Afghans. His voice faded to a whisper, and Parsaa moved close, trying to comfort Paul while holding more towels to the wound.

In the background, the clinic was in shambles. Paul groaned, but he had more to say to Lydia.

"You loved me like a mother. Michael loved me like a brother. I don't know why I did what I did." His voice broke as he slumped in the chair.

"Please." His voice broke. "For . . . give me."

Lydia could not speak. She had nothing more to say to Paul Reichart.

~~~~~~

Lydia called out for Kashif to join her on the porch. She no longer had reason to hide the translator. Kashif surprised Parsaa with a respectful greeting in perfect Dari.

The Afghans spoke back and forth, with quick translations for Lydia about how the blind husband had killed his wife in anger over a dead myna bird. Paul was unfortunate to be caught by stray bullets. Parsaa assured Lydia that others in the room were shaken but otherwise fine.

Lydia talked about reporting the crime. She was a witness, and wondered if Parsaa needed her to file a report. She did not mention Paul's confession to hiring a young Afghan who had killed Michael and Rose.

"It is over," Parsaa said. Afghan judges would not punish a man over an honor killing, and outside authorities would add complications. Parsaa offered to bury Paul near Laashekoh, and she thanked him.

She also asked Kashif to advise Parsaa that a downed helicopter could be somewhere near the canyon. "You can notify the authorities before searchers arrive. Paul thought it was an accident, but there will be an investigation."

Lydia then thanked Parsaa for helping Paul and offering candid thoughts on foreign charities. She asked him to contact her if the village had questions about other groups approaching the area.

He agreed, but was formal. The man would support a relationship that was reciprocal. She went on to ask if he would be willing to chat occasionally over Skype—advising GlobalConnect about how to approach other villages on needs for schools, healthcare, education, even computers.

Parsaa thought a moment, and looked at his son. The boy's face brightened when he heard the translator mention the word "computer."

"There is interest here," Parsaa admitted with a smile. "And my wife would be pleased if a computer convinced my son that reading and education are necessities."

Lydia agreed that the boy would need to read in the fast-changing country.

The group said their farewells. The hour was late in Afghanistan, and Lydia was still shaken. But she also understood why Paul yearned to help such villagers, trying to separate and understand the strands of culture that could produce such hospitality and warmth even as worries about honor and change led to awful violence.

And the same could be said about Paul. An earnest desire to inspire good had led to envy, obsession, and control.

Parsaa mourned Paul's death and offered his condolences to Lydia. "The man was selfless. He saved my son's life, and I'll be forever grateful."

And despite grief about her son, Lydia was grateful, too.

~~~~~~

The call ended. Mohan and Aza told Arhaan about his wife's death, and the man wept, insisting that he had not meant to kill Zahira. Najwa comforted him, and he wrapped his arms around her.

Parsaa turned to the business at hand that required work throughout the night. He ordered his son to leave with Aza and follow her directions on where to dig two graves. Then Parsaa turned to Mohan. With Zahira dead, the caretaker no longer had reason to stay at the compound. The old man would listen to his wife and son and move to the city.

Parsaa was silent, ashamed that he had failed to protect Blacker's daughter, and Mohan read his mind. "It's not your fault. Zahira loved Arhaan in her own way. They fought. They slept with others." The older man looked toward the ground, and Parsaa knew that both Mohan and his son wondered about his own relationship with Zahira.

Parsaa's feelings for the woman were complicated, and he wasn't sure he would ever understand. He had loved her like a sister, yet she had wanted something more. Trying to explain was useless, but he looked at Mohan and firmly shook his head.

Arhaan interrupted, suddenly lashing out in anger, blaming Parsaa and the foreigner for Zahira's death. He swore that Parsaa was no longer welcome to work his land. "And you can tell the village that there will be new lease terms!"

Parsaa sighed and glanced at Mohan. But Mohan was ready to leave, no longer willing to settle compound disputes. It was left to Parsaa to explain that Zahira had never owned the vast holdings surrounding the compound and Laashekoh.

"A debt was settled and the land was transferred before your marriage," Parsaa noted quietly.

"That's nonsense," Arhaan scoffed. "There were annual payments."

"The village provided the compound with a share," Mohan snapped. "Parsaa and I did your bidding to keep peace. You made assumptions, and Zahira did not want to upset you."

And then there was Zahira's money from other sources.

Arhaan went silent as Mohan explained that most of the compound's funds came from foreign donors who had wanted Zahira to distribute contraceptives and healthcare in the region. Occasionally she sold supplies on the black market, but she feared getting caught and the stream of income ending. So she kept most of the drugs and supplies in storage at the compound.

Mohan and Aza did not plan to stay at the compound, and the blind man could not live alone. Parsaa guided Najwa outside so they could talk. "Are you all right here?"

The girl nodded and told Parsaa she had never felt more secure.

"Do you want to stay?" he asked, and she nodded. He mentioned that he no longer had her *peshkabz*, but she didn't care and said she no longer had a need for it. She wanted to forget her past, and she asked him to do the same.

Parsaa advised that she and Arhaan could remain at the compound. "But will Arhaan listen to you? He must be civil with you, the new caretaker, and Laashekoh."

She nodded.

Holding a shovel, Saddiq waited for his father, though Parsaa was in a hurry to return to Laashekoh and show his wife that their son was safe. He asked Mohan to find another shovel so Parsaa could help with digging two graves. The boy insisted on pulling his father aside. There was something his father needed to know, Saddiq whispered, and they could hide the problem by digging a third grave.

Stunned, Parsaa lifted his hand to interrupt. He glanced around to check that others did not overhear. "First I must ask. Do you know where Thara is?"

The boy hesitated. "All I know is that she is not coming back."

Parsaa felt sick, not ready to hear more. "If others ask this question, you do not know where she is." He was stern. "Do you understand?"

The boy swallowed, relieved about not having to explain or lie. "I really do not know," Saddiq offered.

Parsaa asked about the other body, but Saddiq was cryptic. "There is no other body. Someone else at this compound needs our help. A baby girl."

The boy led the way to one of the compound's huts. Inside, a baby squirmed on a pile of bedding and whimpered. Saddiq picked up the child and handed her to his father. "Zahira took the baby from Leila." His voice was firm, and he promised to explain more when his father was ready to hear. "But it is best for the child if Arhaan thinks she died tonight, too."

Parsaa stared into the child's eyes. There was no need for questions. "I see," he said softly.

"I don't think Ali knew about this child," Saddiq said. "But she is ours now."

~~~~~~

The Skype call ended with a click. But the apprehension about witnessing a double-murder and learning why Michael had been killed did not vanish. The group was silent, and Cara recovered first, raising questions about what they should do next. She outlined their options for the recording of the Skype call. She urged copying the files and passing them along to authorities in Afghanistan or India. "Perhaps the US State Department can help arrange the transfer."

Lydia stood and looked out over the front yard and the tree-lined street where Michael and Paul had once played as young boys. Then she gently shook her head.

Cara did not understand and gently pressed the woman, pointing out that Lydia had to hurry with a decision. "The call has a time stamp," she warned. "Any delay will be questioned."

Investigations could be abused. Authorities would pursue the matter only because of Michael's wealth. They would compete to interrogate the Afghans and issue quick pronouncements. Lydia thought of Parsaa and the others in Afghanistan and wasn't convinced that tracing the story to Laashekoh would result in justice. Her son's murderer was dead. The motivations were complex.

The crime was a crisis for the foundation. A key manager had murdered a wealthy man and his wife overseas, and the deaths prompted the creation of the world's largest foundation. Had the killer coerced others? Cara recommended the foundation conduct a thorough audit of Paul's work and connections, checking for fraud or irregularities.

But Cara didn't know Paul and how the foundation mattered to him more than anything else. Lydia turned to Kashif. "Did you sense that the man named Parsaa had any clue about what Paul had done?"

Kashif shook his head. "Paul's admissions were in English. Parsaa thought of Paul as an honorable man and did not realize that Paul had kept secrets from him."

"And what will happen to the man who killed Zahira?" she asked.

The student shrugged. "Without pressure from the funders in the West, nothing," the student said. "And even then . . . The husband talked about his wife having affairs. One of the victims confessed to arranging murder himself. This blind man Arhaan would face no charges." Kashif also trusted that Parsaa would search for the downed helicopter and speak with local authorities.

"The villagers are satisfied." The student shrugged and then excused himself to return to classes on the peaceful campus in East Lansing.

The woman watched him walk down the street amid gold leaves drifting under the blue autumn sky. "So much could go wrong," Lydia said, turning to Cara. "If the video leaves our hands, it will be leaked."

Both women agreed that the only reason an investigation would ensue was because of Michael's wealth. The story would become a media circus, with unwanted attention casting doubt over GlobalConnect and forever changing lives in Laashekoh. "So we agree to trust the Afghan contacts to handle this matter on their end," Cara said. "And we cooperate if they need us as witnesses?"

Lydia didn't want to lie. Still, there were plenty of reasons to hold back. A key foundation employee had committed a crime, but was dead. Authorities in Afghanistan had other crimes to pursue. An investigation and international publicity would destroy the village of Laashekoh. No one in the clinic had known that Lydia and Cara were recording the Skype call. Once the recording was handed over to investigators, anyone in those offices could leak the tape and track down Parsaa, Saddiq, and Arhaan.

Cara continued when Lydia did not respond. "Paul's crimes won't just damage the reputation of this charity. The publicity could damage philanthropy for years to come . . ."

"And so could a cover-up," Lydia added.

The two women stared at each other, and Lydia reached for Cara's shoulder. She would not risk ruining the foundation and Michael's legacy. "The evil is done, and no more justice can be done from here."

Evil must hide, Lydia thought to herself. But all that hides is not evil.

ACKNOWLEDGMENTS

Gratitude to my agent, Alison Picard, and my editor, Dan Mayer, for steadfast encouragement and constant work; the book would not be the same without the contributions of the staff of Seventh Street Books, including Jade Zora Scibilia, Cheryl Quimba, Bruce Carle, Sheila Stewart, and Jill Maxick. This writer thrives on the camaraderie of fellow authors including the fun team at Seventh Street Books and members of Mystery Writers of America, Sisters and Crime, International Thriller Writers, National Federation of Press Women, and Military Writers Society of America, as well as enthusiastic readers including Linda White, Barb Reynolds, Irene Vanh, Joe Malley, Dana Froetschel, Betty Froetschel, and Jennifer LeRoy.

Work at *YaleGlobal Online* and conversations with Nayan Chanda and Rahima Chaudhury have long sharpened my writing on globalization. The countless ideas, experiences, and love sprinkled throughout my books always start with Doug and Nick. And thank you to Afghanistan and Afghan people living everywhere. I have been entranced by the setting, its beauty and history, since 1980. The errors are mine alone, so forgive the wanderings of an imagination anchored in Michigan.

The technology for Photizonet was inspired by physicist Harald Haas and his TED Talk. Details on healthcare in the developing world are from the World Health Organization. The quotations from the Koran are from the University of Michigan's online version; the Dari words are from the Dari dictionary available at http://estragon.100megsfree5.com/dic.htm. Sissella Bok's *Lying: Moral Choice in Public and Private Life* helped with exploring the rationales for lying; *Stanford Encyclopedia of Philosophy* was useful for thinking about the connections behind charity, forgiveness, and wrongdoing.

ABOUT THE AUTHOR

Susan Froetschel writes for *YaleGlobal Online*, based at Yale University's MacMillan Center. Her previous book, *Fear of Beauty*, was nominated for the 2014 Mary Higgins Clark Award through Mystery Writers of America, and it was also recognized by the National Federation of Press Women as a best book for adult readers and by Military Writers Society of America with the mystery/suspense gold star award in 2014. She lives in Michigan.